Praise for *Trigger Point*

"Break out the essential oils, crank up the lute music, Eads is going to massage you until the blood palpates up between his fingers."

—Stephen Graham Jones, bestselling author
of *Mongrels* and *After the People Lights Have Gone Off*

"You may need a massage therapist to release severe knots of stress after absorbing this dark and harrowing story. *Trigger Point* will get under your skin."

—Mark Stevens, *Denver Post* bestselling author
of the Allison Coil mystery series

"With its blistering pace and delicious descriptions, *Trigger Point* invokes a whodunit mystery within the oft-misunderstood world of massage therapy. But this is no light-hearted cat-and-mouse story, and Eads is at his darkest and best when occupying the mind of the story's delightfully disturbed killer. *Trigger Point* will have you burning through its pages and guessing until the very end."

—Carter Wilson, *USA Today* bestselling author
of *The Comfort of Black*

TRIGGER POINT

This is a work of fiction. All characters, organizations, and events portrayed in this book are products of the authors' imaginations and/or are used fictitiously.

Trigger Point

Edited by Rory Olsen
Cover design by Kirk DouPonce and Angie Hodapp
Cover illustration by Kirk DouPonce
Typesets and formatting by Angie Hodapp

A Hex Publishers Book

Published & Distributed by Hex Publishers, LLC
PO BOX 298
Erie, CO 80516

www.HexPublishers.com

Hex Publishers TM is a trademark of Hex Publishers, LLC.

Joshua Viola, Publisher

Paperback: 978-0-9964039-3-1
Hardcover: 978-0-9964039-4-8
eBook: 978-0-9964039-5-5

First Hex Publishers Edition: March 2017

10 9 8 7 6 5 4 3 2 1

Previously published by Musa Publishing March 2012

Printed in the U.S.A.

TRIGGER POINT

SEAN EADS

For Linda Anderson

PROLOGUE

At least this guy's cute, Erin thought, setting up her massage table. His e-mail had said his name was Andrew, and if that was true she figured he went by Andy most of the time. He was a preppy kid in khaki pants and a white Oxford shirt, maybe twenty-two, which would make him five years younger than her. He had a clean-cut look and somewhat shaggy blond hair and a trace of acne on his chin where he hadn't quite surrendered his adolescence. He looked vulnerable to Erin, and she liked that. She smiled at him as she locked the table in place. He smiled back from where he sat across the motel room on an armless tub chair. All the motels she'd ever been in had that type of chair. Was it some sort of requirement, even in a place as foul as this? He sat hunched forward with his elbows on his knees. Erin watched him as she moved automatically with her massage equipment, bringing out small bottles of essential oils, followed by towels. Like a marine, she could have assembled her equipment in the dark.

They felt like props to her now, though. Erin knew that's exactly what they were.

Andy. She liked the sound of the name. Liked the wholesomeness of it. Liked anything that could distract her from the task at hand. She'd felt so unhealthy these past few months, so terribly…sinful, she realized. The thought surprised her. She didn't consider herself religious in any way. No, the dirt she felt was not sin but a sense of self-betrayal. As she finished maneuvering her table, Erin pictured the face of her mentor, Kathy. Kathy had been the greatest teacher Erin ever knew, a woman of knowledge and confidence. Erin graduated massage school with no other thought than to emulate Kathy and make her proud. She'd been successful until the past year. The economy had tanked and times were difficult. Her younger brother finally wanted to start college and needed money.

She had to do what she did.

The expression she imagined on Kathy's face was not one of pride.

I'm betraying her too, Erin thought.

Andy. She looked over at him again. He met her gaze only a moment before glancing elsewhere. *He's so shy.* She liked that, too.

She could already tell his physique was perfect. Of course, a person's looks had never been a consideration to her when she entered massage school. As Kathy had taught her, all people needed to feel secure about their bodies, and massage therapists could help them do that by being professional and nonjudgmental. "There are people who suffer needlessly because they're afraid of going to the doctor and being asked to take their shirt off," Kathy had said. "People are exposing themselves to you because they're desperate for healing. Don't ever fail to honor that. Always use your hands to lift up, not to tear down."

This was different. Erin knew she was here to be feasted

upon. Her massage training and her tremendous skills as a healer were now merely a legal pretense, a cover for this sordid encounter—her tenth.

Once more she pictured Kathy's disappointed look.

"I'm ready," she said.

"The shirt," he said.

Erin looked down at her chest. "O-okay."

His tone surprised her a little. It was direct but not demanding. It carried more suggestion than command, as if they were a couple on a date. Still her fingers had problems with her blouse. They always did when the client wanted her to strip right away. She did not know why she kept wearing anything more complicated than a T-shirt to these sessions. Shirts with buttons just prolonged the agony.

The shirt came off. Andrew still did not move. He was looking at her now, his face still so oddly innocent. Andy. She smiled. She so badly wanted him to be different than her first nine creeps. He must be different. Most guys were rubbing their crotch by now, acting like they weren't even going to get on the table. Andy was rubbing his temples like he had a serious headache.

"Are you okay, Andy?"

"What?" He dropped his hands and looked around, as if surprised to find himself in this room. He clasped his hands in his lap.

"All right. I got mine off. How about you?" Erin said. She hardly believed herself. She sounded coy, flirtatious. She'd never acted like that before.

He stood up and unbuttoned his shirt to reveal a deliciously toned chest. She marveled at his physique. Why had he sought out an erotic massage? What had brought him to troll the Erotic Services section of Craigslist? Her previous clients had been horrible losers who e-mailed her fake photos. Andy hadn't even had a photo, making her fear the worst. But he was so attractive. Was he married? Or just a thrill seeker?

Erin pondered these questions as she came around the table. She patted the surface, asking him to approach.

For a moment, he did not move.

"What's wrong?"

"Nothing," he said. "I just wanted to—memorize you. Smile for me."

He made a motion with his hands, as if he held an invisible camera.

Erin shifted a little and smiled. He made a clicking motion with his finger. "There you are. Your picture's developing in my head. I'll never forget you now." He rubbed his temples again and grimaced.

Great. He's weird after all.

"I think you actually could use a massage, Andy. We'll see if we can work out whatever muscle tension is causing your headache, then—"

"Let's just get started," he said.

As he came forward, he unbuckled his belt and unbuttoned his pants. Erin swallowed. All her usual nervousness was there, but this time she actually wanted to touch her client, to enjoy the firm suppleness of his muscles. She could sense his headache and knew she could remove the pain if he'd just let her. But he was not here for that. As he unzipped his fly, she saw a big erection in his underwear. His right hand slipped under the waistband and grabbed it.

"Andy," she said, her voice trembling, "please at least get on the—"

His hand came out of his underwear holding something. His erection was gone. Erin barely had time to register it was not his penis creating the bulge. He had something tucked in his crotch, something he now aimed at her. A chemical spray struck her face, blinding both eyes at once. She toppled back, clawed hands waving. She struggled to right herself, coughing, sputtering. A strong, implacable grip threw her onto her own massage table. She was choking too much to cry out, even though her terror tried to work itself out in a scream. She heard the rest of her clothes tear even as she felt the room's cool conditioned air shock areas of her body she never thought would be exposed.

Cold steel bit into her wrists.

He was cuffing her and strapping her down!

"Oh please don't! Please don't do this to me, Andy!" She started to scream.

The young man shoved her own shirt deep into her mouth. She tasted traces of detergent and perfume in the fabric. Her vision began to clear. Through tears, she saw him standing there, head cocked as if listening to a whisper.

He looked down at her.

"They told me to tell you that my name's not Andy."

Those were the last words Erin heard.

1

KATHY BARRISTER'S FAVORITE LECTURE ROOM AT THE Academy for Healing Touch could accommodate twenty students and had doors on the side and the back. She was in the middle of answering a question on Monday morning when the back door inched open and a good-looking young man slipped through. He seemed conscientious about his intrusion, as Kathy saw a pained look on his face when he gentled the door shut again. The students did not hear him enter, and Kathy did not interrupt her talk, even as she thought to herself, *Now who is this?*

She was lecturing to a group of twelve eager massage students. The subject was anatomy, and she stood next to three full-scale laminated diagram posters of the human body. The amount of detail the posters presented always astonished and intimidated new Academy students, who never seemed to realize how much knowledge of the human body they needed to be successful massage therapists. Every year, Kathy eased them into the topic by first having her class name the man presented on the posters.

This class had decided on Herbert.

"As you can see on diagram two, Herbert has nearly three hundred skeletal muscles. The body is an integrated system. Disruption in one area will cause poor performance in another. Too often people assume that when their head hurts it is because of a problem in their head. The pain might really be caused from a problem with the muscles of the neck or back. Those muscles can transmit, or refer, the pain to other places for expression, such as the head. As massage therapists and healers, our duty is to bring the body into balance. Balance is wellness."

Kathy fought to keep her gaze trained on each student and not on the mysterious young man lurking awkwardly along the back wall. She loved looking at her students' faces. She enjoyed seeing them smile when they became aware of abilities they did not know they had. Watching students gain self-confidence in their talents and intuition was the special reward only dedicated, compassionate teachers received.

I've seen this man before, she thought, allowing herself a quick glance at him as she kept talking. But when and where? Was he a former student? No, he was too young. She doubted he could legally drink and then she smiled despite herself as she kept talking. *You're getting too old, Kathy.* She was only thirty-eight and the majority of each year's new class looked impossibly young to her. By reflex, Kathy looked over to the left of the classroom where Amanda was taking notes and looking at her teacher with a rare intensity. How old was Amanda? Twenty-two? She had a look that guaranteed she'd be carded in bars until she turned thirty. So young and already developing into one of the best students Kathy ever had the privilege to teach.

Amanda smiled at her.

Beside her, sitting perhaps a little too close, was Jim. He'd started at the Academy last spring. Jim was not taking notes, but he seemed attentive—to Amanda. *Puppy love*, Kathy thought with amusement, and smiled at them both.

"If you remember from our last discussion, each muscle has a hyperirritable spot called a trigger point." Kathy uncapped an erasable marker and began to draw on the glossy surface of the third diagram. "Not everyone agrees on the location of trigger points, but these are the commonly accepted areas." She began to make small circles along the body for the next several seconds. Then she stepped back.

"Poor Herbert must be in a world of hurt if all these trigger points are active at the same time."

The class laughed.

In the back, the stranger shifted uncomfortably. Kathy just knew the young man needed to talk to her and couldn't wait much longer. She checked the clock to her right. She wouldn't be ending the class too early if she stopped now.

"Okay, I think we'll leave today's discussion here for now. I'd like you to go into your study groups for the remainder of the session."

The students broke into their groups as Kathy walked past them. The young man seemed startled by the lecture's sudden end. She thought he was about to run out of the room. Kathy smiled and extended her hand. He offered his. Her initial observation had been right: he was essentially still a kid, maybe nineteen. He barely seemed old enough to vote. Seeing him up close, she became more certain than ever they met before. It had not been recent—six or seven years ago.

"Hello," she said.

He swallowed. Kathy could see the tension in him. She didn't need intuition to discern his agitation. *More than agitated.* The poor kid looked ready for a breakdown.

"Ms. Barrister?"

"Yes," she said, keeping her tone warm and welcoming.

"My name is Brad. You probably don't remember me."

She smiled again. "I was thinking from the moment you came in that I've met you before."

"I really apologize about coming in uninvited. I knew I shouldn't have snuck in."

"But it was urgent. Terribly urgent, isn't it?"

His face relaxed—a little.

"Ms. Barrister—"

"Please, call me Kathy. What's your name? I'm sorry, you're right. I just can't seem to remember who you are."

He squared his trembling shoulders. He was losing his inner battle for self-control, and Kathy's heart broke for him. She wanted to tell him it was okay, to just let his anguish out. She also knew that was likely the last thing a young man wanted to hear. He started to speak and his breathing hitched up and his face paled. Kathy reached out automatically to soothe him. The moment she touched him, he began to cry in earnest. "It's okay," she said.

She put her arm around him and thought to look back. The entire class was silent and all of her students were staring at her.

2

KATHY'S OFFICE HARDLY LOOKED LIKE IT BELONGED TO THE Academy's founder and chief academic administrator. It was cozy and not ostentatious, the walls lined with pictures of previous students in moments of professional success. In fact, that very morning she printed off a photo from a student who had just opened her own private studio in Boston. It was a fantastic, inspiring picture, but Kathy still wasn't sure where to tape it.

She opened the Academy for Healing Touch seven years ago, sensing that her highest duty was to pass on what she had learned from her own dedicated instructors and train a new generation of massage practitioners and healers. It had been a bold and difficult move at the time, especially since she was regarded as one of the top therapists in Pennsylvania. She even sat on the state's licensing board for massage practitioners, a thankless task that gave her a sickening sense of the politics behind even the simplest decision. She regretted that the rigors of teaching and administrative work, combined with her state obligations, took so much time from her private practice. She missed healing people directly but knew her students would go on to help more people than she ever might alone.

Kathy brought the young man to her office for privacy. Her office featured a large window that looked out onto the school's central hallway. She liked to be visible and approachable in her office, but now she lowered the blinds. For the first several minutes he just cried, and she had excused herself to get him water and let him find his composure. When she returned she was surprised to find Amanda loitering outside the closed door, looking worried.

"Who is he?" she said, coming forward when Kathy came into view.

"I don't know."

"He looked so hurt," she said. "It wasn't just the crying, either. There's something deeply wrong. I'm sure about that."

Kathy smiled and nodded. Amanda's own sense of intuition was powerful. Combined with a quick intelligence and an outgoing personality, she would become a very skilled massage therapist and a vital member of her community. But right now she was still a student—and perhaps a little too nosy.

"I'll take good care of him for you; don't worry." This made Amanda blush and stammer. Kathy added, "Just return to the study group. It's the best way to help both of us at the moment."

Amanda opened her mouth to reply, obviously thought better of it, and left.

Kathy reentered her office. Her guest stood up. He wasn't crying any more, but his eyes remained red and tear-stained. He now seemed more embarrassed than sad, and Kathy could see he was almost furious with himself. *Boys learn so quickly to never show weakness or pain*, she thought, offering him the water. He took it and drank deep.

"Thanks," he said.

"You're welcome. May I get you anything else?"

"No."

She was not surprised by how gruff and curt his demeanor had become and let the tone pass.

"Okay. Then may I get your name?"

He looked at her in surprise and then more embarrassment. She felt his anger and humiliation ebb. His shoulders sagged and he sat down. Kathy stared a moment. There were two seats on the front side of her desk. She preferred to talk to students sitting next to them rather than from across a barricade. But this wasn't a student. Reluctantly, she sat down in her official chair, and they regarded each other over the clutter.

"My name is Brad. Brad Haley."

Haley She didn't even have to search her memory.

"Erin. You're related to Erin Haley, aren't you?"

"I'm her brother."

She nodded. "Of course. I met you at her graduation ceremony—the Academy's very first." She remembered now how there'd been something unusual about him being there. What it could be she had no idea. What brother wouldn't come to his sister's college graduation? "You've certainly grown up."

"Maybe. I'm nineteen. I was finally getting my act together and starting college."

She shifted forward and crossed her legs under the desk. "You're not now?"

"No," he said, and his eyes became unspeakably sad again.

What could have so devastated this promising young man?

Her intuition kicked in. For one rare moment in her life, Kathy didn't like what it told her.

"Is it…Erin?"

He nodded and stared down at his lap. Soon he was crying again as he struggled to talk. Kathy simply listened, touching the base of her throat and now feeling grateful for the bit of space the desk put between them. Brad looked so in need of mothering she'd already be cradling him if he were within arms reach.

"I guess you don't know," he said. She had to lean forward to hear.

"Don't know what, Brad?"

"Erin…she…she…"

Now Kathy did rise and come around the desk. She sat down beside him and took his hand with a sure grip. Her intrigue and confusion had shifted entirely into dread, and she had a cold block in her throat that made breathing hard. *You have to stay in control or you're of no use to him or yourself.* She took a deep inhale and willed herself to relax and accept the terrible news she sensed coming.

When it did come a moment later, Kathy's self-control was taxed to the maximum. As Brad began to get out the story, his voice became dead and matter-of-fact, terribly toneless as if part of him had died with his sister. No doubt it had.

"And this happened almost two weeks ago? Why hasn't it been on the news?"

"The police won't even tell me anything. I guess they're afraid giving away any details could jeopardize the investigation."

Kathy mulled this.

"I don't even know where or how she got murdered!"

"Edgerton. She was from Edgerton, right?"

Brad nodded. "Sort of. We spent a couple of years with an aunt who lived there. Even our aunt got tired of it and moved away, but Erin really liked the place. I didn't. I hate small towns."

She nodded. She happened to adore them, but she wasn't a nineteen-year-old man, either.

"Small towns don't have much going for them. That's part of the problem I'm facing. The Edgerton Police Force doesn't exactly have Sherlock Holmes on the payroll. I bet they're missing all sorts of clues."

Kathy thought the critique unfair but understood Brad's frustration and said nothing. Edgerton was a township about a hundred miles from the Academy. It was small but not tiny—enough population to get their share of crime. She remembered now how Erin had planned to return to Edgerton and start her practice. She also remembered Erin calling her in the most breathless voice to say she'd gotten her first client—Edgerton's very own mayor. "Look at me with all the political connections," she had joked. There had been conversations about marketing and growing her business. Kathy had listened to her confess fears about getting any more clients and then state her determination to overcome all diversity. Kathy found herself smiling at the memory.

"Is there something funny?"

"No—no. I was just remembering Erin. I'm sorry if I came across as disrespectful. It's the last thing I would want to do. I just regret that I didn't keep in touch with her. She was special."

"She was all I had," Brad said.

Kathy thought about that and remembered what had made Brad's presence at Erin's graduation so unique. Their parents had been killed when Erin was fifteen and Brad was seven. A car accident of some sort. His sister had practically raised him. Kathy could hardly imagine such a childhood. Her own father died when Kathy was seventeen. His death made the bond between her and her mother passable—a considerable achievement considering they'd never seen eye to eye on anything.

"I'm so sorry, Brad."

"I'm not after pity!"

"I don't pity you, but I am sad for you. I remember your situation. I'm trying to understand."

"I want to know who killed my sister. I want to know why Erin had to die."

She nodded but said nothing, at a loss as to what she could do.

"Erin made everyone happy. She was the only person in the world who never made an enemy. So why her?"

Kathy swallowed. Her throat was dry.

"I wish I had an answer for you."

Brad balled his right hand into a fist. Kathy tensed a moment.

"She loved you," he said.

Kathy blinked, not sure she heard right.

"I don't know if she told you. I don't know if you can really understand how much you meant to her. Erin and I, we didn't have much in the way of role models. Some days were pretty depressing. It made us close. She'd hug me at night while I cried because I didn't understand why Mom wasn't coming back. Do you have any idea what that was like for either of us?"

"No—and I won't pretend to. I wish more than ever we had stayed in touch after she graduated. We did for about a year, and then I heard nothing from her. I assumed she was busy with her own practice."

"She was doing okay. It got hard, especially with this economy. Edgerton's no place to get wealthy."

Kathy mulled this remark, uncertain about Brad's tone, which suddenly added a terse quality to its prevailing despair.

"She was one of the most gifted students I ever had. She told me a little about the struggles the two of you had. I thought maybe she saw me as something more than a teacher, but I didn't want to be presumptuous."

Brad laughed. For a moment, she thought he was mocking her. He had a wonderful laugh all the same, and Kathy was glad to hear it despite his sorrow.

"There was a time when you were all she talked about. I used to be sort of jealous she had such a cool teacher. I hated school."

Now Kathy laughed, but it sounded forced. She found herself suddenly overwhelmed with thoughts of Erin as a student. Kathy was a person to cherish most memories, but not under these circumstances. Thinking of Erin now was like enjoying light from a star she knew to be dead.

"Thank you for coming here, Brad, and telling me. If there's anything I can do—"

"There is," he said flatly.

"What? Name it."

He grabbed her hands. "I want you to help me find Erin's killer."

3

KATHY GOT LOU, HER BEST AND MOST EXPERIENCED instructor, to teach her afternoon Massage Ethics class and went home after getting Brad's contact information. When she learned the name and address of the motel where he was staying, she almost dropped her pen. Not the best part of town. Only a nagging, last-second doubt kept her from extending an invitation to stay at her place. A woman approaching forty, attractive but unfortunately and hopelessly lovelorn, bringing an emotionally vulnerable and rather cute, near-twenty-year-old man into her house—What could be wrong with that?

Tension throughout her back and neck muscles had brought on a headache. The massage teacher needed a massage herself, but for once it would have to wait. She had too much to ponder.

Kathy's house was a one-and-a-half story redbrick bungalow with earth-toned accents. It had needed major renovations when she purchased it nine years ago against the advice of her realtor. Something about the house had called to her. It was the first time Kathy's intuition ever sparked with an inanimate object. She simply knew she needed the house and the house, in a sense, needed her. Her boyfriend at the time, Dave, had thought this to be very weird until she pointed out he'd had the exact same reaction to his rusted 1969 Mustang.

"That's different," he had said, "because that's a car and I'm a guy and guys just know when it comes to cars."

The difference was that Kathy's house was now looking terrific, due to hard work, trial and error, and more than a few seminars at Home Depot. Her ex-boyfriend, wherever he was, was no doubt still driving a clunker. She should have known they were not a match. His favorite movie was probably *Christine*.

Unlike her office, the only mess in her house when she entered was the mail. She had a letter slot in her front door and envelopes were constantly spilled across her foyer when she came home. She stooped to gather the numerous letters and proceeded into the living room. Her furnishings were an eclectic mix and match of decorating designs, furniture and art that appealed to Kathy's sense of balance and calm rather than any specific style. She knew she'd starve to death were she forced to make it as an interior designer. She'd never liked uniformity or thought of buying furniture in sets; she knew of no such thing as a completely uniform taste. She was a just a mutt when it came down to it and had long since quit worrying about whether a vase she liked went with the foyer table it was to sit upon. Life was too short to bother with such concerns.

She thought of Erin.

Life was much too short.

Kathy tossed the mail on the coffee table and went upstairs. Half of the upper level had been remodeled into a home office and private practice area. It was three hundred square feet and cozy, perfect for her bamboo massage table and product storage. The business aspects, her computer and work desk, were concealed behind an elegant partition, leaving the practice area uncluttered and streamlined. Not that her clients would particularly care. Since starting the Academy, her private practice now consisted of a few close friends and ten original customers who came to her for their appointments.

She stopped at the top step and looked around. Had something in the room changed? It only took a moment to realize the difference was in her. *One of my students is dead. One of my students has been murdered.* Kathy could hardly conceive of it. She'd never considered the fact that something so awful could happen to someone she cared for. Perhaps like a mother thinking of her children, she'd just assumed her students would all outlive her. A foolish thought, she realized. Massage therapy attracted people from all walks and demographics. While most were younger, several of her students had been twenty or thirty years her senior. They were men and women burned out by their old careers and seeking something more rewarding and spiritual. But as far as she knew, her older graduates were all still alive.

Kathy went around the partition and turned on her computer. Brad mentioned some scant local news coverage of Erin's murder. She now sought it out on Google. A string of false hits came up—websites for a country musician and a molecular biologist; Facebook and Myspace pages; other random things. Her fingers trembled as she realized she needed another keyword. For a long moment she just sat there, unable to type anything. Then she added, after the words Erin Haley: *murdered.*

She could not stifle a small cry at the new results. There were not many. Kathy fought off an involuntary anger at that fact—did no one care about her death? But the pain ran deeper than that. A few hours ago she hadn't even known. Kathy knew she'd been the closest thing Erin had to a mother. *I wasn't there for her,* she thought, taking a deep breath. She fretted over the fact. Students came and went, no matter how special they were. She'd heard teachers talk about how being an educator gave you a special awareness of time. One day you were teaching your first class of children and then suddenly you were teaching their grandsons. You did what you could for each student, and then you moved on.

Life moved on.

Not for Erin. Not anymore.

She remembered Brad sobbing and suddenly imagined Erin crying in the last seconds of her life. A deep chill shook Kathy's body. One reason Brad had seemed so immediately familiar to her was his resemblance to his sister. Same eyes, same mouth, same dark hair. His entrance was like that of a ghost. Now Kathy realized how appropriate the comparison was.

At last she brought her attention to the screen. The first link was the *Edgerton Gazette*. It provided only sparse information. Small town, small paper, small blurb. She did note one thing that struck her as immensely odd. Erin died in a motel room. Why? She'd lived in Edgerton, why would she need a motel room? Kathy was shocked by the number of assumptions she'd made about Erin's murder. She'd imagined a jealous ex-boyfriend or a random act of violence—nothing she could associate with a motel.

In Erin's own hometown.

She pushed back at her troubling thoughts. She had to focus on the task at hand. Realistically, though, what could she do to help Brad? She knew nothing of forensics or criminal investigations. In Brad's plea for help, there seemed to be something else involved. Did he think Kathy knew something about his sister that he could only guess at? Was that why he had played up the past bond between Erin and herself, to goad her into revealing something crucial? Suddenly, Kathy felt more ill than she had in years, sick with both grief and confusion. Sick above all because she knew absolutely nothing that could help Erin's brother.

She scanned the few other search results, frustrated by the meagerness and repetition of the details. Even the motel's name was not provided. Finally she turned the computer off and went around the partition into her practice room. The light was dim and soothing. She turned on a CD of delicate music she normally used as background for her massage sessions and sat down. *I'll drive to Edgerton.* Wasn't that the only possible thing she could do? Even if it accomplished nothing else, she might find some closure for a wound she'd only just discovered. She closed her eyes, aware that her thoughts were spiraling down a dark and bottomless drain.

4

KATHY SET OUT EARLY TUESDAY MORNING WITHOUT telling Brad. Keeping him in the dark had seemed ridiculous to her at first, and she wasn't entirely clear on her own motivations. She'd had a dream last night. In the dream she and Brad walked into the motel room and found Erin's body on the bed, like it had never been discovered. Brad fled screaming, ran into the road, and was struck by a car. More nightmares followed. They all involved the discovery of Erin's body and Kathy being somehow unable to keep Brad from dying as a result. She woke half wishing she still kept a dream journal by her bed. She'd given it up years ago after deciding her subconscious was just too embarrassingly mundane to commit to paper. What was it telling her now—that she felt responsible for Erin's death? She knew she felt guilty because she had not kept in touch with Erin. Her failure to protect Brad in the dream was an extension of her fears that she had failed Erin as a mentor.

It took her a little over two hours to reach Edgerton. The

drive itself was more relaxing than she expected. Normally Kathy hated to drive. Cars sometimes seemed designed for space aliens with bizarre spines. Her personal motto was cars are terrible for massage therapists but terrific for their business. Some of her first clients were people with back pain caused by long driving commutes. Quite a few of them had been auto mechanics as well. She'd won a marketing award from the area Chamber of Commerce for one of her earliest advertising spots about being "the auto mechanic's body mechanic." She'd started her practice by offering fifteen-minute chair massages at auto repair shops and dealerships. It was, in fact, how she'd met her previous boyfriend, Dave-of-the-rusted-out-'69-Mustang.

She smiled and turned on the radio. The highway was not busy, and the sparsely populated land on both sides afforded gorgeous views. Kathy could almost believe that she was going on some journey of personal discovery or driving to visit an old friend. She tried to direct her mind toward anything other than the reality of driving to locate a crime scene with absolutely no plan to follow beyond a printout of every motel in the area.

Kathy was fine until she saw the first sign announcing the Edgerton town limits. Then dread crept upon her, as if she sensed being unwelcome here, and the heavy weight of her task settled onto her chest. Edgerton was not a sprawling community, but even it boasted almost a dozen hotels. Before she realized it, she'd passed the first on her list and slammed on the brakes to turn back. It was a Motel 6.

Kathy parked by the reception office and stared. *Am I really going to do this?* The building didn't look seedy enough to be a murder scene. It would be nice to think murders happened in designated places that most people with common sense avoided. Instead you could go stay in the nicest hotel in the world and maybe someone got raped on your bed the night before. She shuddered. *Nice, positive worldview, Kathy,* she told herself, and got out.

There were only three other cars in the lot. When she entered the office, the counter clerk said, "Hello!" with an overly attentive friendliness that suggested desperation. Kathy cringed. One of the first business lessons she taught her students was the art of polite confidence. There was a world of difference between making a customer feel wanted as opposed to needed. Or as she had quipped in the first industry article she published about creating a private massage practice: "Make your customer feel wanted, and they'll walk away feeling kneaded."

"Hi," she said.

The clerk leaned forward. "How many rooms would you like?"

Kathy looked around to see if other people were behind her. The clerk smiled like he was ready to wash her car to make the deal.

From pity, she reached into her purse and pulled out a credit card without even asking about price. She saw herself doing this and wondered if she'd gone mad. She didn't plan on spending five hours in Edgerton, much less the night.

"Just one for the night," she said. When the clerk handed her the key, she stared at it as if it were a relic. Kathy became flustered. Why in the hell was she renting a room she didn't need?

"I'll swing by for it later," she stammered, pushing the key across the counter. She was very sure she'd never be picking it up.

The clerk looked puzzled and simply shrugged. With her money now his, he just looked bored. Kathy hurried out to her car and returned to the road becoming increasingly upset with herself. *Are you going to buy a room in every single motel in the area that looks like it's about to go under? You didn't even find out if Erin died there!*

"Stupid."

She drove to the next one on the list. This time she pulled in and went right to the desk. She encountered the same I'm-begging-you-to-rent-a-room demeanor from a much older clerk, but this time she steeled herself. *Sorry, Charlie.*

"No, I'm not looking for a room. I need information, actually. It's sort of delicate."

"Delicate?"

"A colleague of mine—an ex-student, actually—she—well, I learned that she—" Kathy wondered if she should have been surprised the words flowed like her throat was a clogged pipe. The clerk furrowed his brow like he was listening to a foreigner.

"My friend was murdered." There. She had said it. She thought she could say anything now, no matter how improbable. "I don't have much information, only that it happened in Edgerton. At a motel."

Kathy was on completely alien ground as the clerk ducked his head a little as if stung. Kathy felt the impulse to apologize. It felt like she'd accidentally insulted him or something.

"That little girl was your friend?"

Kathy didn't much care for hearing a late-twenties woman called a little girl, but she considered the clerk's age and let it pass. "Yes, she was. Her name was Erin Haley."

"That sure is sad," he said. "The world's just a horrible place sometimes."

Kathy hated that the past twenty-four hours were starting to make her agree.

"I just need to know where it happened."

"Well, it sure wasn't here!"

"Good," she said quickly. "This is such a nice place, I'm sure nothing like that would ever happen here. But can you tell me where it did happen? I couldn't find out anything on the news."

The clerk frowned.

"Please. I drove a long way."

He slapped at the countertop. "Why? Hell, you could have just gotten a phone book and called around."

Kathy had already considered that option and rejected it. Too easy to lie over the phone, and bad economy or not, a murder wasn't the sort of advertisement anyone wanted. But mostly the idea of just calling felt like shirking her responsibility. She couldn't begin to address her emotions in the impersonal brevity of a phone call. She needed to be in Edgerton doing legwork. She needed to earn her information—for Erin.

"I needed the air," she said with a small smile.

The clerk stared at her. Then he tore off a piece of office stationary and wrote on it. He handed the paper to her. Kathy saw an address and a crude road map.

"That's where you want to go. You'll see a sign that says Jim's Motor Inn. Those in the know call it The Johns Motor Inn, though."

"Why?"

He just laughed.

"Because it's where all the hookups happen. Prostitutes meet their clients there."

"Thanks," Kathy said, barely able to get out the word. *She couldn't have possibly heard him right.*

"You won't find that kind of crap here, though," the clerk added as Kathy reached the exit. "Just in case you're looking for a safe place to stay tonight."

"I already have a room," she said and left.

5

I'D HAVE NEVER FOUND THIS PLACE, KATHY THOUGHT AS she parked in front of Jim's Motor Inn. It was on the other side of Edgerton, almost beyond town limits. And it wasn't on her printout. The promised sign was more like a wall plaque. Despite the inn's apparent obscurity, the parking lot, though small, looked full. Clearly, this was a place that some people knew about. She felt uneasy as she stared at the rows of doors. Was prostitution happening behind them right now? Surely the old man had exaggerated its reputation a little. But even so, why had Erin come here? Kathy hated even allowing herself a suspicion.

Edgerton was founded and incorporated just over a hundred years ago. Jim's Motor Inn looked almost as old. It seemed almost historically dilapidated, and yet it had a tacky freshness to it as well, as if built to be always just out of style and out of place. The exterior walls had a distasteful stucco texture that reminded her of wads of chewed gum. The building was painted an odd version of beige, the color of a water-damaged book. Kathy didn't think she could find such a pigment anywhere even if she wanted it. It was the type of tint that only came from terrible fading and neglect. Probably the building once possessed a cheery yellow appearance in a brighter decade. Based on the clerk's innuendo, Kathy doubted the people who came here cared much for the sunshine hours.

Despite that, however, the overall area seemed struggling toward respectability. There were new corner shops and young trees here and there. People who looked anything but lewd walked about, passing the building without a glance at it. Did they not know about it, or had they chosen to ignore it as an embarrassment they couldn't eliminate? Kathy began to hope that the old man just didn't know what he was talking about or had lied to her. There was no reason to feel especially worried that Erin died here. Despite appearances, it was probably a very respectable motel.

Kathy got out and walked into the main office, where the hopes she entertained dimmed again. The inside was even more of a wreck than the outside. Three acoustic tiles missing directly above the check-in desk revealed ancient ductwork. The vinyl floor was cracked and peeling and had odd blister bubbles, as if exposed to great heat. The real disaster, however, was the woman behind the desk. For a moment Kathy was not entirely sure she was alive. Her face had a heavy makeup matte applied poorly so that it accented rather than disguised her wrinkles, which crisscrossed her face like dusty spider webs. She had a stoop, yet despite the worn and haggard appearance, Kathy sensed she was not terribly old—perhaps sixty. She could almost feel the poor woman's muscle knots in her own back and shoulders as she watched her head droop toward the countertop.

"Hello," Kathy said.

The woman raised her head and smiled. It was a cunning expression that made her eyes eerily hard and beady, like a very hungry person too proud to ask for food.

Kathy came up to the desk. "I'm sorry to trouble you. A good friend of mine had some trouble—" She looked down and gave a little laugh at the absurdity of the phrase. When she looked up again, she squared her shoulders confidently and said, "My friend Erin Haley was murdered in one of your rooms."

The woman blinked once and exhaled like someone who has always been a heavy smoker. Kathy could easily imagine two white plumes coming from her nostrils. When she finally spoke, her voice was gravelly and dead. "That a fact?"

"Yes, I believe so."

"Well, I didn't do it."

Kathy nodded, startled.

The woman raised her hands. "Well then? You got something else you want?"

Before she could even think of it, she said, "I want to see the room."

Am I crazy?

The woman chuckled a little. She reached under the counter and retrieved an unlit cigarette. "Can't do that, I'm sorry to say. Crime scene. Your little friend's death is costing me quite a lot, you know that? She died in one of my best rooms—I like to think of it as my suite. Until the police finally take the thumb out of their ass and finish whatever it is they're looking for in there, I can't make a dime off it."

Kathy gaped at the woman, appalled. "Sorry to see you're so put out."

"Put out." She laughed. "That's a good way to describe everything that happens here, I suppose. Guess your friend learned that shit happens outside the toilet sometimes."

Kathy backed up a step, actually afraid of the confusion and rage building inside her. She'd never met anyone in her life that she hoped to never meet again—until now. But she kept control, aided by a rising sadness for this person who seemed so beaten down by life. The woman so obviously had nothing left inside, so she lashed out at anyone who did. It was as close as she could come to feeling.

"Which room was it?"

"Number eight, if it means anything to you. Curtains are drawn; door's locked. But put your ear to the door. Maybe you'll hear a ghost."

Kathy turned without another word and gulped air as soon as she was outside. The whole world seemed different after her encounter with that woman—somehow less bright. She had been drained, of course. The old woman was an energy vampire, the type of abusive people-user she so often warned her students about. Kathy closed her eyes and summoned herself back to balance through force of will.

Room Eight.

She came to the door and stopped to stare at the number. The door was the same impossible beige as the building. This was the color of sadness. And behind it, horror. She shook her head and hugged herself. *Well, at least I've accomplished this much. I've found where she died.* But where was the closure she hoped to achieve? Her psychic wound felt even wider now, and she knew she'd never have peace until she got into the room and saw exactly where Erin died. And then what? Did she really think just standing there would make things better? Kathy suddenly felt compelled to go on seeking Erin's murderer, seeking something nameless that had haunted her dreams without her even being aware of it. She wished she could define what it was.

She moved forward to put her right palm flat against the door. This was as close as she'd get. It was as close to putting her hand on Erin's coffin as she could come. "I'm so sorry, Erin. I don't know what happened or how you came to be behind this door. But I know you were a good person. I wish there was something else I could do."

"Who are you?" Kathy jumped and turned to find a man holding up a gold police badge in her face.

6

T HE PLAIN-CLOTHES OFFICER LOWERED HIS BADGE AND stepped back. They were both studying each other closely. Kathy blinked in a swirl of confusion. She knew this man.

The detective was evidently thinking the same thing. He smiled and said, "Kathy? Kathy Barrister?"

"Greg!"

An excited psychic hug was exchanged between them even though neither moved. *Greg Beacon*, she thought in amazement as she looked up and down his sturdy, six foot three frame. He wore dress slacks and a blue shirt, the long sleeves rolled up halfway to his elbows. He still looked as boyish as ever, despite a few strands of gray in his brown hair.

"You shave now!"

Greg grinned at her, and Kathy smiled back. The shift in her emotions was so powerful that she felt dizzy. Finding Greg alive and in front of her was nearly as great a shock as learning Erin had been killed. When they were best friends in high school, he was just a tall, lanky kid who perpetually looked in need of a Norelco. He was clean-shaven now. The lankiness was gone too, she noted with approval. He filled out that shirt nicely.

Kathy watched him put the badge away. Despite their initial friendliness, he seemed just as confused as she, and when he spoke next his voice had a serious, official tone. "I'm afraid that room is sealed for an investigation—something I hope you have nothing to do with. What are you doing here?"

Kathy had no idea how formal or informal to be with him. She glanced back at the door. "It's not really all that long of a story—so far."

"Have you been in Edgerton a long time?"

"I pretty much just got here."

"There's a café a few blocks north of here. Do you have time to talk?"

She nodded but took another look at the door. When she turned back, she found him studying her very carefully.

"What?"

He offered a grim smile. "Well, Kathy, I hate to say that you're acting suspicious. But, Kathy, you're acting suspicious. There's a murder scene behind that door."

"I know."

Greg raised his eyebrows. He directed her to start walking. She presumed he was leading her to the café—or his squad car. She didn't see either.

"What else do you know?"

"I guess not a lot," she said.

"Just enough to come hang out around a crime scene?"

"Well, Greg, it's not how I get my kicks, I assure you."

They walked the rest of the way to the café without talking. Kathy stared ahead and tried to organize her thoughts. Greg Beacon, a policeman? In some ways, she supposed the career fit. Even in high school he had a superserious side and a fondness for order, if not necessarily neatness. Hard to believe they hadn't seen each other in twenty years. No, that wasn't quite right. They'd reconnected at their last high school reunion ten years ago, but it had been difficult to talk much about anything substantial. He'd had a girlfriend; she'd had a boyfriend. They hadn't even exchanged e-mail addresses.

They reached the café. Greg held the door open for her, and she glanced at his fingers. No wedding ring.

She knew her interest wasn't right. Today was about Erin. Greg was a decidedly welcome reminder of the past, but just now he almost seemed like an obstacle to the day's progress.

Kathy was starting to feel anxious, and she knew it showed. Normally she could hide her feelings well, even though she believed that doing so led to bad health. But in high school, when they were best friends, Greg had always known her state of mind. She'd loved that about him, but right now the memory of it scared her. She doubted his police work had done anything to dull his skills at observation.

They sat down at a table for two. A pretty waitress came over and said, "How are you today, Detective Beacon?"

"Good, Sandy. Can we have a couple of menus?"

"Sure," she said and left.

"Detective?"

He looked quizzical. "I showed you my badge."

"They all look alike to us civilians, I guess. I didn't realize the Edgerton Police Department would even have a detective."

"I'm with the county, actually. Edgerton falls in my jurisdiction. I like to stop in here when I'm around."

And just how often is that? Kathy thought, glancing at the waitress when she returned. She seemed polite, but Kathy thought she looked a little anxious at seeing Greg with company. *Probably how his girlfriend thought I looked at the reunion ten years ago.*

As she started to look at the menu, Greg surprised her. His voice dropped its previous formality, and he spoke exactly as he did at seventeen. "Kathy, do you still drink that soy-based crappola?"

She stifled a laugh and smiled at him. "Yes, as a matter of fact."

"You can actually get a soy latte here, did you know that?"

"I did not."

"Just letting you know."

"I already know what you want," the waitress said, grinning.

Kathy looked between them. Greg was smiling back and the waitress seemed to consider this a small victory. *Nice. Young, pretty, and a mind reader as well.*

"I may need a minute or two."

"That's fine," the waitress said. Annoyingly, she and Greg simply chatted away about affairs in town while Kathy scanned her options. No talk of local murders in the waitress' sunny world.

"I'll have an English breakfast and a scone, please." She wasn't sure she wanted either, but it got the waitress away from them.

Greg leaned forward, and Kathy could tell he had not switched back to his earlier detective attitude. If anything he seemed to be acting younger, closer to her memories of him. *My God, he's adorable.*

"It's really good to see you, Kathy, regardless of the circumstances."

"You too, Greg. I had no idea you were in Edgerton."

"Where do you live?"

He's not subtly questioning me, is he? She shifted from a small internal discomfort and then told him.

"Back in the city? That's fantastic! I didn't realize you were even in the state. For some reason, I thought you had moved to New York."

"That was for college," Kathy said.

He shook his head. "It really has been a long time."

She gave a nod of agreement. She could see the last twenty years pass like a movie. She remembered the final time they got together as kids. It was the end of summer following high school graduation. Her father had died in January, and she'd relied heavily on Greg for support. He'd been there for her, of course. Her relationship with her mother was complicated and both thought it would be better if Kathy went to school out of state. She left for New York to study at CUNY. She already had her major decided—psychology.

Greg had shocked her and everyone else by declaring he had no interest in college. His parents argued about it with him constantly, and she knew he resented the way she took their side. She just cared too much about him and saw not going to college as throwing his life away. In those days, Kathy thought a standard four-year degree as the end-all, be-all of education. Now, of course, she understood that people had their own callings besides some bachelor's degree. The lack of fulfillment her psychology degree gave her was proof of that. She supposed Greg had made this discovery for himself long before she ever did. *Always one step ahead in the game*, she thought.

"I'm sorry I lost touch. Your parents moved away while I was in New York. I thought you moved with them."

"No," he said, grinning. "As soon as you left, I decided to join the army."

This revelation floored her. Greg—in the military? But it did not seem so astonishing when she considered it more. Even his personal disorder and messiness had always had its own arrangement and logic. Giving him another quick once-over, she could see the military training still showed in his body. He was lean and poised. The slouch that typified his high-school posture would never return.

"So what do you do in the city?"

"I'm a massage therapist and healer."

His nose wrinkled a little as he processed this. "Like, alternative medicine?"

She laughed and reached forward to take his hand. "Same old Greg. If aspirin and bloodletting don't solve your ills, you're obviously dying, right?"

The waitress returned, and Kathy noticed her pause when she saw them touching hands. Kathy decided to let her touch linger.

The waitress sat down the scone and tea without making eye contact with Kathy and then put a large glass in front of Beacon. Kathy raised her eyebrows as she appraised it.

"Chocolate milk?"

"What?"

Kathy shrugged. "Milk seems a little wholesome for a detective working a seedy city like Edgerton."

"But it's chocolate milk. See, I'm a bad cop."

"Positively rogue."

She sipped at her tea while he chugged down half his drink on the first swallow. He dabbed at the corner of his mouth with a napkin and said, "Want to tell me what's going on?"

It was jarring how fast he'd snapped into detective mode. It was also a little disappointing. She wanted to talk to Greg, not Detective Beacon. Greg reminded her of happy, mostly carefree times. Detective Beacon reminded her of Erin's murder.

She took more of her tea and sighed. "I know the woman who was killed in that room."

"Oh?"

Kathy looked at the scone and wondered what to divulge. What was Greg thinking about all of this? She'd been able to read him well enough when they were teens, but now she found there was a mask between them. Whether the mask was over his face or hers, she couldn't decide.

Willing to gamble, she said, "Her brother came to see me. He told me what happened."

"What brother would that be?"

"Don't do that."

"Do what?"

"Act like you don't know."

He smiled. "Act like I don't know what?"

"Me, if nothing else," she said.

He took another swig of chocolate milk. She could see him weighing his options. "Okay," he said. "So you were friends with Erin Haley?"

Kathy had to stifle a gasp when he said the name. The separate pasts Greg and Erin represented for her had been coming closer and closer together in the past half hour, but as soon as he said her name they collided. *What have I gotten myself in to?*

"We were colleagues."

"What's her brother's name?"

"You really don't know?"

"I just want confirmation."

She said Brad's name, not confident about anything. It just seemed too late to go back now. Greg only nodded and finished the rest of his drink. "I guess he doesn't have much faith in the police if he went to you."

"What's that supposed to mean?"

"Nothing insulting," he said fast.

"He's frustrated and afraid. And alone in life, I might add. He says the police won't tell him much about Erin's death. I don't know if he means you or someone else. She was his sister, Greg."

"It may seem harsh, but being family doesn't necessarily make someone privy to every detail of a police investigation."

"From what I can tell, you're not saying much to anyone. Is that because you don't have anything to say yet, or is there another reason?"

She thought he looked a touch nervous.

"Kathy, what other reason would there be?"

"I don't know. But something's not right. I can sense it."

"Sense it?"

"Intuition," she said.

He chuckled at this, causing her to frown.

"Don't knock it, Greg. We all have it and that includes you.

We just use it in different ways, depending on our training. Surely a detective knows the body reveals what the mind tries to hide. Sometimes it does so in ways that activate our finer senses and tell our minds to be alert. Sometimes the signs are more obvious. For instance, your personal comfort level has dropped visibly in the last minute. You're a bit paler; you're sweating a little. That tells me I'm on to something when I suggested Erin's murder might be more complicated than I first thought."

He drummed his fingers on the table. The waitress came over again. "I'll have another," he said.

Kathy looked at him, waiting.

"You mean tells, like in poker. Players give away their cards by how they react in certain situations. But I play a lot of poker, Kathy, and I'm pretty good at not revealing anything I don't want to reveal."

"An experienced massage therapist would eat you for lunch in Vegas," she said with a smile. She looked down at the table as Greg's second glass arrived.

"Are you going back to the city right away?"

"I'm not going anywhere until I see inside that room."

"What?"

She shrugged. "You talked about playing poker. So there—I just put all my cards on the table. Erin's brother asked me to help him find out who killed his sister. There's no real way I can do that, as far as I know. I'm sure I told myself I was driving down here to help Brad, but really this is about me. Erin was a student of mine. I want some sort of closure."

"Her body is not in that room, Kathy. What good will it do for you to see where she died?"

She took a deep inhale. "Do you remember my father's death?"

He stiffened. With caution, he said, "Yes. I'll never forget that."

"Remember how I didn't ever want to go into the room where he died? Remember how I said I'd never go in there again?"

Greg nodded. He looked grim.

"You're the one who convinced me I had to do it. Hell, you came over and held my hand. You opened the door to the room and we walked in there together."

He shook his head. "That was different, Kathy. That was your house. You can't live in a house and have one room you refuse to never enter."

"Oh, I assure you, you can," she said. "If it wasn't for you, I'd have never stepped into my dad's study ever again. I cried. God, how I cried."

He reached across the table for her hand. "I remember."

"I came back, after you were gone, and I cried even more. It was one of the most powerful healing experiences of my life. It was far more cathartic than standing at my father's grave. Everything about him was still in that room, Greg. His spirit, in a sense. I'd have denied myself that connection if it wasn't for your help."

She could see he was overwhelmed. She didn't mean to pour so much of herself out—it just happened. And as she talked, she realized that it really was the reason she wanted into that motel room. It was not just about saying goodbye. It was also, in a way, about saying hello.

"Kathy," he said, "I don't think you'll find much of Erin's spirit in that motel room. Not anything you'd want to know about, anyway."

"I'd like to be the judge of that."

"Damnit," he said, voice dropping. She looked at him and he smiled. "You're sizing me up again, right? Looking for my tells. I admit I'm on edge."

"So there is more to Erin's murder than what's being said."

"Don't jump to conclusions." The waitress came back again

with a third glass of chocolate milk even though Greg hadn't asked for one. This one looked far larger than the last.

"Just in case you get really thirsty," she said, and left.

"Someone's sweet on you," Kathy said.

"Your intuition tell you that?"

"No, but that liter of Nestlé Quik on the house does. You come here a lot, Greg?"

"Best chocolate milk in town," he said with a grin.

Pity then about their scones.

They walked back to Jim's Motor Inn and their cars without talking, though the silence was not uncomfortable. Their high school days had been a mix of loud get-togethers and tomblike study sessions. In a way, Kathy felt like the entire time in the café had been a study session, except this time their subject was each other. She certainly wanted to quiz him more about his life. He wasn't married—that much was clear. What happened to that woman he brought to the high school reunion? They could still be together but not married. There seemed no way to bring up such a question and wished she wasn't so desperate for an answer. She supposed some tests ultimately judge the giver rather than the taker.

They stopped in front of Erin's door. Kathy fell back into a somber mood. She knew Greg understood, which is why his smile puzzled her.

"What?"

"Do you remember when you broke into the school gym on a dare?"

She did as soon as he brought it up. "Eleventh grade. Me and Elizabeth. You chickened out."

"It wasn't the right thing to do," he said.

"Well, boredom was our punishment for doing it. Our entire goal was to get into the boys' locker room. I guess that seemed like forbidden fruit at the time," she said, laughing. "But when we got in, we just stood there. It looked exactly like the girls' locker room, in fact, except with fewer stalls—and a different odor. Why do you bring that up?"

"Two reasons. That gym was a hell of a lot harder to get into than this motel room, I can promise you that. In fact I'm sure a few people have already been inside. I've been doing a bit of surveillance on the side. When I saw you, I naturally assumed Glenda gave you the key—for a price."

"Glenda?"

"I saw you come out of the office. You must have met her."

Kathy shivered just remembering her. "I did. I thought Glenda was supposed to be the good witch."

"Not a thing remotely good about her," Greg said. "When we told her we needed the room sealed off, she got this look in her eye, the kind people who turn their homes into haunted houses in October and charge their neighbors an admission fee. Pissing off the police is pretty ballsy for a woman in her occupation."

"What occupation would that be?"

"Never mind," he said and looked embarrassed. Kathy let it pass. "My point was a simple one. You can get inside this room if you really want to. No city has the manpower to enforce every ordinance on the books, even when it comes to a small town like Edgerton. They sure can't spend time staking out a door every minute of the day—even if what's behind the door might be more important than they know. But that's not all I'm getting at. Let's say you do get in. Is it going to be like the gym? Are you just going to stand there, shrug, and leave?"

Kathy thought about it and came up blank. "I don't know. If it's all I can do for Erin, then I at least want to try."

"You can't help Erin, Kathy."

"It's her brother than concerns me."

"He concerns me too."

Kathy stared at him hard. "Why?"

Greg smiled. "Just a hunch."

"Some would call that intuition," she said.

"Maybe."

"My intuition tells me you're going to let me into this motel room."

He nodded. "Your intuition is pretty presumptuous—and also damn good. I can't let you in yet. I need to clear some things first. And I want to talk to you some more."

"Anytime, Greg."

"This evening. Over dinner. Now don't get a strange look in your eye, I'm not trying to hold you hostage here. It'll take a few hours to get the paperwork done. And since you and I both have to eat, we might as well do it together."

"Do it together," Kathy said, feeling every bit of her mischievous high school personality roar back to her.

Greg looked mortified and defenseless—as he'd always looked when she teased him. Kathy thought if she pushed, he'd have let her into the motel room then and there. But she didn't. It would be wrong to use his embarrassment like that. She also knew her emotions were jumping too quickly between extremes right now. She needed to be as clearheaded as possible when the time came. And it will come, she told herself. She had to be patient for herself, for Brad, and for Erin.

They had dinner together at a little mom-and-pop Italian restaurant that bested anything Kathy had tried at restaurants three times as expensive. They talked about almost nothing but his plan to take her into the room and the procedures he had followed for clearance. He would allow Kathy access but he wanted Brad there too. He confirmed Brad's story about not telling him where his sister had died. "The kid was a wreck. Keeping some information from him is probably for his own good. No need to tell him where she died. It would only hurt him more."

"How would knowing where it happened hurt him more? He'd already been told she was murdered."

Kathy observed Greg's gaze dart down to his plate. He

seemed uncharacteristically shy, and she realized her stupidity. *The notoriety of the motel, of course*, she thought.

She said, "I don't know a lot about Edgerton, but I thought in most small towns everyone knows everything that's going on in just a few days anyway. No real secrets."

"Oh, there are plenty of secrets. And when it comes to The Johns—sorry, that's what the Edgerton PD calls Jim's—people don't seem to say a whole lot. Half the town doesn't want to acknowledge it exists."

"There must be some people who want it closed down. A murder would surely be ammunition enough—"

"Edgerton is trying to revitalize itself, but The Johns is still on the very edge of town, in the bad neighborhoods. Think of it like a wart, Kathy. If you get a wart on your face, you get it removed real fast. If the wart is on the top of your foot and isn't causing any real grief, maybe you leave it alone. Maybe you even forget that it's there most of the time."

Kathy nodded. They ate a few moments in silence.

"Why do you want Brad there now? Surely he isn't a suspect."

"Edgerton's not some backwater that's never heard of a DNA test. He's cleared of the murder so far just on lack of evidence."

"Then why bring him—"

Greg leaned across the table at her. He'd been half in Greg mode, half in Detective Beacon mode most of the dinner. Now she saw him going full detective. "You were right, Kathy. Erin's murder is big—I think. Not everyone else does. There is a lot of stuff I'll probably never be able to share with you. I have to stress that. I don't want you to think that I'm being a bastard on purpose."

She nodded, stunned by his admission. What could Erin have been involved with? Kathy knew so little about crime that her imagination created scenes she knew must be ridiculous. She saw Erin as a spy or a gun smuggler. Perhaps as outrageous as either scenario was, they were preferable to what she'd been steeling herself to hear. The Johns? Greg had yet to say anything explicit but even a neophyte could make an inference.

Greg's cell phone rang and he excused himself. While he was gone, Kathy took out her own phone and called Brad. He answered right away. His voice was shaky as he responded to the information she gave him.

"I can come and pick you up if you think you'll have trouble driving," she said.

"But you're already in Edgerton."

"It doesn't matter. Greg—Detective Beacon—wants us to meet at ten. That's plenty of time for me—I get up early. The main thing right now is safety. Do you feel like you'll be able to drive?"

"Yes," he said after a moment. She told him to meet her at the Motel 6. She didn't know if he knew about The Johns or not, but she didn't want to risk it. *Looks like I'll be sleeping there after all.*

"Thank you, Kathy. I can see why Erin thought so much of you."

She was contemplating that with some sorrow when Greg returned. It amazed her how fast her spirits could lift just by seeing his face. She told him about her phone call to Brad and he nodded. He did look very tired, and she could intuit that his own phone call had been important and troubling. So much responsibility rested on his shoulders now. The burden of it radiated off him in such a mature, adult way that Kathy found it difficult to reconcile against the lackadaisical teenage boy she'd known and liked. *Liked*, she thought, looking up so suddenly it caused Greg to notice, smile, and glance down shyly at his plate.

They finished their meal and lingered in the restaurant for over an hour, talking about anything other than the murder. Greg's parents were alive and well. He asked about Kathy's mother.

"Too stubborn to die," she said. Her mother was actually in excellent health and happy in a retirement community in Florida.

Finally they both seemed to run out of steam at the same time.

"It's been a long day. We should pay and get out of here," Kathy said. She started fishing through her bag for her credit card.

"I don't suppose you have a place to stay?"

She pulled out the receipt from the Motel 6 and showed it to him.

"As a matter of fact, Greg, I do."

7

SHE HEARD BRAD'S KNOCK. IT WAS HALF PAST NINE AND Kathy's was thinking that on normal Wednesday morning she'd be teaching her Anatomy class right now. She'd already gotten other faculty to cover for her on Friday as well—just in case. She welcomed Brad inside and sat him down. Based on appearance, there was no way he had slept last night.

"I'm sorry I didn't tell you I decided to come to Edgerton. It was a spur-of-the-moment decision."

"That's fine. I really appreciate the help."

"I'm not sure how helpful this will be, to tell you the truth."

"I'll take anything I can get, Kathy."

She nodded and noticed him looking around. He seemed almost too tired to be anxious. Maybe in a way it was good that fatigue had deadened his senses. The idea ran completely contrary to all of Kathy's beliefs about the body and awareness, but her beliefs had never come up against a murder before.

"We're going to take my car, Brad. It's not a far drive."

He inhaled and held it a moment. Kathy watched with

concern. He's not going to be able to handle this, she thought. I'm probably not going to be able to either.

"This is really happening," he said.

"It doesn't have to. We can delay. I can't imagine the amount of stress you're under. I don't know what we're about to see."

He shook his head. "I don't want to wait. The police have already kept me blind long enough. I hate them."

Stay gentle, she told herself.

"I think you'll find Detective Beacon is a very helpful man. He's not exactly with the Edgerton police, so I don't know if you've ever met him before."

Brad laughed.

"What is it?"

"Beacon," he said. "Sounds like bacon. You know, like a pig. Police, pig."

Kathy waited a moment, gathering herself. In a quiet voice, she said, "I don't approve of comments like that, Brad."

His expression changed immediately to embarrassment. "Sorry."

Kathy sat down next to him. "I actually went to school with Detective Beacon, so I can vouch for his character."

"I didn't mean anything by it. I'm just pissed off. My sister's been killed. I should know anything the cops know."

"I think sometimes the police really do have reasons not to share everything, Brad. We'll get through this."

They left her room and got in Kathy's car. Her dread built as they drove and she cast sideways glances at Brad to see if he showed any reaction to the change of neighborhoods. The houses got worse, dumpier, neglected. The yards became more a composite of assorted weeds rather than grass, and all the fences seemed to either lean in toward the houses or fall out toward the street. Nothing about the next few hours was going to be straight. But Brad showed no reaction until they pulled into The Johns' parking lot.

He ducked his head and squinted at the horrible building. "Is this—is this the place?"

"Yes," she said. "Are you familiar with it?"

He shook his head. "Like I said before, I didn't have much interest getting to know this town."

Thank God. They got out and she looked around for Greg's car. A moment later, she saw him driving in. Behind him was another vehicle, an Edgerton police squad car. Brad tensed and shoved his hands into his pockets as they parked.

"What's going on, Kathy?"

"I don't know. Greg didn't say anything about an extra person."

Greg and the second officer walked over to them. The officer said, "Mr. Haley," and extended his hand at Brad. Brad didn't shake it right away.

"I'm sorry our last meeting was under such bad circumstances. I guess our second meeting isn't much better."

Kathy looked at the second officer. He was young, maybe right out of training, and had an overly officious look to him. His body was tight, and his movement economical. He seemed built for a much larger city and knew he was just biding his time in Edgerton until something better became available. She noticed he carried a clutch of latex gloves and some sort of clear baggy that might fit over their shoes.

"This is Officer Porter," Greg said, introducing Kathy in a formal, stiff manner. Kathy took this as a cue to act like they barely knew each other.

"Officer Porter," Greg said, "is your official chaperone for the next thirty minutes. I'm here to maintain the integrity of the crime scene. And this is a crime scene—as you're both only too well aware. Once inside, your emotions may get the better of you. They may cause you to do something that is unacceptable. Unacceptable in this case has a very broad definition. Don't be surprised if you find your actions severely restricted. Is that clear?"

Kathy and Brad looked at each other. Both nodded.

Officer Porter said, "Mr. Haley, Ms. Barrister, I cannot stress this last point enough. Contaminating the crime scene is a damn easy thing to do. Defense lawyers head straight for it as a way to challenge evidence. Messing up here could impair our ability to bring Erin's killer to justice—so do exactly as I say."

They waited until Kathy and Brad had nodded again.

"Officer Porter—the door."

Entering the room was one of the most difficult experiences of Kathy's life. Going into her dad's study after he died paled in comparison. She went in third, after Officer Porter and Brad. They wore plastic covers over their hands and feet, though after being warned about contamination Kathy had expected to don a HAZMAT suit. The officers weren't joking about their freedom of movement being restricted. Officer Porter was already telling Brad exactly where he could step. She looked at Greg, who held the door for her. He just nodded for her to proceed.

The room had a musty, unidentifiable odor. The doors and windows had obviously been shut a long time. The nasty scent seemed to be an amalgam from a whole range of filth emanating off the carpet, walls, even the sheets. Kathy had a sickening, hollow gut sensation when she realized it might also include lingering traces of Erin's death. It was not a large room by any stretch. She remembered the old clerk, Glenda, referring to it as her suite. Her idea of a joke, Kathy guessed. The lights were not on and the dirty carpet and dull paint, a beige not far removed from the exterior color, combined to give the area an oppressive murkiness. She jumped a little when the door shut, despite Greg's gentleness with it. Officer Porter gave her a warning about not straying from his designated path.

Greg turned on the light. She blinked once and decided she liked the room better in the dark.

I am a fool. What closure could she find in a room that reminded her of a body ripped apart? The carpet was stained in layers of filth like tree rings that indicated nothing but bad years. The last ring, the most visible stains, were clearly from blood. It was evident even to an untrained eye. Erin's blood. She put a hand over her mouth.

Officer Porter let out a sigh. He glanced around in a respectful but bored manner, as if he'd been forced to bring students to an art exhibit he'd stared at one time too many. She did her best to understand his reaction, as inappropriate as it seemed with Brad in the room. She looked over at him. Brad seemed very lost as he stared around. She couldn't read his expressions at all. *If I stay too long in here, I might never be able to feel happiness again.*

Still, she stood firm. She owed that much to Erin's memory.

"Greg—Detective Beacon, I mean—" she started. She didn't get to finish. Brad let out a wail and seemed to go insane in front of her. He ran over and kicked the cheap, rickety dresser along the far wall. His foot bashed through the decayed particleboard, splintering it. The protective plastic hung from the wood shard like a flag of defeat.

Officer Porter was on him in an instant. He was shouting and cursing at both Brad and Greg. In an instant, she realized the two of them were not at all friends and that Porter was Greg's subordinate. He was yelling at Greg, saying he knew letting them in here was a mistake. Greg shot past her. The problem was subduing Brad without contaminating the crime scene further. Kathy could see they didn't want to just take him down on the carpet. They seemed to be wrestling and steering him toward the door, avoiding the bed and other furniture as best they could. Kathy jumped off Porter's declared safe area and into a corner. Meanwhile, Brad refused pacification. He escaped Porter's grasp and moved like a wild animal trying to avoid a cage. He shot toward the back of the room screaming Erin's name over and over again.

Kathy stood paralyzed. She had a clear run for the door and knew she should make it. As is, she was just another unwelcome body taking up precious space. But she couldn't stop watching. She worried about both Greg and Brad. The two men were squaring off across the broken dresser with Officer Porter coming in from the right. As he made his lunge, Brad hurled himself over the cracked dresser and scrambled directly at her. Kathy opened her mouth to scream but nothing came. Brad was looking right at her but not seeing her.

Kathy dodged in the last moment and to her utter horror landed atop the nasty mattress, its old, disturbed sheets flecked with blood. *But not enough blood*, she thought, a flash insight that didn't matter now. She screamed once from disgust, kicking herself away and distracting Greg, who pivoted to help her. As he did, Porter lunged past and took Brad down near the door. He drove his right knee into the boy's back, driving the oxygen out of his breadbasket. Shaken, Kathy listened to the small hitches of Brad trying to get his breath back. He was still trying to say, "Erin."

"So much for not disturbing the goddamn crime scene," Greg said, brushing Kathy off. "Are you okay?"

"Yes," she said. She fixed her attention on Brad. Officer Porter still had his knee in place. Brad looked like some abused puppy under the policeman's intimidating presence. Porter unhooked wrist cuffs from his belt and opened them.

"Officer, is that really necessary?"

"Your damn right it is," Porter said.

"Kathy—"

"He's out of his mind with grief. My God, his sister died here. His only family!"

She stared hard at Greg, hoping to sway him despite thinking it would be easier to bring Erin back to life. But he surprised her by saying, "Let him up once he's cuffed, Allen."

There was a small silence before Officer Porter complied with a crisp, "Yes, sir." Kathy had never heard two syllables convey so much contempt.

Brad got his breath back and winced loudly as Porter

hauled him up. He couldn't straighten his back. "Goddamn pig!" Porter's expression went murderous in a flash and Kathy jumped forward to avoid a second crime scene. Greg was at her side and together they separated them. Kathy helped Brad lean against the wall. He was doubled over and panting from pain. Near them, Greg and Officer Porter were in a quiet shouting match.

"What the hell is all this?"

Kathy turned to the door. Glenda stood there like some awful demon. She pointed at the broken dresser and started to curse a blue streak. Greg turned to her with almost the same expression Porter had for Brad. She and Brad seemed not to exist to the rest of them.

"I—I can't straighten my back," Brad said, barely audible. "I think it's broken."

"It's not broken," Kathy whispered. "I'm going to lift the back of your shirt. I need to get a sense of the muscle damage, okay?"

He nodded, gasping with the pain. She raised the shirt about halfway up his torso and made a fast but delicate assessment. Porter's knee had left an obvious, angry red impression on his pale skin. Under normal circumstances, lacking a massage table, Kathy would have put him on the bed or floor. She shuddered at the idea of him stretching face down on either in this disgusting room.

"Hold very still. I know it's difficult, but try to ease your mind. I'm going to extract as much of the pain as I can."

"E-extract?"

Kathy placed her right hand on his back and closed her eyes, summoning her own energy toward her palms. The argument raging behind warred with her concentration. Gradually that noise faded as she became one with herself. She moved her right hand in a series of delicate gestures and arrangements as she sensed and scanned the damaged tissue.

Brad became very still. She sensed his pain. Her thoughts

went out from her own quiet mind, and she sensed the sudden tranquility of the room, this horrible room that had soaked up such amounts of negative emotion and energy that its very air was polluted by it.

"Beacon, what the hell is going on?"

"Don't know, Allen. Kathy, what are you doing?"

She broke her meditation a second to scold them. "Please quit talking. I need all of my concentration to sense how deep the damage is."

"I can tell you that it's pretty goddamn deep. I kneed him real well."

"Quiet, Porter."

The two officers kept bantering until Kathy gave up and turned to them. She was most disappointed in Greg, but knew he didn't understand. "You're making it extremely hard to undo the damage you've done."

"The damage I've done? He's destroyed the crime scene. I don't believe this, Beacon."

Before Greg could intercede, Kathy said, "I need quiet so I can intuit the exact nature of the physical stress on his body."

"Intuit? What, you got Spidey Sense or something?"

Kathy and Officer Porter glared at each other. She could see Greg looking anxious. Maybe he was in serious trouble because of Brad. Kathy couldn't let that distract her now. Brad's pain was almost calling to her. She turned back to him after giving Greg a pleading look.

"I'll handle it from here, Allen."

"This is total bullshit."

"I'm still officer in charge."

"Yeah, until you're not," Porter said.

The door shut behind them, leaving Kathy alone with Brad and Greg. Porter took his condescension with him, an immediate boost to Kathy's concentration. She held her palm above Brad's skin, about half an inch from touching. As her hand moved, Brad's sharp intakes of breath ceased and he became very still as Kathy completed the task over the next five minutes. "Okay," she said. "See if you can straighten your back."

Brad tried, tentative at first, then with increasing confidence as he found himself pain-free. He reached around to touch the small of his back and beamed at her.

"That was amazing! What did you do to me?"

"It's called Reiki," she said. "It's a type of energy healing. It takes quite a long time to learn. Even longer to master."

"You must have done it."

She smiled.

Brad continued to rub and probe at where the pain had been. "I'm completely pain-free. I can't believe it, after the way that pig—"

She caught Greg's glare and said, "Quit using that term, Brad. I don't approve of what Porter did, but he was trying to bring you under control. You were out of it. Look."

They stared at the dresser. Brad looked all around the room like he was seeing it for the first time and his arms came up to hug himself.

In a very small voice, he said, "Erin was murdered here."

Kathy didn't think twice this time about hugging him. She put her left arm around his shoulder and drew him close to her. He was a sturdy, well-built young man, but just then he felt like a fragile bunch of sticks against her torso.

She released him when Greg cleared his throat. Brad swiped at his eyes and could barely meet Greg's stare. "I'm sorry," he said. "Have I ruined any chance to catch Erin's killer?"

"We'll have to determine the extent of the contamination later. Your back seems better."

Brad gave Kathy a sheepish smile. "I don't know how to explain it. Fifteen minutes ago I thought I'd be paralyzed for life. Now the pain is gone."

"You still need to be checked out," Kathy said. "Reiki is

a powerful tool but it's not designed to cure your ills in ten minutes. You may wake up with more pain tomorrow."

"I'll make arrangements for you to get it checked," Greg said. "You'll have to come with me."

"Why?"

"Apart from the general paper work I need to fill out about…this mess…you've just destroyed someone else's property."

Brad's voice rose. "I was upset!"

Greg shrugged. Kathy didn't like the dismissive attitude it conveyed but realized she could help best by shutting up.

"Am I going to jail?"

"Yes. But you're not being booked."

"Then why am I going to jail?"

Greg sighed. "Kid, the police have to keep their computers someplace. Now go outside and wait with Officer Porter. I need to talk to Kathy alone."

8

GREG SHUT THE DOOR AND LOOKED AT HER. HE ADOPTED a smile of disbelief as he raked his fingers through his short hair. "This might end up being the worst mistake of my professional life."

"Your professional life? Does your private one have a bigger doozy?"

"No comment."

Kathy said, "You were right about everything, Greg. I thought the idea of not telling Brad where his sister died was callous. I now see I didn't understand what I was talking about. I've never seen anyone react like that."

"You don't think he was faking?"

Kathy's eyebrows shot up in astonishment. "No! Do you?"

Greg seemed to consider, then shook his head.

"You already said he definitely wasn't guilty, Greg."

"Of the murder. But maybe he was an accomplice. Don't scoff at me, Kathy. Family members manage to off each other all the time. Most murder isn't random."

"What motive would he possibly have?"

Greg conceded that at the present he had nothing in mind. "But he's not as squeaky clean as he looks. He did some time in juvie for repeated vandalism. His psych profile isn't the happiest reading material either. He—"

"I don't want to hear any more. It's none of my business, and I don't want to feel prejudiced against him. He may be a troubled kid. I don't doubt it, considering his circumstances. But it's got to be a gigantic leap between breaking someone's window and killing your own sister."

Greg walked past her and around the bed. Kathy followed his progress, studying the room again. She no longer felt overwhelmed by its atmosphere. She looked at the bed again, seeing the rumpled area where her own body had fallen in the melee. Not enough blood, she thought again. Suddenly she asked, "Where was Erin's body found?"

"What?"

"Where was she killed, Greg?"

"In this room," he said with cautious intrigue. "Isn't that enough for you?"

Kathy stepped toward the left of the room, on Greg's opposite side. The bloodstains were heavy and more pronounced here. The stains were not in a splatter pattern. It was as if the blood had dripped off a long straight edge. It reminded Kathy of a time in the early days of remodeling her house, when she had placed a bucket of paint on a wide board suspended between two ladders. The bucket was mostly empty when she accidentally tipped it over, and the paint had dripped from the board edge to the floor in a similar line.

"Something else is gone besides Erin's body, isn't it, Greg?"

She studied his reaction, knowing it was the truth. She waited for him to speak, curious to see if he would lie or not.

"Yes," he said.

"There was a massage table here."

He smiled. Kathy thought he did so against his will. "How the hell did you know that? More so-called intuition?"

"No," she said, not liking his tone. "It's simple so-called observation. Erin brought her massage table here. She must have been meeting a client."

"Something like that," Greg said.

"A massage client."

He chuckled.

"Goddamnit, Greg! I taught Erin how to be a massage therapist. She was great at it. She came to Edgerton to start a legitimate practice. We're not just a bunch of girls working in some parlor waiting to jerk a guy off."

"Kathy—"

"Maybe whoever did this told her he was a business traveler. I don't know. But if Erin brought her table with her, she must have thought she was here to give an actual massage. Simple as that."

She could tell Greg was on the verge of challenging her, and she had her blood up to defend Erin's honor to the end. Instead he pointed at the carpet.

"We noticed the odd blood pattern too and thought he must have placed her on some sort of structure. But we didn't find a table, Kathy."

Kathy processed this and looked down again at the stains. A moment ago she had felt excited by the observation. Now she only felt sadness and horror. Erin's blood. Erin's passion—smeared into that nasty carpet.

"These massage tables, they fold up, don't they? Are they easy to carry around?"

"Yes, but you'd definitely notice someone toting one. They—"

Her gaze returned to Greg, who reacted to her trembling. He reached out to her.

"What is it, Kathy?"

"Erin was one of my favorite students. I knew she had no money. It was my gift to her."

"What? What was your gift?"

"I gave her my old massage table as a graduation present. I was just wondering if she still used it—and if she was killed on it."

9

Her name was Melissa but all her friends called her Missy. She was twenty-four years old with a college degree that had nothing at all do with her day job as a jewelry clerk at Sam's Club.

It had nothing to do with her second job, either.

Her night job.

She had never heard of Erin Haley or her murder, but they both lived in Pennsylvania. Melissa lived in Brunz, eighty miles northwest of Edgerton and even smaller in size. She was just one of a population of around five thousand, and at times she felt she was the only person around who didn't make and sell clay pots or wood figurines. Some pronounced the town's name to sound like "bronze." Others, to sound like "Bruins." But Melissa always made it sound like "brunts," as in "bear the brunt of." Her entire life here had felt like she was bearing the brunt of a lousy upbringing, a lousy economy, and a lousy life. She knew there was a whole world outside of Brunz that one day she would taste. One day—once her mother died.

"Mom, I'm going now. I won't be back until very late."

She said this for her own satisfaction. Her mother was unconscious, knocked out again by the pain medication that kept her cancer bearable. She would not wake up for hours. Melissa shuddered to think what would happen if she did. Last week she had returned at two in the morning to find her mother weakly calling out her daughter's name. She had been saying it for hours. After that, guilt-ridden, Melissa had upped the dosage. She didn't think it fair that she felt guilt. As a child, Melissa remembered the times she woke from a nightmare and called out for her mother. She wasn't there, having snuck out to some bar as soon as she got her daughter tucked in. Why should Melissa feel guilt about the tables being turned?

After locking the apartment door behind her, she pulled a piece of paper from her purse as she headed outside to the parking lot. The paper had driving directions followed by more personal instructions. Her client tonight promised to be strictly vanilla in terms of his needs. No handcuffs, no spanking, no weird mommy issues to work out in some role-playing fantasy. *No, I guess the mommy issues are all mine tonight*, she thought and slammed the car door.

She advertised herself on Craigslist as an erotic masseuse. Almost everyone online did because it provided legal cover. The e-mails back and forth about the type of massage being solicited was just a game, more mutual protection against a prostitution charge in case either party turned out to be a cop. Tonight's john actually seemed to really want a massage. Surely he wasn't that clueless, but it was going to be interesting either way. Melissa bet he turned out to be a seventy-year-old man who hadn't been touched in five decades.

What a life. Sam's Club all day, whoring all night. That was the price she paid for having a useless college degree in history. She still blamed her high school guidance counselor on that decision. You didn't secure your future by majoring in the past.

She turned onto a main traffic artery and checked the

directions again. Light traffic on the roads. Normal for a Tuesday night.

He'll be a gross, fat dweeb. Of course, he hadn't described himself that way. They never did—but they all were. Despite her degree, she'd never studied the history of prostitution. It fascinated her now that it had become her night career the past several months. The Internet and Craigslist had really revolutionized the process. She knew she'd never make it the old-fashioned, street-corner way. Her computer was her street corner and her Comcast high-speed connection was, in a manner of speaking, her pimp.

She laughed to think about it. After the drudgery of Sam's Club and dealing with her mother, her night job excited her with its illicitness, if not its realities.

What Melissa truly wondered about was the nature of johns in the computer age. Were her Craigslist clients exactly the type of men—and, once last month, a woman—she could expect if she did go hook on a street corner someplace? So far, excluding the one woman who was by far the best-looking of her clients, she'd gotten nothing but a string of depressingly lonely and obese men in their sixties whose lives seemed to revolve around doing the one-handed dance with their keyboards. Was the reward for the risking exposure on an actual street corner the chance of landing someone at least moderately successful or cute?

She had a desperate fantasy that one of her clients would end up being really hot and wealthy and they'd fall in love. Tonight's john said he was well built and handsome and twenty-five. The chances were good he'd lied about all three since he didn't provide a photo. Most of them never did, for all the obvious reasons. Hopefully he wasn't lying about his age like the guy two nights ago did. *Thirty-five years old my ass.* More like fifty-five. Tonight she just felt more like touching someone her own age, even if everything else looked like a disaster.

She pulled up at the specified motel and checked herself in the mirror, her mind almost entirely on accounting as she dropped her gaze to look at the gas tank indicator. Travel was such a terrible business expense.

Melissa got out and walked. The motel was built with an open courtyard. She crossed it and found the designated door. Right next to a vending machine, like he'd said. The one window was lit up but the curtains were drawn. She took a deep breath and knocked.

The door opened, revealing one of the cutest guys Melissa had ever seen.

"Andrew?"

He smiled at her. Behind him, further back in the room, she saw a massage table set up and waiting.

10

"This door's almost harder to face than the motel room."

Kathy wasn't looking at Greg as she spoke, but she felt the flat of his palm touch her back. They stood in a hallway right outside of Erin's apartment on Wednesday afternoon. Greg explained that Erin had lived here for two years and had no known boyfriends during that time. He said Brad had occasionally crashed with her when he passed through. Then he added, "In fact, I'd call him a serial crasher. Whatever friend offers him a couch is where he spends the night."

"You really don't like him, do you? I'm sure he's not a bad kid."

"It's not that."

"Then what is it?"

"The chaos," he said after a moment of thought. "You look in his eyes and you see someone with no plan for their life. Hell, the kid doesn't even have a plan for his day. Guys like that wake up and just do whatever, which usually translates into doing nothing good."

Kathy suppressed a smile but Greg caught a trace of it. "What?"

"It's just that I can see how you'll be as a father, that's all. Plus I don't remember you always being a hundred percent on point at that age."

"You're wrong there. At nineteen, I was in the army. I guarantee you I was on point every second of the day."

Greg produced a key. Kathy wasn't sure what to expect as the door opened. Obviously the police had already been inside. She half expected the apartment to be empty. They entered a clean, if slightly dusty, living room. There was a small bookcase in the corner and a metal-frame futon against the wall. She walked gingerly and heard Greg chuckle. "It's not like the crime scene. You don't have to tiptoe here."

Kathy nodded but kept her careful motions. *I feel like such an intruder.* She passed the kitchen and saw a few dirty dishes. The cozy, round dining table had two chairs. Kathy found herself staring at them and hoping Erin had not eaten alone too often. Greg said she hadn't dated in two years, but what about friends? Kathy remembered her as one of the most popular students in her school. How could she have no social life here? How could someone not miss her? Kathy hated where her mind was, trying to reconstruct Erin's emotional life from a few superficial glances at her kitchen. Still she sensed loneliness here, like an echo trapped in the walls.

"Kathy, look at this."

She followed Greg's voice down the short hallway leading toward the bed and bathroom. The walls were lined with pictures—not framed art, but personal photos just taped or thumb tacked together in a magnificent collage. The first were fading Polaroids. Erin must have been three or four years old in some of these, a serious-looking little girl standing alone. As Kathy and Greg progressed down the hall, the photos became crisper and the scenes changed. The Polaroids were now 35-mm prints. An older Erin held a little baby in her hands. *Brad's on the scene now.*

The scenes changed with greater frequency. How many different places did they live growing up? Who took these pictures? Erin was now seventeen or eighteen. Stunningly attractive and with hopeful eyes. When Brad appeared, he seemed sullen and moody. They continued down. The photos became still more modern. Digital photos she'd produced on a color printer. She gasped and covered her mouth, staring. Greg leaned closer.

"Kathy, that's you!"

"These are photos of her when she attended my school."

Greg looked at her. "I thought you said you were a massage therapist."

"I am. Bodyworkers aren't just people who come up and start karate chopping your back, Greg. They're trained professionals. They go to school. I decided to develop my own institution. My students learn anatomy and physiology. They learn modes of healing, ethics, business skills."

"No, seriously—you have your own school? You're like a dean?"

She smiled. "Just a little project I maintain on the side."

He whistled, causing Kathy to blush. She knew he was teasing her a little, but he was also genuinely impressed. "When you said she was your student, I just thought it was like a tutoring thing. I didn't know it was so…sophisticated. How come you didn't tell me more about this?"

"I don't know," Kathy said, touching the first picture. It showed her and Erin sitting together and smiling. There were more photos of the two of them, sometimes alone, sometimes with other students. The last photo with Kathy was a group shot. *My first graduating class*, she thought, looking at their happy faces as if they were all ghosts. How many had she kept in touch with? There was Lisa and Claire. She hadn't caught up with them in years. There was Michael, who had sent her two successive Christmas cards before falling off the face of the Earth. She'd heard from various others at random times. *I hope you're all well. I hope you've all found more happiness in life than you ever imagined for yourselves.*

"Are you okay?"

"Just a little overwhelmed," she said. Greg's hand rubbed her on the shoulder.

"She really did look up to you. You can see it in the photos, especially when it is just the two of you. She emulates your body language. I don't think that's a coincidence."

Kathy saw that it was true. *But I always knew it.*

"Why didn't I keep in touch with her? What was I thinking?"

"Hey there," Greg said. She only realized she was trembling because of how steady and firm his hand felt on her body. He led her back into the living room.

"It is okay to sit down? Will it mess up anything?"

"It's fine," he said. He sat down with her, his right hand never losing connection with her shoulder.

"I'm such a failure."

Greg's tone was sharp. "Why? This isn't your fault."

"It sure as hell feels like it is. I keep wondering how Erin could be so stupid. One of my specialties is massage ethics, Greg. Hell, I'm on the state licensing board for Massage Practitioners—another little side project. I drill into my students the importance of ethics and safety."

She saw Greg's confusion and explained.

"Had The Johns been a nice hotel, I would have expected Erin to tell the concierge desk that one of their customers had booked a massage with her and that she had arrived for the appointment. That's just what you do. It keeps everyone safe. Obviously The Johns doesn't have a concierge desk. But she was doing an outcall massage at a seedy motel. She should have let someone know the exact details of the appointment—

where she was at, who her client was, what she was going to do. You document everything. I stress all of this now. But Erin was in my first class of students. I got better over time as a teacher—a lot better. Maybe that first class got cheated."

"I think that's ridiculous," Greg said.

Kathy shrugged and rubbed at her temples.

Greg started to say more when his cell phone rang. He frowned at the screen. "I've got no choice but to take this, Kathy. I'll go in Erin's bedroom. I'll be right back."

She stared at the carpet as he left. The bedroom door opened and shut and she heard his muffled voice. Sighing, Kathy got up again. She wondered if the television worked. Any distraction would do. She went to the bookcase. It had two shelves and held about twenty-three titles. Most were trashy bestsellers. Kathy gave a wan smile.

Erin shared my reading tastes as well.

The second shelf was geared toward professional books. Kathy saw titles like *Basic Clinical Massage Therapy*, *Trigger Point Therapy Workbook*, and *Therapeutic Massage in Athletics*.

Kathy went rigid as her gaze locked on the last book.

Touching on Massage Practitioner Ethics: Building Your Business Right.

It was Kathy's second book, published just last year. Her right hand shook as she took up the text. She opened it and gasped. Page after page was highlighted and the margins were filled with notes. A deep sense of honor and confusion swept through Kathy. She could not have imagined anyone responding so completely to her work. Erin had studied all two hundred pages with the attention a lit major might give a poem. *But why didn't she call me? Why didn't she come see me even once?*

Why didn't I contact her?

The bedroom door opened. She returned the book and stepped back as he came into the living room. His face was a puzzling mixture of concern and something unexpected—excitement. She decided against asking him about it.

"First things first. Do you feel okay?"

"I'll survive," she said.

"They're through with Brad down at Edgerton PD. I've still got my report to write, but I can do it later. You want to see him?"

"Yes."

"Good," he said. "I may have something else to show you afterward."

11

Brad seemed steady in the small lobby after his release but he looked dazed. Kathy stepped forward and gave him a hug. He hugged her back with equal force. *He is a good person*, she thought. Erin's photos had jogged other memories for Kathy, one being a reminder of her hugs. Brad's embrace was so similar to his sister's in its genuine affection. Kathy felt in a way that she was hugging both siblings at the same time.

"Is your back okay?"

He nodded. "Thanks to you."

She handed him two sets of keys—for her car and her motel room. "My car is outside. Drive yourself back to the Motel 6. You're welcome to stay until I get back, or you can leave. If you leave, just toss my car keys on the bed and give the door key to the front desk. I'll pick it up later."

"I just want to get as far away from this town as possible."

"Are you sure? You're alone back in the city."

"I'm alone here too. Thank you so much for helping me, Kathy. Today was hard, but I needed to go through it."

She nodded. "You can thank Detective Beacon too."

His expression soured automatically at that, but he nodded in Greg's direction. Greg had distanced himself several yards to give them some privacy.

"He seems okay," Brad said. "Hell of a lot better than Officer Back Breaker."

"He was a little intense. Drive home carefully. Stay in my room if you feel like you can't go home right away. I may not be back until very late."

She saw Brad cast another glance at Greg.

"Okay," he said.

Greg came over as Brad left. Kathy smiled at him.

"You were talking about showing me something?"

He nodded. "Come with me."

She followed Greg through a door and into several corridors. The police department and jail were housed in a single building that didn't look very spacious on the outside. The labyrinthine interior surprised her.

Greg said, "When we investigated Erin's apartment, we removed certain things for further research."

"Her computer?"

"That's right. Clothes too."

"I get the feeling you're not going to be showing me Erin's wardrobe."

They stopped at a red, unmarked door. Greg produced a key to open it. "Wait here."

While Greg was inside, Kathy saw Officer Porter coming down the hallway. *Great,* she thought, thinking about ducking through despite Greg's order. When Porter saw her, he raised his hand up and made an ongoing circle about his ear with his index finger. The crazy motion. He passed without even a word.

No love lost there.

Greg stepped out. "Something wrong?"

"Nothing at all."

Greg had a laptop computer tucked under his arm. She saw it was a Mac.

They walked on until coming to a nearly empty office with no windows. Its only contents were a plain desk, an undersized chair, and a PC that might have been cutting-edge in 1998. It was hooked up to an even more ancient printer. Greg ushered her inside.

"This is where they've stuck me while I work on the case. Edgerton PD isn't too fond of a county investigator muscling in on their turf." He laughed. "After this morning, they're not getting any fonder."

"Your boyish charms haven't won them over?"

"I can't even get in on a game of poker with them. Too bad—I'd enjoy taking their money. Of course, in their opinion that's what county law enforcement does anyway: take funding away from the municipalities."

Greg plugged the Mac in and turned it on. "I hate these damn things," he said.

"Computers?"

"Macs." He gave her a sly look and added, "They're like the alternative medicine of computers."

"I'll take that as an extraordinary compliment to both alternative medicine and Macs. They both leave you with fewer problems with viruses."

"You have one, don't you?"

"A Mac, or a virus?'"

"Wisenheimer," he said.

She nodded and smiled. "Yes, I'm a Mac girl."

"Figures."

The computer came on. Greg sighed, referring to notes someone had written in a nearly illegible hand. Kathy squinted, following along. The notes were clearly guiding him through the unfamiliar operating system. Kathy watched screens pop up and change. Suddenly Greg stopped and turned to her.

"Showing you this was a difficult decision for me, especially after seeing the photographs in the apartment. But the one thing I know about you is you always value the truth."

She straightened sensing something horrible was at hand.

"I do," she said.

Greg nodded and proceeded. Kathy stared at the screen. Greg was going through Erin's browser cache, sifting through websites she'd been on. Suddenly the screen changed.

She bent over and leaned down, glaring. "What?"

They were looking at an Internet site. She recognized it at once—Craigslist. She'd sold her used car on it last year. This particular advertisement seemed to be selling something else. She only skimmed it. The words were familiar: massage, erotic services, trained massage therapist. She knew these ads existed, of course. The sex industry had been sullying the name of legitimate massage therapy for years. But this particular ad came with a picture.

Erin.

Kathy slapped the desktop. "I don't believe this! Someone used her photo."

Greg's voice maintained its calm. "You value honesty. Be honest with yourself, Kathy."

Her chest hurt. What was the difference between a heart attack and heartbreak? She gripped the edge of Greg's desk and stared at the floor.

"She posted ten identical ads over the past several months. That's not many."

"What the hell do you call many, Greg? Fifty? A hundred?"

"Kathy, there are people who post ads like this three times a day every day. Erin's pattern suggests she only did it when she was absolutely…desperate."

"Desperate for what? A customer? Erin was a massage therapist. A real one. She'd never—"

Greg sighed. "In bad times, people do what they have to do. Sometimes that involves making horrible choices."

"God, why didn't she call me? Didn't she even think I might be able to help? That's what I told them all when they graduated. I'd be there for them—I'd do anything I could. I would have given her money. It wouldn't even have been a loan!"

"Don't beat yourself up, Kathy."

"I was her teacher."

"Students sometime fail their teachers."

Kathy grimaced. She was a little stunned by Greg's accepting attitude. She read the ad again. Erotic massage. From an LMT—Licensed Massage Therapist. That's what infuriated Kathy the most. Erin had not only trained at her school, she was licensed to work by the very state board Kathy served on. And she turned around and used that hard-earned legitimacy as cover for work as a glorified prostitute.

She knew Greg was watching her. He said, "I think your jaw could crack a walnut right now."

"I'd like to crack a head."

Greg started to speak but Kathy waved her right hand to silence him.

"You have no idea, Greg. This type of stuff is used against massage therapists all the time. It gets in the public perception that massage is just a cover for sex. Ads like this poison the entire profession. People walk into a regular spa, a wholly legitimate business, and think they're going to get jerked off. I hear complaints about it all the time. But to know an actual LMT posted this…"

"It's a difficult economy, Kathy. People have to make choices."

"Erin made the wrong one," she said, and walked out to find a bathroom.

12

KATHY WAS SPLASHING WATER ON HER FACE. SHE FINALLY heard Greg's voice calling to her over the sound of the running faucet.

She turned off the water and leaned across the sink to the mirror straight ahead. She had beads and streaks of moisture on her cheeks. Some of them were tears.

"Kathy?"

Come in here and hold me. More than anything else, she wanted to place her forehead against his chest and go to sleep standing up and leaning into him.

"You okay, Kathy?"

He'd never open the door, not unless she went an hour without answering. And even then he'd probably find another woman to enter on his behalf. All his sense of order, all his desire for boundaries, probably started when he was a serious-eyed little boy being lectured on the strict difference between the men and ladies restrooms. It made Kathy smile to think of it. No, there was no chance of him poking his head in after her. He'd stand out there calling her name until his voice went hoarse.

She dried her face. She felt better. Better but drained. She opened the door and Greg was right there, backing away to give her space, looking too pensive and nervous to be a police detective. In fact he had an expression she'd could only remember seeing on one other person—Nick, her date to the junior prom. He had it when he arrived to meet her parents. It should have been Greg all along. In her heart of hearts she'd known it then just as she knew it now. *Another blind spot in my past.*

"Do you forgive me for showing you?"

"Of course. It was not about you, Greg."

That hadn't come out right, but she couldn't think of how to correct it.

"What will you do now?" he said.

She considered a moment and shrugged. "Go home. Meditate. Write another worthless book on ethics."

"Come back into my office."

He led her in and closed the door. She wouldn't sit down until he slapped the laptop closed and implored her.

"I decided to show you Erin's ads after the phone call I got when we were at her apartment. I think the call confirmed your suspicions—and mine too. There's much more to this than one murdered woman."

She shook her head in complete weariness. "I don't see how you can do this job, Greg. I'm sure it has its rewards, but right now it seems the nastiest, most depressing career in the world."

"Sometimes it is. You see, the phone call I got was telling me there's been another one."

"Another what?"

"Killing—of a sex worker. It was the same kind of setup. The victim offered 'erotic massage' on Craigslist. Her body was found last night."

Kathy nodded. She couldn't speak. Another Erin, she thought.

"They want me to see the crime scene as a special consultant."

"Special? I thought Edgerton was entirely in your jurisdiction."

"The murder didn't happen in Edgerton, Kathy. This one happened just outside of Brunz."

13

To her regret, Greg had to leave right away. She returned to her motel room. Brad's car was gone, and she found her keys on the bed. Picking them up, she understood his sentiments exactly. She didn't want to spend another minute in Edgerton either. She'd just lie down for a second and rest.

She woke up just after nine on Thursday morning when the cleaning maid knocked.

Dazed, Kathy stepped outside. Thursday. How could she have wasted so much time sleeping? She rushed to settle her bill and sped off toward the highway. She felt like she was fleeing a haunted town. Unfortunately she drove home with Erin's ghost very much in her car.

She entered her house in a rare attitude of defeat, ignoring the mail spread along the foyer floor. Her house seemed unwelcoming to her now, as if someone else owned it. Her body and mind were poisoned by fatigue and sadness. She desperately needed a massage to restore her depleted energy.

After all you've seen, you think about a massage? She disliked the scolding nature of her thoughts. Too many people thought of massage as some sort of luxury service, something trifling, unserious and even decadent. If she of all people started feeling that way, how could she help convince anyone otherwise?

She called her best friend, Sharon. They had both graduated from the Institute of Therapeutic Touch in Philadelphia, where they met as study partners. There had been talk of creating a business together but in the end Sharon had other goals. When Kathy went scrambling for work to build her practice, Sharon got a job in a day spa. She'd married and had twin boys. The marriage hadn't lasted but her tenure at the spa did. She now owned it. Kathy had been trying to get her to guest lecture at the Academy for the last two years.

Sharon's office phone went to voice mail. Sharon was seldom in her office. Kathy decided to give her spa some business anyway. Anything was better than being here. Part of the problem was her anger and regrets about Erin. Another part was the short but intense time she'd spent with Greg. She found herself missing him a great deal and wondering when and if she'd see him again. She just didn't want to be alone right now.

Sharon's spa had become one of the largest and most popular in the city. It was a relatively small operation when she started there, its success a tribute to her hard work. Kathy knew it would be busy but when she pulled up she was astonished to find an angry mob besieging its doors. Kathy squinted, her mouth open in shock. Sharon was standing at the doors engaged in a shouting match with the crowd.

What the hell is going on?

Kathy got out and looked around. She saw three vans from local news stations and now realized that camera crews were filming the chaos. Kathy stepped closer until she reached the periphery of the crowd. Suddenly a woman just ahead of her raised a placard. One cameraman pivoted to record Sharon's reaction.

"Lady, that is absolutely disgusting and defamatory!"

Kathy circled to the left in an attempt to read the sign. She ran into a young man, about twenty-five, who was tapping into his iPhone.

"Excuse me," she said. "Are you a reporter?"

"Hell no," he said with a grin. "I'm a lot better than that. I'm a blogger. You can find me at badpenny.com. My name is Scott Carson—remember it, because I'm going to be big. I go around covering stuff in the city, getting the scoop."

That sounded like a reporter to Kathy. Annoyed, she said, "So what is the scoop?"

"This? You know. Concerned Citizens Brigade. Moral Majority."

She repeated this to herself. "Whose morals are they concerned about?"

"Hers, I guess," he said, nodding toward Sharon. "Massage parlors and prostitution."

Kathy tensed with another flash of anger. *See what you've done, Erin?* She blinked away tears and regret. It wasn't fair to lay the blame there.

"Why would they target this spa? It's the largest in the city."

Carson returned an incredulous look. "Can you think of a better way for them to get their point across?"

"These people really can't tell the difference between an aboveboard business and a seedy prostitution front?"

Kathy knew it was a naive question. Her work on the state licensing board had exposed her to the political game. Many elected officials abused the legitimate concerns of the public, pumping up outrage and misdirecting it at minorities of all kinds. The irony was real massage therapists and these protestors essentially were on the same side. That was especially true for Sharon, a dedicated Christian very proud of her faith. Politics had once again turned potential allies into adversaries.

Kathy started moving. Her goal was to reach Sharon and stand shoulder to shoulder with her. Before she could go much further, though, police sirens grabbed everyone's attention. The news crews began to pack up as the mob started to thin out. She watched the blogger pocket his iPhone and go to his car. So much for this scoop. By the time the squad cars arrived, there was almost nothing for the police to do. Kathy stared at the cars and vainly wished Greg was in one of them. Was he already in Brunz?

Kathy turned to find she now had a clear, straight path to Sharon. She was talking to a reporter in an animated fashion, touching the fingers on her left hand as she forcefully made her points.

"There is absolutely no relationship between a legitimate massage business and an undercover sex shop. We're professionals licensed by the state after taking strenuous amounts of classes at accredited colleges. Our operation could not be more ethical or respectable."

Kathy smiled as she listened. Sharon was as fierce an advocate for her profession as anyone could want. Hearing her powerful arguments was almost as revitalizing as the massage she had come to receive.

Sharon went on a minute longer. She glanced over and saw Kathy. They smiled at each other. "Does that answer your questions?"

The reporter put away his recorder. "I'll make sure your side gets in the paper too."

He left, and Sharon came over to her.

"Hey, you!"

Kathy smiled. "You know, my offer still stands. If you ever want to moonlight as an instructor, I know the perfect school. Students need to hear from advocates like you."

They embraced each other like dear friends who'd been apart for ages. That was somewhat true. Though they talked by phone or e-mailed almost every day, it had been over a month since they'd last gotten together. She hugged Sharon even tighter.

"Something wrong, Kathy?"

"Just missing a friend," she said. Sharon patted her back and then they went inside.

The spa was gorgeous and comforting, a total credit to Sharon's stylistic sense and awareness of what put people at ease. There was a Roman elegance in the marble floors and columns, but lush plants and soft lighting removed the cold feeling stone might convey. Soft, delicate piano music soothed Kathy as soon as they were in the reception area.

"Peter Kater?"

"His latest CD," Sharon said.

They went into the heart of the spa, an expansive arboretum with soothing stone and water elements, highlighted by a central fountain. A little boy, about ten, was there staring down at ornamental goldfish. Sharon bent down next to him. "Where's your brother, Jacob?"

"Ryan's in the storage room playing with the massage lotion."

"Playing?" Sharon's eyebrows shot up. She and Kathy exchanged glances. "Well, go watch him. Remember, you're his big brother."

"Only by two minutes," the boy said, but ran off toward a room on the other side.

"They've gotten so big," Kathy said. "I guess I haven't seen them since last Christmas."

"Time really flies."

"I don't need any reminders about that," she said, causing Sharon to look at her again.

"What's wrong?"

"Nothing."

Sharon smiled. "You're so tense. I can see the anxiety all over you."

"It's been a very long forty-eight hours."

"All bad?"

She smiled, thinking of Greg. "No, not all."

Sharon took Kathy to the woman's locker room. Kathy changed, swapping her clothes for a soft terrycloth robe and comfortable sandals. When she finished, Sharon returned and took her out a secondary exit and opened a door that led into one of the most cozily secluded environments Kathy had ever seen. She knew it was one of the spa's luxury suites. Three wall lamps lit the room in soft yellow and the floor was bamboo. A corner wicker chair hosted several inviting cushions. On the ground in front of it was a plush folded towel that had a deep wooden basin sitting on it. Kathy felt Sharon's hand on her shoulder, guiding her toward the chair.

The cushions were as soft as they looked. Sitting, she saw the basin was filled with water. Rose petals floated on the gossamer surface. The water itself has a soothing lavender tint to it.

"Kick your shoes off and start soaking."

"Oh, Sharon, this is too much."

"Don't be ridiculous. Besides, my intuition tells me you need way more than a simple massage right now."

"Intuition is a hell of a thing," she said with a laugh. It surprised her how natural the reaction was. In the last two days she felt like she'd lost the ability to feel true joy.

Sharon went to a cabinet and retrieved another cushion. This she placed on the floor by the basin and took a seat. "Let me work my magic. This is my favorite type of service."

"Because of the bible?"

"Yes," Sharon said, smiling. They had discussed religious faith many times. Kathy's beliefs were more Buddhist but she was moved by Sharon's devotion, especially her love for the sequence where Christ washes his disciples' feet. She had declared many times how she felt closest to Jesus when she was emulating that scene from the Gospels.

Sharon dipped her hands into the water and started working the tension out of Kathy's body. Reflexology had been a specialty of hers. She understood how palpating specific areas of the hands and feet stimulated corresponding reflex points in other parts of the body. Kathy had always marveled at the body's unity. Demonstrating it to her students was among her greatest rewards as a teacher.

But there was nothing quite like having it demonstrated on yourself by an expert!

"I'm giving you the works today, Kathy. Lavender foot soak, Thai massage, a facial. Have you ever done a seaweed wrap?"

"Just this is more than enough, really," she said. "After what I saw when I pulled up, I feel like I should be taking care of you."

"Oh, that crowd? They're just misinformed."

"I prefer the term idiots," Kathy said.

"That's seems a little harsh for you."

"Guess I'm not in the most understanding of moods," she said, and closed her eyes to let the negativity drain out of her.

14

"Ms. Barrister?"

Kathy looked up with her hand still on the doorknob to her office. It was Friday and she'd just returned from lunch. Amanda was coming toward her. Kathy smiled, slightly surprised by Amanda's formality.

"Is something the matter, Amanda?"

"I just wanted to apologize about Monday. It was none of my business."

About Brad. "You saw someone was hurting and you wanted to be a part of healing him. I hope you never feel the need to apologize for that."

Amanda gave a big smile. "Thanks, Kathy! Is he okay now?"

"Unfortunately, I don't think so."

Amanda looked more stricken by this than Kathy would have supposed. She started to say something when another student called Amanda's name from down the hall. It was Jim, he of the puppy-love expressions. Right now he was barking for Amanda's attention.

"Yeah, I'll be right there," she said.

Jim went on. Kathy looked at her.

"We're taking the Cranial Sacral Therapy class with Mr. Roberts together."

"And my Anatomy class," Kathy said.

Amanda nodded, and Kathy detected some tension there. She opted not to question her about it. Amanda shifted her weight and didn't seem to know what to say next. "I guess I better get going."

Kathy smiled. "You definitely don't want to be late. That would be a Cranial Sacrilege."

"Wow," Amanda said, reacting to the pun by dramatically backing away from Kathy. But she seemed more at ease— exactly as Kathy had intended.

Kathy entered her office. Her desk was a field of kudzu paperwork, though most of it required little more than her signature. Her administrative assistant, Brenda, had taken care of the dirty work with her usual excellence. A light on her phone blinked, indicating waiting messages.

One of them was from Greg.

He was in Brunz still and wanted to see her. The message was rushed and cryptic. He sounded almost breathless. Kathy frowned. Could the new murder be related to Erin's? She dialed his cell phone number but only got voice mail. She didn't leave a message. He would see that she called. That was enough for now.

She spent the next two hours struggling with the paperwork that did require more than just her signature. The Academy for Healing Touch was due for its ACICS accreditation review soon. No independent college or school could operate legitimately in the state without its stamp of approval. Kathy knew the Academy exceeded the Accrediting Council's expectations in every way, but she wanted to be prepared. The school's annual institutional report was due in a few weeks and she had already redrafted it twice with Brenda's help. There were so many times when she wished she could just be a teacher with nothing else to come between herself and her students. Reflecting on Erin's death had strengthened this desire. Could she really be a great educator if most of her time was spent as a pen-pushing administrator?

Maybe Sharon had made the better choice, she thought. Kathy pushed the stacks of paper away from her and sighed. She didn't really believe that. They had each made decisions best suited to their desires. The real question, Kathy realized, was whether or not Sharon had the better desire. Her thoughts were too muddled to follow. On the subject of desire right now, neither massage nor instruction were the first things that came to mind.

She thought of Greg.

A moment later she was dialing his number again. This time he answered.

"Kathy! I saw you called earlier. Sorry, I couldn't pick up."

"That's okay." She kicked back in her chair and sort of slid down in it. *So this is what people mean when they say someone's voice makes them melt.*

"How's the investigation?"

"I can't explain over the phone. That's why I need to see you."

"When will you be coming my way?"

There was a pause on his end. "I guess my message didn't make things clear. I need you here in Brunz."

"What good could I possibly do?"

"The police force here is even smaller than Edgerton's. They're good people, long on training, painfully short on experience."

Kathy laughed. "Any experience they have is bound to trump mine."

"Not necessarily. Not in this case," Greg said, and she detected a darkening in his tone.

She wanted to see him so bad.

"I'll head out after my last class."

15

KATHY TAUGHT HER ETHICS CLASS IN THE LATE AFTERNOON with a particular vigor, as if it would be the final thing she ever said to them. They all looked like Erin to her. She had to make sure she wasn't failing them.

She arrived in Brunz at dusk after some confusion with a MapQuest direction that proved wrong. Brunz was a quiet town known for its arts and crafts. She thought it had originated as some sort of colony of artists who shared broad sympathies with the Quakers. Driving up Main Street, lined with cute shops she hoped she and Greg might visit together, Kathy thought Brunz the most unlikely place in the world for a murderer of any type—much less a prostitute. She had come prepared to be depressed, a realization that upset her. She did not believe in expecting the worst. She couldn't let recent events change that philosophy.

She located the Brunz police headquarters. It didn't look much different from the storefronts she had passed. It was situated on the end of the central strip like an afterthought. She parked and got out. A few passing people smiled and nodded at her. She detected no trace of stress or tension in their faces. *The murder must not be public knowledge yet.*

She entered the HQ and asked for Detective Beacon. Greg came out with another man, about her age but rather short and plump. He looked like he might have spent the last several hours pulling his hair out. He didn't have that much to spare.

"Kathy, this is Detective Dwayne Robinson. He's in charge of the investigation."

Detective Robinson extended his hand and they shook but there was little friendliness in it. *I hope this isn't going to be another Officer Porter situation.* Kathy wondered if he felt threatened or diminished by her presence. She just wanted to help. Though how exactly she could help eluded her.

She exchanged glances with Greg, who smiled. "I was telling Dwayne about your prominence as a massage practitioner in the state. Even on the state board of certification, isn't that right?"

Kathy nodded. "I don't know if any of that helps you."

"Probably doesn't," Robinson said. Kathy detected a New York accent in his voice, gruff and unsparing. This made her jump to the conclusion that he'd once been some big city cop. It took her a moment to walk back from the assumption.

"We'll see," said Greg.

"Let's get going," Robinson said. He coughed once and left. Greg grinned at her.

"I don't think I should be here," Kathy said.

"Just trust me."

They went out the back exit and got in his car. They followed Robinson's vehicle down the street and out of town. Neither spoke.

After about five minutes, Kathy said, "Are we're leaving Brunz?"

"Very nearly. Sorry to tell you that tonight's destination is another motel. At least it's a lot nicer than The Johns."

She thought of Erin again and the hurt renewed itself. "Does it annoy you to know that prostitution goes on there and they do nothing to prevent it? Why isn't it shut down? Why isn't Glenda in jail?"

"They make raids sometimes."

"They need to make them more often. Maybe it would have saved a life or two."

"Hey, now," Greg said. "There are a thousand laws on the books that we can't really enforce."

"Well, prostitution should be at the top of the list of the laws you can. It's stupid to make a law if you can't enforce it."

"Stupid is just another name for government," he said. Kathy turned and found a big grin on his face. She remembered it from their high school days. It only came out under very specific circumstances. He was obviously very satisfied with his response. She found her annoyance level dropping despite herself.

"They could at least shut that place down."

"They could. Then people would go somewhere else and there'd be secrecy for a while. Secrecy just adds to more crime. Sometimes it's better to know where the crimes are happening and tolerate it a bit than risk being totally blind."

"I would think that idea offends your holy sense of order."

Greg turned the wheel, following Robinson. "Are you pissed off at me, Kathy? If so, I want to know what I did."

She sighed. "Sorry," she said after a moment. "I'm just frustrated."

"I understand that, Kathy. I really do."

They pulled up to the motel. It was nicer than the one in Edgerton, and Greg told her it had no reputation as a hookup spot beyond area high school kids out on prom night. They got out. Robinson went to the clerk's office and returned with a keycard.

He swiped it through the magnetic reader and opened the door. He stepped through without a moment's pause. Greg was about to follow. Only Kathy seemed to notice the change of protocol. She knew she was intruding, but she cleared her throat anyway.

"What about the protective clothing? Won't this disturb the crime scene?"

Robinson laughed. "Right now the only protective gear within thirty miles of us are the condoms at Rite Aid. You're sharp, though. All caught up on your *CSI* episodes."

Kathy blushed.

"It was still a great observation, Kathy. I told you she doesn't miss much, Dwayne."

"We'll see," Robinson said. They entered.

Kathy gasped.

Perhaps it was the relative freshness of the scene compared to Erin's that overwhelmed her. The blood, though dried, was more striking in its color. *And there's a lot more of it,* she thought. There were no lines here, just blotches and splatters.

"It's even on the walls," she whispered.

Greg moved closer to her.

The walls were stained with thick streaks that reminded her of how she'd sometimes try out paint samples to see which color worked best. She glanced around further. At the bedside was a lamp that had been knocked over. Its white shade had a delicate red handprint on it. *She struggled.*

Did Erin struggle too?

"Didn't anyone hear anything?"

Robinson looked over at her. "Doesn't seem like it."

Kathy nodded. "Has she…been identified?"

"Yes," Greg said.

"How old?"

"Midtwenties. I can't give you her name, you understand."

Kathy nodded. She was afraid to know. Part of her was convinced it would be another former student.

"You'll find out soon enough, like everyone else," Robinson said. "We're going live with the media tomorrow."

And then this town's innocence ends. She stepped here and there, dodging obvious bloodstains. It was only when she turned back for a more encompassing view of the room that the blood splotches seemed to organize themselves into a pattern that caught her attention. As a girl, like just about every child, she sometimes stared at the sky and made objects from the clouds. There had always been a terrific thrill whenever a cloud became something so recognizable that it seemed real.

She felt that thrill now.

"There's something here," she said.

The detectives looked at each other.

"There's lot of stuff here," Robinson said. "Care to be a little more specific."

Specific, Kathy thought. Yes, that was exactly the word she was looking for. It wasn't just her imagination. There really was a picture on the carpet. More specifically a drawing.

A symbol.

She brushed past Greg and got to the left of the bed. She knelt, twisting her head. Up close the details were lost to her. She had to use memory and focus to find it again. There, beginning almost at wall, was a sort of flag, somewhat like the top of a music note, except the staff went left rather than the right. She pointed it out.

"Okay, Kathy," Greg said. "What is this?"

She pointed with her finger to keep all eyes focused. A single line of blood extended from the staff. The line fragmented in placed where the carpet fibers were less saturated but otherwise it was clearly present. The line ran about three feet and disappeared along the edge of the bed frame.

Kathy stood up, gasping.

"What is it, Kathy? Intuition?"

"Intuition?" Robinson's tone even more skeptical that Porter's had been. "What are you showing us, exactly? There's a line of blood here extending from a funny blotch hear the wall. So what?"

"The killer drew something," Kathy said.

"Excuse me?"

Kathy stepped back again, staring. Robinson's negativity was hurting her clarity. There was an arrangement of rough circles, also drawn in blood, intersecting with the straight line. The circles were not independent of each other but part of a single spiral that extended out from the line and got wider and wider. Only the first two turns were visible. At the third, part of the spiral swept under the bed itself.

"Help me, Greg."

He came forward. "Tell us what you're doing, Kathy? What is it?"

"We have to move the bed."

"Move the fucking bed?" Robinson said. "Why?"

Now Kathy looked at him. "Because there's something here I guess you all didn't see. Maybe it's a clue."

"Dwayne, perhaps we better do it."

"Why not," Robinson said with a sigh. "Crime scene probably can't get more destroyed than it already is."

The men bent to take the bottom edges of the frame and shifted it to the right. Kathy stared at the revealed carpet. No pattern. The carpet was untouched. It even looked new.

"Did you think someone was hiding out under there or something? Was there a point to this?"

"Kathy?"

She looked at Greg, momentarily confused. Her intuition spiked. Someone who would draw a symbol like this wouldn't leave the job unfinished. She looked at the sheets.

Of course.

"Reposition the bed."

"Oh, come on!"

"Just do it!"

Even Greg looked doubtful. This hurt her a bit. He'd trusted her enough to call her down here, hadn't he? Why lose faith in her now? She nodded as they moved the bed. She told them to shift it down a fraction and stopped when the alignment was right. The spiral jumped off the floor and onto the side of the mattress. Kathy bent and pulled the top sheet away.

Portions of the spiral arcs were there too.

"Son of a bitch."

Robinson pulled out a flashlight, keying in on the pattern now. Greg saw it too. Kathy watched them trace the spirals even further out. She looked down at the central line, studying the points of intersection. She noticed something in the carpet where the spiral started. It was a little particle. In her haste, she almost picked it up. Instead, she pointed it out.

Robinson dashed into the bathroom and came back with a wad of tissue. He used it to make the retrieval. It was small and bloody. Kathy didn't know exactly what to make of it.

Breathing heavily, Robinson said, "It's just like your case, Greg. Goddamn."

"What is it?"

The detectives looked at each other as if psychically trying to decide what they should reveal to her.

Then Greg said, "It's a tooth."

16

R OBINSON WAS SO EXCITED HE ALMOST SHOUTED INTO THE phone. Kathy decided she disliked his voice. It seemed to only show enthusiasm for unpleasant things.

Greg reentered from outside.

"Do you need some air before we start?"

"No."

He had gone to his car for a roll of blue tape. At her direction, he proceeded to outline the bloody symbol, laying down the tape in small strips. Kathy swallowed hard. The tape made the pattern even more distinct and identifiable. It took Greg half an hour to get the outline set.

"It looks Chinese or something," Robinson said.

"It's Japanese, actually."

"What does it mean?"

"Cho Ku Rei."

"Okay. So what does that mean?"

Kathy inhaled.

"Power."

The detectives looked at each other again. Kathy glanced at a bulge in Robinson's pocket. Greg had given him the bloody tooth wrapped in toilet paper. Just like his case. Just like Erin.

Greg hadn't mentioned anything about a tooth.

She stepped about, looking at the symbol from all sides. "It's a symbol used in Reiki."

"Reiki?"

Kathy smiled grimly despite herself and gave a quick explanation. She was getting the opportunity to educate law enforcement one detective at a time.

"Reiki uses certain symbols. A practitioner might draw one to boost their own healing energy before treating a patient. They can also be drawn for protection. Cho Ku Rei is a very important symbol."

She looked up and found Greg was taking notes.

"It sounds like witchcraft," Robinson asked.

"No, it's nothing like witchcraft," Kathy said with obvious annoyance. "Cho Ku Rei is supposed to be a positive symbol, a way to enhance your abilities and focus your energies."

Robinson elbowed Greg in the ribs. "Sort of a psychic Viagra, I guess."

Kathy pressed her lips into a thin line and stared him down. "No, that's not what it is at all."

Greg finished writing. "Dwayne, this is obviously a major breakthrough. Just from what Kathy has said here, we can start a significant psych profile."

Kathy held up her hands. "I don't know about that! Like I said, whoever drew this clearly doesn't understand the true meaning of the symbol. It's been perverted—horribly so."

"That's just as useful to know," Greg said.

Robinson patted his pocket bulge. "I'm going to get this sent off to the boys in the big city," he said, and with his accent Kathy again thought he must mean New York. It dawned on her that he probably meant her own.

New people in uniform arrived. A woman took photos of

the pattern. A patrolman dropped in, seemingly with no other goal in mind besides shooting the breeze. Kathy felt nauseated and rushed outside.

She breathed deep. Suddenly, two hands gently touched her shoulders. "You did great in there," Greg said. "I doubt we could have discovered the symbol without you."

She nodded, staring at the cars in the lot, her back still to him.

"Reiki," he said. "You know a lot about it, don't you? You used it to treat that kid's back."

"Brad's back. Yes—it's used to heal."

"How does it work? You didn't even seem to touch him."

She turned to face him. "For the first time in my life, Greg, I really don't feel like explaining it any further than I already have. It's an old technique."

"I'm just saying it sort of looked like you were using the Force or something," he said, and he gave her the same big grin he'd given her in the car. Kathy didn't think it appropriate, but she knew she couldn't ever be truly mad at him when he smiled like that—even if part of her did want to slap him silly.

"What did Robinson mean, about the tooth?"

Greg pulled back. "I don't think I can say."

"Even after I gave you a major lead?"

"I can't even begin to thank you for that, either. But I told you before, there are some things I just can't divulge."

"Maybe I should go ask Dwayne. He seems a little more talkative."

Greg pursed his lips and glanced down at his shoes. Finally he looked at her and said, "This particular killer seems to rip teeth from his victims."

Kathy's body jolted with shock. She saw Greg wince at her reaction.

"I thought I better not tell you. Knowing your feelings about Erin, I thought it would…brutalize you."

She nodded. He was right. Even now she imagined

Erin's mouth being forced open. The bastard wasn't content just taking her life. Kathy closed her eyes and hoped Erin was already dead when it happened. Cold comfort was still comfort.

"How many teeth?"

"Come on, Kathy—"

"How many?"

"Two," Greg said. "Apparently one for himself, the other— for us. I found it placed perfectly under the pillow in Erin's room. It startled all of us. The coroner confirmed two of Erin's teeth were missing. We were never able to find the second. We already knew this victim was missing two teeth as well. We just hadn't found them."

The motel room opened and closed again as Robinson herded the photographer and the patrol officer outside. He checked the lock. He looked too damned happy for Kathy's tastes.

"Edgerton and now Brunz. Jesus Christ, Beacon, I think we're looking at a serial killer." He patted his pocket bulge again. "Considering his MO, maybe we should start calling him the Tooth Fairy. What do you think? Catchy, right?"

"Thomas Harris already took the idea," Greg said in a sour tone, and he and Kathy got into his car.

17

B RUNZ WAS A TOWN THAT ROLLED UP ITS SIDEWALKS BY nine o'clock. There was nothing open when they returned to Kathy's car at eleven. The main strip was deserted. Greg parked and they got out.

"I'm sure Brunz won't feel as sinister to me in the morning," Kathy said.

He came around to her. "It's a great place morning and night. You're just creeped out, that's all. With good reason."

She nodded and the two of them leaned against her car. This felt like high school. Their weekends often ended outside of his house or hers, the two of them talking as they leaned against their cars. She realized when she started dating and had obligations to hang out with a boyfriend just how much she missed those talks. It had made her not always mind breaking up.

"Look at us," he said. "Near midnight and we're hanging out by our cars—again."

"I was just thinking about that."

"What else were you thinking about?"

"You. Tell me about yourself, Greg. I feel like I know nothing."

"What do you mean? We know everything—"

"What happened when you were in the army? What happened there? How long were you in the service?"

"Ten years," he said. "I was stationed all over. Saw a little time in Germany. I even got to go to South Korea."

"A girl in every port?"

"You're thinking of the navy. But yeah, there were girls. None of them measured up."

"To what?"

"To who," he said, giving her a serious, steady glance. A thrill shot through her.

"What happened then?"

"I got interested in police work while I was in the service. I thought about joining the MPs, but civil service was more my thing. And I fooled someone into thinking my mind was sharp enough to solve puzzles. I went through police training in Miami."

"Why so far away?"

"It wasn't far away at all. I finished up my last deployment there. I though it was where I wanted to live. Miami certainly offered a challenge—they need good cops."

"Why didn't you stay?"

He smiled. "After all those years, I was missing home."

They returned to his hotel, where Kathy got her own room. Greg said nothing about this, though she detected a certain disappointment from him.

She felt it inside herself too.

18

K ATHY'S CELL PHONE STARTED VIBRATING ON THE NIGHT-
stand too early on a Saturday for her liking. She pulled it
to her ear.

"They found it, Kathy!"

She sat up. "Found what?"

"Your symbol. At The Johns. I had Edgerton PD and the
county crime lab go over the photos again. It was very hard to
detect. The carpet in that room was much darker than the one
here in Brunz. A computer imaging scan found it."

They met in the hotel lobby and ventured out for breakfast.
We could have had it in bed, Kathy thought wistfully. She woke
up four times last night to find herself reaching across the
mattress for him.

Greg wasn't dressed for duty. He wore a blue short-sleeved
Polo shirt tucked into khaki pants. He looked like a handsome
tourist without a care in the world. The shirt showed the
suppleness of his arm muscles and accentuated his chest.

Why, why did I sleep alone last night?

They had a light breakfast. More correctly, she had a light breakfast. Kathy smiled when the glass of chocolate milk came Greg's way. She had a cup of coffee and a bowl of granola. Greg's plate was piled high with hash browns, scrambled eggs, and sausage links. Kathy found herself getting as much pleasure watching Greg eat as Greg got from the food itself. When he finished, she was astonished to see him pick up the small laminated dessert card that was tucked behind the condiments holder.

"You're serious?"

He looked at her innocently. "You don't like pie?"

"It's eight in the morning." She looked at her watch. "Almost."

"It says available at any time."

Undeterred, he ordered a piece. Kathy practically saw his metabolism kicking in, like a steam locomotive being fed a particularly rich vein of coal. She couldn't remember how big an eater he'd been in high school. Here, at any rate, was a potential snag in the domestic happiness she'd started to entertain with him. Kathy was not a baker. She was not a fryer, boiler, or broiler for that matter. Greg coming home to a plate of microwaved steamed vegetables didn't seem like a scenario he'd accept. She laughed out loud imagining it.

"What?"

"Finish your pie," she said.

She learned he essentially had the day off unless another break presented itself. After breakfast, he and Kathy toured the shops. She'd not mentioned wanting to do so, and Greg suggested it like a genuine interest. Perhaps it was or perhaps his own intuition told him what would please her. It certainly wasn't a recommendation from any insight into her past. In high school, Kathy could have cared less about a bunch of rustic shops. Back then, a vase was a vase—just something her mom cared about.

They held hands halfway through their tour of Main

Street. She found it was too easy to imagine a life with Greg. They went from shop to shop in bliss. Each storefront seemed managed by a different grandmotherly woman who gave them an approving smile. Kathy wondered if this was because they looked like they belonged together. Maybe it was just a marketing ploy. If so, it worked. Kathy bought a little something from every place they visited. Greg also got in on the act, even though he seemed unlikely to care about ceramics, blown glass, or knickknack metalwork. When they reached the last store, he seemed to have even more bags than she did.

"We've certainly done our part to stimulate the local economy," he said.

It was after twelve when they finished. Kathy felt a twinge of sadness, like something more than the shopping was over. In the last twenty minutes, the people had acted a little differently toward them. It was as if there was a friendly half of the strip and an unwelcoming, suspicious half. She noticed a change in Greg's demeanor as they loaded their purchases into his trunk. When they got in, he didn't start the engine.

"News of the murder will have hit the press now."

She sat back. "It happened a while ago," she said, realizing. They'd literally seen the change it caused in the town as they shopped and news of the murder spread. Toward the end, the shopkeepers had looked at them as strangers rather than customers. As potential killers. Kathy lowered her gaze. For a little while, at least, the peaceful waters of Brunz would be poisoned by doubt and fear.

"I'm afraid there'll be a media rush," Greg said. "Robinson's exactly the sort of policeman you don't want anywhere near the press. He's too sensationalizing. There was nothing I could do to stop him. Truth be told, though, it's the bloggers who present the bigger headaches these days. They don't have the tools and presence of a newspaper or TV station, but they're a hell of a lot better at putting two and two together than the average reporter."

"Unless Robinson purposely linked his investigation with yours, they probably still need to put one and one togeth—"

Greg looked at her when she stopped.

"Your intuition telling you something new, Kathy?"

"Yes," she said. "Erin wasn't the first murder victim—and you've known it all along."

19

"**E**RIN WAS THE THIRD."

Of course. Four murders—two and two together.

Kathy stared blankly ahead of her at the world through the car windshield.

"Why didn't you tell me?"

"Partly because I didn't think much about it myself until yesterday. I'd entertained some ideas, but I thought they were far-fetched."

"What changed your mind?"

"The removal of the teeth. I confirmed from other investigators that their victims' had teeth removed as well. Now I'm just waiting to hear back on any symbols drawn in blood."

"Where did the first one happen?"

"Up in Patterson."

"That's the far eastern side of the state," Kathy said.

"It didn't get a lot of media attention. None of them have. Unfortunately, police departments aren't always so great about talking to each other and sharing what they know. I'm working to change that. A little cooperation can go a long way."

Maybe it would have saved Erin's life. Caught this bastard before she stumbled into his trap.

"Turn the car on, please."

"Why?"

"Because it feels depressing sitting here talking like this while people walk around us under the bright blue sky. Even the engine running would make me feel…I don't know. Active."

Greg nodded and turned the ignition. The air conditioner, on its lowest setting, sighed against her skin.

"How many Reiki symbols are there, Kathy?"

"Why?"

"The killer may not be drawing the same one every time. I'd like the other departments to look for as many different patterns as possible."

She nodded. "There are four symbols."

"Good," he said, sounding relieved. "That's not many. I was expecting you to say something like four hundred."

She smiled. "When you're dealing with a healing source as powerful as Reiki, four is all you need. Technically, of course, you don't need any. Our energy is our own to direct as we choose."

"But the symbol in the motel room—you said it meant power."

"Cho Ku Rei is the symbol for power, yes."

"Personal power? Like domination?"

"No, no," she said, shaking her head. "It's about enhancing your personal energy in order to direct it toward someone in need. A Reiki practitioner will draw the symbol because they want to amplify their healing session. The symbol itself is a sort of trigger—like all symbols. It's something that centers and focuses your thoughts just by looking at it."

"Can you draw the other symbols for me? I'd like to fax them in."

"I can. But you can get them online easily enough. Did you know the symbols used to be strictly forbidden to write down where non-Reiki practitioners could see?"

Greg now looked more interested. "You mean like secret-society type stuff?"

"I suppose. But I doubt anyone would hold that view now. The symbols are on the web, after all. And any local library will have books on Reiki with the symbols there as well."

"I'm just thinking of all the angles for a psychological profile. If our suspect has a warped view of these symbols, perhaps it warps in other ways as well. Maybe he does want them secret. Maybe he also believes in secret sects like the Illuminati too. These are patterns of behavior that can help us down the road. Tell me about—"

"Wait a minute," Kathy said. "I want to ask some questions."

"If I think I can ethically answer them, I will."

"I want to know if it's always the same teeth."

Greg smiled. "That's a very brilliant question, Kathy. No, he's taken different teeth each time."

Her voice became small and whispery. "Which of Erin's did he…?"

"Don't torture yourself by asking."

"I have to know."

Greg frowned. "Her uppers," he said. He opened his mouth and pointed, touching his two front teeth.

They became silent, contemplative. After a minute, the quiet became unbearable to her.

"Are you staying longer in Brunz?"

"No," he said. "I don't think there's much else here for me to accomplish. I'm going to start working with the State Bureau of Investigation to develop our profile. A lot of it will be derived from the information you've provided."

Kathy smiled. "The Bureau is headquartered in my neck of the woods, isn't it?"

He smiled. "As a matter of fact, it is. I'll be there for most of next week."

She leaned forward and kissed him on the lips. "I know a place where you can stay while you're visiting. It's got a kitchen that'll serve cold chocolate milk all night."

They kissed again. It was the best kiss of her life. She believed that when a couple really belonged with each other, their kisses had a certain dynamic. They actually traded energy back and forth in the most intimate way, balancing one another. She'd come to realize most of her past boyfriends had been the exact opposite. They kissed very forcefully, in a way that suggested passion. But it was a disguise. She could feel them taking energy from her, draining her and giving nothing in return.

They lingered for another thirty minutes, neither wanting to initiate the inevitable. Finally, Greg said he could delay no further. They followed each other down the interstate until Kathy parted company at Exit 57 to get to her city. Greg continued toward Edgerton.

Coming home from Brunz, she felt the exact opposite of how she'd felt returning from Edgerton. She cleaned house with gusto, feeling as if she had reclaimed her life. She did not allow herself to think of Erin just then. She didn't allow herself to think of anything except Greg coming to stay with her for a week.

She began her cleaning in the bedroom.

A few hours later, satisfied with a job well done, Kathy turned on her computer to perform a task that had been on her mind since the drive to Edgerton. Her fingers raced over the keyboard as she described the Academy's first year of life. All of her students were special, but those first twelve would always be especially dear to her. Now there were only eleven of them. They all deserved to be celebrated. A school memorial service for Erin would be that occasion.

Kathy finished typing and read over what had started out as in memoriam e-mail and became an invitation to a celebration—of Erin, of the Academy, of their very profession. She would use this moment of terrific hurt to remind them all about their commitment to healing.

For you, Erin.

She sent the e-mail.

20

THERE WAS SOMETHING LIKE PANIC AT THE ACADEMY when Kathy arrived Monday morning. She'd allowed herself to sleep later than usual and tune out the world's gibberish since Sunday, and had no idea what could cause such chaos. Her students seemed pale and nervous. Arriving at her office, she found even Brenda looking vexed.

"I think Lou's teaching a relaxing class on Hot Stone Massage at eleven, if you'd like to be a guinea pig for the students."

"It's hot enough around here as it is. Thanks, though."

Kathy had never heard such tension in Brenda's voice. She'd been her assistant for five years.

"It's not the e-mail I sent out Saturday night, is it? I don't intend to dump the organization of a whole memorial service on you—"

Brenda shoved the newspaper at her. Kathy took it and looked.

Her mouth dropped open.

As she was about to speak, her cell phone rang. She saw it was Greg.

"Excuse me, Brenda, I have to take this."

"But—" Brenda began, saw it was futile, and left.

"Greg."

"—and that fucking Robinson—" She heard Greg say.

"Greg?"

"Kathy! I'm at the Bureau now. Have you seen your daily paper?"

"Only just now," she said. She looked again. The headline "Massage Killer" almost bulged off the paper. She could hardly scan the accompanying article.

"It's not just here. Most of the state papers are running something similar. The AP picked it up as well. It should be on Yahoo! by now."

The article appalled Kathy. It was a mishmash of innuendo and sensationalism with an occasional lapse toward truth. Quotes from Detective Robinson were liberally sprinkled throughout the piece. Kathy rubbed her forehead with her left hand. She wondered if the other articles were as bad as this. The writer blatantly conflated massage practitioners with sex workers. That was terrible enough—and then she read down further.

"Good God!"

"What is it, Kathy?"

"Have you read the article, Greg?"

There was a long pause. "Yes."

Robinson had named Kathy as a consultant in the case. The article made it sound like Kathy was claiming the killer must be a massage therapist. Reiki was described in terms more appropriate for a sinister occult.

She threw the paper away in disgust.

"Kathy, you still there?"

"I'm here. Barely."

"Please don't worry about the article."

She laughed. "Are you kidding? I have to send out a press release right away to clear this up. The paper makes me sound like a nut that doesn't know what the hell I'm talking about. Never mind me. This could damage my school. And anything that damages my school damages my students. I won't allow that."

She hung up and went to her Anatomy class. She stood in the back entrance. The students were huddled around looking at copies of the paper. None of them knew she was there. Jim and Amanda were standing apart, looking at the paper as a couple. Jim leaned forward and Amanda elbowed him back a little and tried to concentrate. Rachel, Kelly, and Paul were shaking their heads. Paul was sort of the class father figure. As a student he was as inexperienced as anyone else, but at nearly fifty years of age he was easily the oldest person in the room. She listened to them talk. Their voices were a mix of fear and sarcasm and a little confusion about the words the article had put in their instructor's mouth.

"Newspapers are getting desperate," Paul said. "The blogs are killing them and they're losing money, so they make stuff up."

The younger students nodded.

Paul laughed. "You don't seriously think Kathy would say anything like this, do you? I know lumberjacks who'd be proud of the hatchet job this writer did."

Kathy beamed and came forward. "Thank you, Paul. I appreciate your level head and leadership."

The class turned to her as she assumed her position in the front of the room.

"I want to clear up some misconceptions in what you're reading. First, the true parts—this will be quick. Did you all receive the e-mail from Saturday about my plans for a memorial service for a former student, Erin Haley?"

The students nodded.

"I was called to help investigate her murder. That part of the story is true. The rest is pure trash. I was asked some questions about the murder in Brunz, but I was in no way a consultant, as the paper implies, and I have never made a statement to the media nor have they contacted me for my opinion. I would have no opinion to offer if they did. I have no theories about the nature of the murderer. I certainly don't think he—or she—is a massage therapist! Most importantly, the victims were not massage therapists—"

"But Erin was, wasn't she?"

"She was not—she was not killed in that capacity."

An embarrassed silence filled the room, and Kathy wished she'd taken another approach. She saw from their expressions that bloggers were not the only people able to put two and two together.

Kathy found the class's collective stare upon her in a way she had never experienced in all her years of teaching. She realized she didn't know what to say. Any comment seemed like it would compromise Erin's memory even more.

Quietly, Paul said, "Why don't we focus on today's lesson, everybody. The best way to beat this is to learn to be the best therapists we can be. That's all there is to it."

A general murmur of agreement spread through the classroom. The newspapers were abandoned. "Thank you," Kathy mouthed at Paul. He smiled back and she confidently began to teach.

21

When the door opened, Allison smiled with some confusion. "I might have the wrong address. I was meeting a man named Andrew…"

"I'm Andrew. You're late."

"I'm very sorry," she said. She was thrown off by his tone and quickly stepped inside at his invitation. She was also thrown off by his appearance. He'd described himself over the phone to her as being thirty-five and husky with "some stretch marks." He'd said this last part in such an embarrassed tone that she felt the immediate need to reassure him. Money was money. But nothing about him matched his self-description. Allison was used to that. She just wasn't used to the reality being so much better than the description. He'd answered the door wearing no shirt. His body was fit, toned but not overly muscled. A classic beauty.

Allison got nervous once she stepped inside. She always did with her customers, but this was different. The house was vacant, not a piece of furniture in sight. The windows didn't have blinds. That made her feel more secure. She could see the neighbor three houses down mowing his lawn.

There'd been no For Sale sign in the front yard.

"You just moving in or moving out?"

"In," Andrew said, smiling.

"It's a beautiful house."

It was a nice, upper-middle class home. Just the type of place she saw for herself in the future if she kept the money coming in. Empty or no, it beat the hell out of some of the nasty motels she'd traveled to before.

"In here," he said.

She followed, watching his smooth, inviting back. His elbows dropped down closer to his waist. His fingers were obviously working his belt buckle.

Am I going to have to blow him in the middle of an empty kitchen? It seemed the only place in the house without carpet. But it also gave the most privacy. The windows were higher and smaller.

"Did you bring your table?"

Table? Then she realized. "Well, I don't actually have one."

He turned on her. His expression had changed to show confusion.

"You said you did."

She laughed before she could stop herself. "You weren't really expecting a massage, were you? I mean, that's not what you actually—"

"You said you were a massage therapist. With a table."

He unhooked his brown belt and slid it from around his lean waist.

"I can massage you," she said quickly. "Is there any furniture left at all? That's all I need."

"No."

"The floor," she tried. "I know it's not the best, but I can make you forget all about that. I'll start with your back. Then I'll turn you over."

He took the belt and folded it. Stretching its halved length between both hands, he made a quick jerk. Crack! Allison tensed, wanting to run. Her feet betrayed her.

"Here, just turn around. Let me try your shoulders. You'll see how good I can be."

He rubbed his left temple. "I don't know if it works if you're not real."

"Look, Andrew, massage therapists just rub on you. There's no real talent invol—"

She saw him whirl toward her. He smacked her to the ground. She cried out once, cringing away, shaking.

"Oh God, don't kill me! I—I'll do whatever you want. I won't even charge."

He stood over her, cracking his belt again. Allison tried to pull herself onto her knees in front of him. She'd always thought of it as a humiliating position. Now she'd pray on her knees to him if he wanted it. Her mouth opened; her hands rose to touch his blue jeans and his stomach. He backed away before she could do either. She froze, waiting. The belt in his right hand was raised over his head, ready to strike. Instead it was his left hand that moved. He reached toward her with his index and middle finger. He put them into her open mouth. Allison misinterpreted his intent and began to lick and suck them. She looked up, certain she'd pleased him. His expression was not glad, and she simply opened her mouth again for instructions. He moved his fingers around. He seemed to be scratching his fingertips on the crowns of her teeth.

Then he gently tugged at one of her molars. She started to gag. *Bite him. Mash down until he's blinded by pain and get the fuck out of here!*

She was about to, but she delayed a second too long. His confidence unnerved her as he brought his fingers out. Her saliva dripped off them and onto the floor.

"Wipe that up."

She was crying now. "I don't have any tissue!"

"Use your shirt."

She obeyed him. Anything to keep him happy.

"Stand up."

Here's your chance. All those windows. All you got to do is get in front of one. Bang on the glass. Scare the hell out him.

Allison stood.

He cracked the belt in his hands again. She flinched. It dawned on her she wouldn't run to a window. She wouldn't do a thing. Andrew already owned her.

He took her from the kitchen to the living room. Her gaze darted to the front door. So close. What came next made her wince inside. Oh God. Oh God, no!

He pointed up.

That's where he'll kill me. The thought was so surreal it had the perverse effect of deadening her to the reality. Her damn feet started lifting, taking her up. What would he do to her? How would she die?

He shoved her on the last step so that she fell forward on her hands and knees. "Please God! I'll do anything!" she shrieked, turning over to look at him. His chest had a sheen of sweat now, and if anything he looked, repulsively, even better looking than before. There was a film of sweat on his chest that in any other circumstance she'd have thought the hottest thing ever. He towered over her and pointed. She saw the door down the hallway. It was open. The room inside had barely any light. It might have been painted a summer blue but now it looked gray and hopeless.

She nodded and started to stand. Crack! He snapped the belt close to her ear. She'd started learning its language.

It told her to crawl.

Allison did. The carpet stung her knees. When she dared stop to rub them, Andrew drove the toe of his shoe into her thigh. She cried out, falling on her face. He cracked the belt two more times, but she just lay there, sobbing. Her eyes were shut tight but she sensed him moving around her. Suddenly he seized her hands and dragged her. The awful carpet burned the length of her torso, and she began to kick at the floor.

Then she was in the awful room. The door closed. For a moment Allison didn't think he'd stayed. She heard nothing but her labored breathing. She looked over and saw something in the darkness. It looked like a cabinet—a piece of furniture. He was standing by it, staring at it, running his fingers along it.

Her voice was very weak and timid. "What are you going to do to me?"

He came over and lodged his arms underneath her. He could have lifted her easy, even if she did struggle. She did not. The heat of his body was scorching. He laid her out on top of the cabinet, on her stomach. She now saw it wasn't a cabinet at all. It had a comfortable surface and a sort of open pillow to cradle her face. *It's a massage table. He had one the entire time. But why—*

In the next moment, she realized he was strapping her down. The table had been modified with braces and restraints. The final strap came over the back of her neck, shoving her face deep into the cradle. The table itself was open here, and she found her gaze locked on the floor. The table was maybe four feet tall, but to Allison that carpet seemed a hundred miles distant.

She jerked and spasmed in the restraints. She wrestled until the bindings rubbed the skin of her wrists raw. She cried. Tears fell through the opening to darken the carpet. How long was he going to let this continue? After several minutes, she ran out of tears. She just laid there, her dry, hyperventilating sobs the room's only sound.

He touched her.

"You're muscles are tense," he said. He'd been silent so long his voice startled her even more than his touch.

His hand probed along her back. His touch was gentle—even respectful. He seemed to be seeking out her aches and pains. He should know where they all were. He'd caused all of them.

He touched her thigh where he'd kicked her. Allison winced.

"This is a tender spot."

"No shit!"

"I'm going to end it," he said. She broke into a fresh sweat. His tone was a little too encompassing.

He worked her thigh. His touch was rough and harsh, his fingers pinching. His strokes drove pain into her rather than removed it. She winced, hoping to endure it. Then she screamed. Or tried to scream. Her voice was now as fleeting as her hopes.

"Does it feel better?"

She sobbed.

"Does it feel better?"

"Yes," she said, "yes!"

"I gave you pain, and now I've taken it away."

"Yes," she whispered. Her mouth made many pleas and whimpers. "You took away my pain. You took it away."

His hands left her body.

"They said you'll take away my pain now. They said. They said it. They said."

22

THERE HE IS, KATHY THOUGHT, SEEING GREG'S CAR COMING up the road. She'd stationed herself upstairs with her phone to her ear as she stared across at her yard through a raised slat in the blinds. The scene below reminded her of the mob that had surrounded Sharon's spa. But this time all the participants were with the media.

"Nice house," Greg said. "Too bad about all those weeds in the front yard."

She smiled, holding the phone closer. "I don't know what's holding up the police. I called them a half hour ago. These people are trespassing."

"That's okay," he said. She watched his car stop. He got out, still talking to her. "The gardener's just arrived."

He kept his phone on and in his palm as he strode into them. Kathy smiled. She could barely see him as he waded into the crowd. She just listened.

His voice boomed. "Back off, everyone! Right now!"

The networks had established some sort of base camp in

Kathy's yard. It happened before she got home and made no sense to her at all. Her instinct was to stand before them and answer every question. The cameras would make sure she wasn't misquoted this time. But she called Greg first and he advised her to call the police. She sensed he knew more than he'd say over the phone. He sounded rushed, like he didn't even have time to talk.

Something had happened.

Below, the reporters had pivoted on him. She heard them interviewing him. Greg looked like a man who'd jumped into shark infested waters to save her and now had to fight off becoming a meal.

Kathy listened to the feeding frenzy in amazement.

"What are your comments on the Edgerton case?"

"We heard you brought Ms. Barrister into the investigation. How do you know her?"

"Do you think Ms. Barrister is right that the killer will strike again in two days?"

"Two days?" Greg's voice was sharp and arch through her phone. "What in hell would make anyone think Kathy said that?"

"So it's a first name basis, is it?"

He sounded like he was pushing closer and closer to her porch. *Oh God. He doesn't realize I'm not there!*

"Greg!"

He couldn't hear her over the noise. She shouted his name again and again. She could just hear the sound of him knocking.

Eventually he said, "Kathy, I'm at your front door. Can't you hear me ringing? Come down let me in."

She laughed. "I guess I wasn't clear. I'm at my neighbor's house. On your right."

"Shit," he said. "You could have divulged that sooner. Now I'm going to look really weird wading back to my car."

This time he hung up. Kathy opened the blinds all the

way and pressed up against the window, trying to see. She could just see his car and the edge of the crowd on her yard. She waited. He was probably stuck answering more of their questions. Then she saw him cross the street to his car. He got in and drove off past the neighbor's house and out of sight.

"No, damnit, that's too far," she said. She called him again but just got his voice mail.

"Honey," an elderly voice called from downstairs. "Is everything okay?"

"I think so, Betty," she said, going to the top of the steps. She descended into the living room, experiencing the same momentary disorientation she always felt at Betty's. Their houses had identical floor plans but vastly different furnishings.

There was a sharp knock on the door. She looked at Betty, who nodded. She was seventy years old, hale and hearty for her age, but not enamored with getting up when she didn't have to. Kathy went to the door and peered through the spyglass.

"Greg," she said, working all four of Betty's locks. A moment later she was in his arms, half in and half out of Betty's house.

"I saw you drive so far out of sight—"

"I was going to go further, thinking at least one of them would tail me. I got three blocks before I realized that wasn't happening. I just parked there and hoofed it back."

She brought him inside, watching Greg's reaction as he peered around. Half of Betty's house looked like an armory, and that included the living room. She had guns of all shapes and sizes. Greg whistled in admiration and seemed to forget he had a host to meet. Kathy cleared her throat and prodded him. He looked down, breaking into a wide grin when he met Betty herself. She was polishing a rifle in her lap.

"You must be Annie Oakley," he said, his tone playful and coy. Kathy felt tense for a second. Then it became clear that Betty liked playful and coy—at least from strapping policemen.

"Greg," Kathy said, "this is my neighbor, Betty. Betty collects guns."

"I can see!"

Betty stood with the rifle still in hand. She looked him up and down. "You're a police detective?"

"Yes, ma'am. With Foster County, in the Edgerton area."

"Betty and I have been friends for years. She was actually one of my first massage clients too. I'm glad she was home—"

"I'm almost always home," Betty said.

"If you weren't, I was afraid I'd have to spend the night at the Academy. I wasn't about to pull in my driveway and let them know who I was."

"It's disgusting," Betty said. "Those people stalking a nice girl like you."

"It's a hassle, but they're just exercising the First Amendment," Kathy said.

Betty was having none of that. She showed off the rifle with pride. "Sometimes the Second Amendment has to come forward and make the First Amendment shut its damn mouth." She went past them into the kitchen.

Kathy found Greg grabbing her arm and grinning. "I love that woman."

"Betty's a little extreme about her guns. It used to bother me a little, to tell you the truth. I'd never given an in-home massage surrounded by so much…firepower. I can't say I really like them."

"I can definitely see why you came here," he said, looking around again. There were guns mounted on the wall in places where most people would put family portraits. "The Terminator would have trouble running this gauntlet."

They entered the kitchen. Betty had stowed her gun safely and stood cooking. Kathy took Greg to the window, which looked south. The angle was bad. She saw her back yard but none of her front.

"I'm really sorry about this, Kathy. Robinson really screwed us by getting the media involved."

"Nothing to be done about it now. But why haven't the police come?"

His reaction—a halfhearted shrug—told her the police had more pressing matters. But what?

"You'll stay for dinner, won't you?"

"I'd love to but tonight has to be a rain check," Greg said.

"Are you sure? I'm trying out a recipe for my Thursday book group. I could use guinea pigs."

They looked at each other again. Greg was in a hurry, she just couldn't tell why. Her intuition told her it involved more than just rescuing her from some reporters and she knew he wanted to go.

"I'd love to," Greg said, stunning her. Kathy saw his mischievous smile.

They ate. Kathy was fascinated to listen to Greg and Betty talk. She thought she knew a fair amount about her neighbor. Betty had developed worsening symptoms of rheumatoid arthritis over the last several years, and Kathy's massage sessions granted her considerable relief without need of medication. Betty distrusted medicine of any sort beyond vitamins and chicken soup. They'd always managed to steer clear of talk of religion and politics. These were not subjects likely to promote a relaxing massage session under the best of circumstances. Her political work with the state had exposed her to a wide range of views. She considered some people to have ignorant beliefs, and she knew some people considered her own opinions to be stupid. She agreed to disagree and moved on. Better yet, she never brought up the topic at all.

It was this aspect of her personality that had kept her from thinking about Greg's politics. As they talked, Kathy felt like a Republican convention had sprung up around her. Betty talked freely to Greg in ways she never had to Kathy. And why not? They were under her roof. She loved the NRA—no surprise—but she also had fierce antiabortion views, dogmatic notions of sin and retribution, and an unfortunate attitude toward gays. Kathy felt sick having to listen to it. Several times she wanted to challenge Betty's statements, only to retreat. It was her house.

Greg, however, was another story. He nodded too much in agreement with her. Kathy studied him closely. *He's just being polite. There's no way he could actually agree with her on all that.*

But her intuition and her hearing told her otherwise. There seemed no question about it: she was in love with a Republican.

Had he changed? She couldn't remember exactly what his views on social issues were in high school. Probably he didn't have any. *Maybe the army did this to him.* Kathy's previous boyfriends had mostly been apolitical. She told herself to stop overreacting, but for the first time Kathy felt glum about the long-term potential of their relationship.

Greg's cell phone rang and he answered at once. He stood up and walked into the living room. Through the kitchen window, Kathy heard a new commotion—van doors slamming, people hustling. Had the police finally arrived? She got up and stretched.

Greg came back.

"I think they're leaving," Kathy said. "Guess they got bored."

"I wouldn't bet on that," Betty said. "They're always feeding."

"Betty's right. We're going to have to leave right now, Kathy."

She looked at him. "Where to? Home?"

"No," he said. "The new hunting ground."

She sighed. "Where is it this time? Brunz again? Edgerton? I don't think I can do a long drive."

"You won't have to. Based on the directions I was given, I'd say where we're going is about four blocks away."

23

"THE POLICE HAVE BEEN THERE SINCE THREE," GREG SAID in the short drive over. "That's how I knew you were being left out to dry on the trespassing."

"Oh, fantastic."

"This town has great cops. Don't blame them. I was coming over to get you anyway and told them not to send any more manpower. I intended to get you back over here right away, but I didn't take Betty into account."

"She utterly loves you."

He smiled. "I've always had that effect on grandmotherly types. There were two things that told me we had a little time to sit down and eat with her. First, all the camera crews at your place. The media's watching the police really close right now. Serial killer stories bring out their ruthlessness. There's always an informant or two on the inside. I barely got the call before they did. But I knew if I heard them start packing up, then we'd need to wrap up dinner and go."

Kathy listened to this with her head leaning against the passenger window.

"You feel okay?"

"No. You're saying the guy who killed Erin and the others has struck again, in my city—four blocks from where I live?"

"We don't know that yet. We're just hoping."

"Hoping? Good God. Look, Erin's murder has hit me pretty close to home. But four blocks away is close to home, Greg!"

He nodded.

They pulled up several houses down and idled. The vans were everywhere, interspersed with squad cars. Neighbors gawked on all sides.

"I told them I wasn't a consultant," Kathy said, almost to herself.

"What?"

"My students. The article made it sound like I was heavily involved in the investigation. I told them I wasn't. I guess that's no longer true."

"No," he said. "It's not."

They got out. Greg pushed into the crowd of media that was pivoting on them fast. She looked at the house. Its exterior appeared much nicer than hers, even after the remodeling. She was always amazed at the leaps in income required to live in certain areas that weren't even half a mile away from what she could afford. Though she hadn't had time in months, Kathy liked taking evening walks in her area. She'd passed this house before on different occasions. She thought she remembered a child playing in the yard. The surrealism of the media horde trampled that hazy child into the back of her mind.

Greg pushed through. More police came out to clear a swath to the porch. They reached the middle of the yard.

"House has been on the market for a few months," Greg said.

"No one's living here?"

"That's right. Do you know the owner?"

"No," she said. She remembered something. "They liked Christmas lights, though. Everyone on this street did. The houses were beautiful in the winter."

How horrible it seemed now, though, dark and lonely, full of strangers who looked like astronauts. Police moved around inside wearing full protective gear. Bureau investigators, she thought. Dazed, she stopped and glanced about. The media had huddled up by a police spokesman who was giving information in a quiet voice. She appreciated the tactic—talking low forced them all to shut up and listen. She wondered if the spokesman had anything legitimate to say or if it was just a distraction to let her and Greg pass. She blinked. Half this crowd had been in front of her house only a few minutes ago. For a moment, the two houses merged in her mind and she was standing in her yard waiting to enter her empty house where she had been murdered. Kathy shuddered, nauseated, and thought about just running away.

Suddenly, a voice said, "I know you!"

She turned to find a young man approaching cheerfully from her left, oblivious to an officer's call to halt. Kathy recognized him—the blogger from outside Sharon's spa.

"Who is this?" Greg said.

"Scott Carson," he said. "I'm a blogger."

Greg studied him a moment.

"I've been here an hour," Carson said. "Long before those jokers showed up. They probably learned about this scene from my coverage."

"What do you cover?" Greg said.

"Anything of local interest. You're Detective Beacon, aren't you?"

"Get lost," Greg said.

"And you're Kathy Barrister."

"Yes," she said, "I'm Kathy."

"So what's inside has to do with the other murders?"

"None of your business," Greg said, pulling on her arm.

"Anything that happens in my city is my business," Carson said.

"Not right now," Greg said, summoning an officer over. "Get rid of this guy."

The officer started pushing Carson toward the driveway.

"I have a right to be here!"

Greg took Kathy onto the porch, grumbling about rights all along the way.

"Do you know him?"

"Not really," she said. She did her best to explain. "I guess he must sound like a real pain in the ass."

"Frankly, he sounds like a suspect," Greg said. Kathy opened her mouth in surprise. Greg smiled. "I'll make sure we keep a tab on him, that's all."

They were ushered into the empty foyer and the door closed behind them. Immediately they were ordered into more elaborate protective clothing than she'd seen before. They both put on what looked like clear rain slickers, followed by pants and shoe coverings. Kathy began to sweat in her new uniform. The layers were not designed to let the skin breathe.

"Greg."

Kathy saw an imposing man coming toward them. Greg introduced him as Detective Mark Rierdon with the Bureau. Rierdon's expression changed once he learned who Kathy was. He took Greg aside, and they began to powwow. Kathy tensed, unable to hear their exchange. Her attention drifted to all the activity around her. Several people wandered about dressed in outfits even more elaborate than hers. Actual crime scene investigators, she thought. She realized her imagination was stuck at some point in the 1930s, because she'd always pictured such an investigation to involve people holding up magnifying glasses to every spot of interest. Two people were taking photographs. Their cameras made a delicate, prolonged sigh after each shot. There were three open laptops on the ground nearby, running some sort of architectural imaging program. Closest to Kathy, a woman swabbed the stairway banister with cotton balls. Kathy guessed she was DNA.

Greg returned.

"Is there a problem?"

"The Bureau isn't as open to having outsiders standing in their crime scene. But I've explained your importance."

"Am I important?"

He smiled. "I think you are."

"Upstairs," Rierdon said, coming over.

Kathy looked at Greg, who nodded and took the lead. They eased around the swabbing woman and climbed to the top.

"Best we can tell, this happened yesterday evening. The girl's name is Allison—her roommate reported her missing."

"What do we know about her?"

"Another Craigslist whore," Rierdon said. His crudeness jarred Kathy. "Her roommate claimed to not know anything about that. Maybe she's telling the truth, but I doubt it. Looks like they shared a computer—we've already seized it. Techs are going over it now."

They came to a bedroom door. Rierdon paused, looked briefly at Greg, and then leaned toward Kathy. "I want to give you fair warning. Allison is still in there."

Kathy started to nod, and then froze. *I can't do it.* Her gaze darted to Greg. He looked anxious. What had he said to Rierdon? Had he told him she was necessary to the case? *Am I?* The idea that Greg had championed her steeled her resolve. *If I can contribute in any way, then I've got to go in there.*

She squared her shoulders and said, "I'm ready."

Rierdon looked doubtful. He turned the knob, and the door opened with a low groan coming from its dry, arthritic hinges.

24

THEY STEPPED INSIDE. KATHY KEPT HER GAZE DOWN. THE carpet was a pretty blue until it suddenly turned red. She broke into a shiver. Greg's warm hands touched her back, steadying her but also moving her forward.

She saw the body in her peripheral vision. It seemed simply suspended in the middle of the air like a magician's trick. The effect was unnerving and paradoxical. She didn't want to see further and yet she had to understand the body's odd arrangement. Rierdon went past her toward it. Greg stood at her side. Like someone getting acclimated to very hot water, Kathy eased closer and closer until she gained a tentative comfort. Then she forced herself to look.

Dear God.

Rierdon's attention snapped over at the sound of her gasp. Kathy pressed her lips together, aware of his curiosity. He seemed to be deciding whether or not she'd run away. *I won't do that.*

Swallowing, she took one step forward.

The naked body—Allison, Kathy thought, Allison—was stretched out and bound on a massage table just a few feet ahead of her. Kathy's pulse increased. Her respiration followed suit, her quick and shallow breaths sounding explosive to her. She dared not look away from the body to judge what the men were thinking. Kathy let her gaze linger without processing what it saw. After a minute, she thought she'd convinced both Rierdon and herself that she could handle the situation.

She turned from the body to examine the room. The Cho Ku Rei symbol was drawn on the wall behind the body, but this time the killer had expanded his interests. The remaining symbols were also painted in blood, one per wall in the same gruesome fashion—Sei He Ki, Hon Sha Ze Sho Nen, and Dai Ko Myo.

Kathy sensed a monstrous pain coming from the symbols, as if they were mourning their own misuse. How could any human intelligence have so misunderstood and corrupted the gentle power Reiki represented? She pitied the killer for his lack of understanding, but she hated him far more. His murders struck at the body. His perverted take on these symbols struck at the soul. Reiki taught a person how to direct their innate energy to the benefit of others, to give their own energy to replenish that of another. The killer obviously feared that. He could not give energy. He could only take.

She looked back at Allison's bound body. She saw the bindings were integrated into the table itself. Straps. These too were a profound perversion. A massage table represented trust and comfort. The killer seemed determined to turn it into a sacrificial slab.

The table.

Against her will, Kathy leaned forward, squinting.

"Greg," she whispered.

"I'm right here, Kathy."

Her hand grabbed his.

"I—I recognize it."

"Recognize what?" His tone rang with excitement. "Another symbol?"

"No. I recognize…the table." She touched the base of her throat with her free hand. She wasn't sure she had a voice.

"It's mine."

Greg swung around her, putting his body between her and it. He put one arm across her chest and he backed her away as Rierdon stepped closer.

Kathy's hand rose from her throat to her mouth. She started to sob.

"This is too much," Greg said. "Rierdon!"

He tried maneuvering her to the door. Kathy would have none of it. She wrestled away from him and stood her ground. They looked at each other. He seemed dark to her, like she could barely see him. She realized she could barely see anything except the table itself. It attracted all the light in the room. It almost blinded her. She came closer to it, no longer afraid or disgusted. She felt only outrage.

I gave it to Erin, and the bastard killed her and took it as a trophy. She vividly remembered presenting it to Erin. She'd seen so much of herself in that girl, so much dedication to massage and such a kindred healing spirit. Kathy would've given it to Erin regardless of need. It had been like an inheritance and an acknowledgement of their special bond. Kathy did not know the sad woman tied to the table now, but she could not avoid imagining Erin in her place.

"Kathy?"

"Look…look at the bottom right corner. There should be a small brass plaque."

Rierdon knelt down and looked. "I see it. For Erin from—"

"Don't read it!"

Rierdon stood up. "Looks like we've found your missing table, Beacon. This is excellent."

Kathy blanched. "Excellent?"

"Agent Rierdon means that the murders are now

incontrovertibly linked. The symbols and the teeth were one thing. This is another level."

Another level? Greg sounded like he was talking about a video game. Kathy stormed out. She ran down the steps, almost slipping in her plastic shoe covering. The techs on the ground floor stopped and stared at her. She shook her head at them and stepped onto the porch. There she faced the lingering media. Two officers were talking to each other on her right. They stopped to glance at her.

Short of running home dressed in plastic, she realized she had no place to go.

Across the street, apparently relegated to the confines of his car, Scott Carson looked over and fixated on her. His right hand tapped into his phone.

"Hey," Greg said in a quiet voice. "Come back inside, Kathy. Please."

"I need air."

She heard the creak of floorboards. He was leaving.

"Greg."

"Yes, Kathy?"

"What's going to happen to my table?"

There was a moment of contemplative silence.

"It'll be held in evidence until the killer is found and brought to trial. It's possible that you never get it back."

She turned around in astonishment. "I don't want it back!'

"What do you want?"

She didn't even need to think.

"When this is over, I want it burned."

25

Kathy sat in her living room watching the television. The news was all about the new murder. She'd just sat through a string of neighborhood interviews. They were faces she'd seen during her walks. How bizarre to see them in this context. *The world is falling apart.*

She straightened and sat up when Bernard Morrison came on the screen. Bernard was her representative in the state legislature. He'd run for Congress twice, almost winning the last time. It didn't surprise her he'd use the murder as a chance to preen. She'd squared off against him more than once because of her role on the State Board for Massage Licensing and Ethics. He was a tricky bastard. At first he'd claimed to oppose a regulatory board, saying it wasn't the government's business. Now he argued it didn't go far enough. His definition of massage was self-servingly inclusive. He now expanded it to include every permutation of the sex industry.

"This is another case of massage being a front for

prostitution and illegal sex," Morrison said. Kathy moaned, unable to stomach more. The public was already disposed toward believing Morrison's nonsense. Another murder and he'd have them convinced every massage therapist in the state should be shipped to a gulag.

Greg came downstairs. He'd showered and changed to a pair of sweatpants and a T-shirt. His hair was still damp and messed up from being towel dried. Kathy thought he looked the picture of comfort, but as he sat down beside her, he winced.

"What is it?"

"My lower back is stiff. It happens when I sit too much. All the recent fieldwork has been a blessing, actually, since most of my detective work gets done in an office. I guess I pulled something."

"Well," she said with a smile, "you happen to be sitting next to a damn good massage therapist, if I do say so myself."

He smiled with a combination skepticism and shyness. "That's okay."

"What?"

He settled back and reached for the remote control. She snatched it before he could get it and leaned toward him.

"Don't tell me you've never had a massage?"

He shrugged. "It's really not my thing."

She started to tease him but thought better about it. There were too many emotions surrounding the very idea of massage for her right now. Could she even go upstairs and look at her table without feeling nauseated? She dropped her gaze.

I can't let myself be bullied and psyched out. I can't run from what I value most. She thought of her students. How were they doing tonight? How could they make it if they knew their teacher was surrendering?

Greg shifted again, frowning. "This is a damn lumpy sofa."

Kathy stood up. Greg stared at her.

"Upstairs, big boy. Now."

She marched past him and went up, confident he would follow.

Less than a minute later, he did.

Facing the massage table was just as hard as she thought it would be, but it seemed even harder for Greg. He blinked as if confronting some new and exotic kind of animal he'd been asked to saddle. Kathy found her haunted feelings being replaced by amusement.

Kathy knew he was afraid. She half wished her new students could see his face. Everyone loved massage once they had one. Getting clients onto the table was the toughest part. All businesses had to deal with customer psychology, but massage therapists had to overcome a vast array of public neuroses. Most people's image of massage came from some movie they saw as kids on HBO or Cinemax. Many feared disrobing and thought they'd be forced to lay naked with no covering. For some this fear came from imperfect bodies, for others uncertainty about intimacy and any number of mitigating factors. It boiled down to trust and respect. The massage therapist had to be the agent of both.

"Do I have to—take my shirt off?"

She went to a cabinet and got a loose garment. It was made of soft terry cloth and had interconnecting zippers all over it. "You can put this on if you want to, Greg. It means I only have to expose the particular area of the body I'm working on. The rest of you will stay covered."

"It's not that," he said, blushing. As if to prove his point, he suddenly whipped the T-shirt over his head, revealing the torso she'd been imagining the past several days. He was toned and defined, dusted with hair on the pectorals and a darker swirl that started at the naval and disappeared into his sweat pants. Kathy just stared. Had her class been watching, they'd have given her a failing grade for lack of emotional detachment.

Greg for his part just looked innocent and shy. She stopped

to wonder if he was hiding his own amusement. Was she being played? Did his back actually hurt? She thought she knew him well enough to tell. He was not good at suppressing a grin.

She pointed to the massage table.

Now he did come forward, smiling a little as he approached. But it was not the coy or knowing expression she might have thought. He really was facing something strange to him. Was it the therapy or the therapist that made him uncertain?

As an ethicist, Kathy knew the situation was wrong. She'd spent so much time railing against the conflation of massage therapy and sex, and here she was blurring the lines herself. *Ethics, hell. I crave him.* She watched Greg walk around the table, touching it, probing to see if it would be hard or soft, warm or cold. She now wanted him on that table more than anything in the world. She wanted to rub deeply into his muscles and feel all of his body, its combinations of hard and soft, its radiant heat. She wanted to find the places that hurt and pour her energy into them.

"Greg," she said, "please don't be nervous."

"I've never had a real massage before," he said. "A shoulder rub from a girlfriend. Nothing this elaborate."

She nodded.

"I don't…I don't like the idea of laying on my stomach while someone stands over me. It makes me feel defenseless."

"Part of getting massage is letting your guard down. It's how you learn to trust. But if you want, you can start off on your back."

"That's not a good idea," he said in a low voice and blushed, a flush of red that colored his face, neck, and the upper part of his pectorals. Then Kathy saw that both his hands were cupped near his groin, as if he were naked. She realized what he concealed and also blushed.

She took a very deep breath. "Maybe you're right. I shouldn't—I shouldn't do this when my mind is thinking about you in a way that isn't professional."

They looked at each other. Greg's throat worked as he swallowed.

"It can't always be wrong. Not when…we're a couple."

Her blush deepened. "I think that even then it can be dangerous. Intimate massage in the bedroom is one thing. The table means something else. It's always got to represent a professional standard. The table really is a symbol. I think I was letting myself forget that just now."

"I'd never ask you to do something you don't feel comfortable with," he said.

"I know that. I feel completely comfortable with you. Better than comfortable. I trust you. I always have," she thought to add.

He nodded, pausing. In the next moment, he climbed onto the table, on his stomach. She went speechless watching him take up its space.

He looked over at her.

"Trust to me is about love. I trust you too, Kathy," he said, and put his face into the mattress pillow.

26

On Tuesday morning, Kathy selected a group of students for quick individual meetings with her. She'd always favored private checkups, but she'd let the practice slide too much. Recent events reminded her of their importance. Her college memories centered on shuffling between vast classrooms for impersonal lectures. Few professors ever bothered to learn names. She'd never let the Academy become so depersonalized.

Her last morning meeting was with Amanda. She asked again about Brad.

She'd only spoken with him once since Edgerton, but it happened to be that very morning. She'd called to tell him about the massage table and to see if he needed anything. News of the table upset him at first. Then he latched on to the idea that it meant the killer was closer to being caught. Kathy agreed with little conviction.

"You really liked him, I take it?"

Amanda smiled. "I guess so. I can't stop thinking about him."

"It's important that you keep your emotions in check. You're very empathetic, Amanda. The ability to sense hurt will make you a great massage therapist. But it also means you'll be in danger of getting sucked in to someone else's suffering."

She nodded, looking at her lap.

"It must be very hard on him, knowing his sister was murdered by a serial killer. It makes it worse somehow."

Kathy nodded. "But how does it make you feel? How do you think your classmates are reacting to yesterday's news?"

She thought a moment and shrugged. "Okay, I guess. It's awful. All we can do is work hard and try to help."

Kathy smiled. Most of her students had said the same thing.

"Of course, it's a little scary," Amanda added. "To think someone could book you for a massage, have you come to them, and—" Her voice drifted.

"Don't be frightened. Massage therapy isn't an isolated work environment. You have the power over your safety. Remember that these victims are being conflated with us. But they're not us."

Amanda said, "My mom called from California. She read about the killings online. She read massage and murder and immediately thought I was lining up to be killed. 'Is that what you'll be doing, just going to someone's hotel to rub them?' How am I supposed to answer that? In California, you can't go a day without hearing about the police closing a 'massage parlor' down. That's where my mom thinks I'm going to be working for a living." She laughed without mirth.

"Massage therapists don't work in secrecy and shadows. It's vital that all of you remember that."

"I'll never forget. But when people like Bernard Morrison start saying their garbage, I don't know what to do."

"I wish I could offer you all a class on how to deal with

bullies and thugs. Just remember that what you said before applies with people like him too. Maybe it applies even more. Work hard and try to be helpful. People will see that and be swayed. We're the ones who must ultimately change other people's perceptions."

Amanda nodded again and gave a confident smile.

"How about your classes—are they going okay?"

"I'm still trying to figure out which modality works best for me. Myofascial just feels right. It just seems so…obvious. But then other techniques appeal to me too. Sometimes I just want to mix them all together in a bag."

Kathy smiled. "I encourage you to! Be creative. Find the technique that best addresses your client's needs. Let your imagination and your intuition meet in the body of your patient."

Amanda seemed very excited. *She'll work wonders for people one day.*

She was about to end their meeting but thought of one more thing. "I haven't had a chance to talk to Jim yet. Is he still working out as a study partner?"

Amanda's smile ebbed. "He's okay. I don't want to talk bad about him or anything."

"Oh?"

"He probably doesn't pay as much attention as he needs to. He's afraid to follow his own path. When I said I liked Myofascial, he started getting into it himself. But he doesn't seem suited for it. Sometimes he'll just sit and complain about the terminology."

Kathy nodded. She already knew memorization was not one of Jim's strong points.

"Please don't think of complaining about him or anything. He's a supersweet guy, and a really good friend. You can tell him anything. Maybe there have been a few times when I told him a little too much!"

Kathy considered this and remembered Jim's puppy-love

eyes from last week. *Probably the same eyes I was giving Greg in bed last night.*

"If it gets to be a problem, I'd like you to tell me."

"A problem? With Jim?" She laughed. "It's okay, really. He just needs a little extra help. I don't think he's got any real support structure in his life. No family nearby, few friends. It's because he's so shy. Otherwise, he's pretty adorable—he's just not right for me," she added quickly.

Kathy nodded. She made a note to talk to Jim as soon as she saw him. She already felt like she'd completely ignored him since he started last term. *Otherwise, he's pretty adorable.* Kathy smiled. She felt that way about all of her students.

27

S HE AND GREG MADE LOVE ON TUESDAY NIGHT AFTER coming back from dinner, where they spoke little about the case. Greg said he'd spent most of the day clustered with a group of specialists cobbling together a psych profile. "Tedious work," he told her. "The majority of it always ends up being bullshit thrown in for padding."

The comment didn't faze her until later as they snuggled next to each other. She asked him what he'd meant.

"Why?"

"I guess I wondered if you thought Reiki is the bullshit," she said.

He rolled onto his back.

"Serial killers almost always fit a few basic categories you can feel accurate about. A certain age range, a certain personality type—controlling, aggressive. In most cases, once you stray beyond those parameters, a profile is just guessing. I've read some that looked like wholesale creative writing."

"But isn't this killer different? I mean, with the Reiki—"

"An interesting variation on a theme. The symbol the killer focuses on is power. It goes back to the basics—control, possessiveness, domination. To read any more into his interest in the symbol may be pointless. But some psychiatrists will write a hundred pages on it just to make their analysis seem more impressive and alternative."

She thought his voice changed at the end. "Alternative. You really don't like that word, do you?"

He shrugged. "I don't think I've got anything against it."

"Let me ask you something. How is your back?"

"Best it has felt in years."

"What did you do to ease the pain before I massaged you last night?"

"I took some Advil, had a hot shower, and cursed my mattress."

"Wasn't last night's massage a better—dare I say it?— alternative?"

He chuckled. "I saw where you were going from a mile away."

"Well, massage is considered to be alternative medicine, isn't it?"

"I guess. But that's different," Greg said.

"Why?"

"Because massage itself is different. Did you ever meet my grandpa Rodney? He once told me about getting a massage in New York back in the 1950s. He said it used to be you went in this steamy room with just a towel and a big Russian guy threw you on a slab and karate chopped your back a hundred times. You felt better because your body was numb. I don't think there was a whole lot of professional certification going on there."

"As opposed to the psychological profilers with their sixth-grade education?"

Greg smiled briefly and drew her closer to him. "What's on

your mind, Kathy? I don't have intuition; I have a gut feeling. My gut feeling tells me you'd like to punch me in it."

She swallowed. "I guess it goes back to yesterday at Betty's."

Greg sat up, rubbing his face. "Now I'm lost."

"I was listening to the two of you talk. It made me a little worried."

"About?"

"Our compatibility—in the long run. Finding you again has reminded me of how much I treasured our friendship. I don't want to lose that to an affair that won't work out."

Greg laughed. "This is the first time anyone ever had sex with me and then said they just want to be friends."

"I'm not saying I just want to be friends. I love you, Greg. But I've been in love before and know that it isn't always enough."

He kissed her.

"You're worried about my politics?"

She nodded.

"Okay. I'm a little conservative. Sometimes a lot conservative. I guess it depends on the topic. That doesn't mean I'm narrow-minded."

"What about religious beliefs?"

"I don't really have any."

"Do you believe in the possibility of past lives?"

She frowned when he laughed. "The possibility? Sure, I can go along with that."

"I take it you you've never heard of the tenth chakra?"

He laughed again. "I haven't heard of the first chakra, either. Does it matter? If you're into chakras and believe certain smells can actually heal you—"

"They certainly can," she said, alarmed.

"Fine. Well, if you believe in all this pseudoscience, be my guest."

"Pseudoscience!"

"I'm sorry. I shouldn't have said that."

"But you did say it," she said.

Now Greg sat up all the way. "Remember *Star Wars*? I'm like Han Solo, okay. Hokey magic is no match for a gun in your hand. I'm not trying to denigrate you. Your methods work for you. I just like the tried and true approach, that's all."

He smiled at her. *It'll always work on me.* Greg, the cop with the get-out-of-jail-free grin. Kathy was surprised at how anxious she felt, as if they were arguing. Aren't we? The pseudoscience remark had started it. He'd shown his true feelings. Why am I trying to get myself worked up? What if he didn't believe everything she did? Just agree to disagree.

She settled back into bed.

"Well, Kathy, I've got a headache now. Do you have some ibuprofen?"

"I don't have any pharmaceuticals," she said in a superior tone. "I can help, though. Would you like to experience the power of Reiki for yourself?"

His eyes widened, and he gave an exaggerated headshake, like a little boy suddenly finding new food on his plate.

She teased him. "What's wrong? Afraid you'll have to change your world view?"

Greg gave her a knowing smile. "I'll just sleep off the pain."

28

Bᴜᴛ ɪᴛ ᴡᴀs Kᴀᴛʜʏ ᴡʜᴏ ᴅɪᴅɴ'ᴛ sʟᴇᴇᴘ. Sʜᴇ ᴡᴏᴋᴇ ᴜᴘ ᴛᴡɪᴄᴇ between midnight and one thirty. Each time she sat up gasping, as if she'd been drowning in her dreams.

She looked at Greg in the dark. He slept soundly on his side, his back to her. She placed her palm just above his skin, sensing his energy. It was powerful and good, balanced and at ease. She smiled. He was such a profoundly good man and she didn't need to sense his energy to realize it. She had always known.

It was almost two. Kathy tried to think of what terrified her in her dreams. Her mind was trying to tell her something important. She believed dreams, especially nightmares, were always the mind's way of serving notice about an imbalance in the body's health. In a sense, nightmares were things to be cherished. They told you to pay attention. They also told you that you always had more information at hand than you realized. You just had to work to retrieve it.

Maybe it's Greg. Could she trust her feelings for him? It

wasn't even a question of his politics or personal opinions anymore. They'd been brought together again through acts of murder. Everything about the case was poisoned soil and the roots of their romance were planted there. How could they thrive?

She turned over and draped her arm over him, putting her face into the heat of his back. *I love this man.*

She closed her eyes and fell asleep. The nightmare wasn't long in returning. Kathy walked down a long and empty hallway with identical doors interspersed on both sides. The hallway was lit by a few dying, flickering bulbs. She kept walking, the atmosphere becoming more oppressive on each step. *So lonely.* The air became chilly. Her bare arms broke into gooseflesh.

"Hello?"

No one answered. At last she heard sound from the last room on the right—a couple engaged in low talk, or a man mumbling to himself. She crept over to eavesdrop.

She put her ear to the door. It was a couple, a man and woman. They were talking about massage. For a moment, everything seemed fine. Then the mood soured. The man started to yell, demanding cash. Then he demanded much worse. The woman screamed. Kathy jerked back, realizing someone's hand was on the knob. The door appeared to be locked.

The woman screamed. The voice sounded familiar, unmistakable. *Erin?* In the nightmare, Kathy knew it was her. The voice screamed again, and Kathy yelled down the hallway for help. The hall seemed so long her voice collapsed and died halfway down it, like an exhausted sprinter.

The knob rattled more. Kathy pressed against her side of the door. "Erin, I'm here! I'm right outside the door, and I've brought the police!"

She almost believed herself. *But you lied. You just gave*

Erin false hope. There's nothing to save her. There's nothing to save you, either.

The door rattled like something very heavy had struck it. Kathy jumped back, hands clasped at her chin, her heartbeat scary. Minutes passed. *What's happening in there? I've got to open the door. I've got to help Erin.*

Kathy tried the knob. The first time her skin slipped from sweat. The second time she got the door open.

The room didn't belong to any motel she'd ever seen. Stepping in, she realized where she was—

The Academy.

She stood in her favorite lecture room. Past and current students filled the seats and stood in silent rows going all the way to the back wall. A massage table draped in black stood in the open demonstration space.

Brad and Erin entered from the side door. Brad was steering his sister, who seemed dazed, almost robotic. They passed Kathy, who tried to say Erin's name. Brad put Erin on the massage table and handed Kathy a scalpel.

"Thank you, Kathy, for today's anatomy demonstration." Brad looked at the students. "And please, everyone; thank my sister for volunteering herself. It's important that her life have meaning."

The students began clapping wildly.

When Kathy didn't move, Brad turned and forced her to the table. She looked at the scalpel in her hand, unable to let go. She started to cry.

"Just look at her," Brad said, putting one hand around Kathy's shoulder. "Erin's so beautiful, don't you think?"

She looked down to discover Erin smiling very brightly at her. Her two front teeth were missing.

As Kathy started to scream, the man who now had those teeth entered.

29

Kathy's scream carried into the waking world. As she sat up, she saw Greg jump off the bed, his body a pulse of reflexes. In the next instant he was shaking her shoulders and peering into her eyes. Seeing his face broke the nightmare's spell. She sobbed with her head in her hands, feeling cold. She warmed as he settled in to hold her.

"Must have been an awful nightmare," he said. "Want to talk about it?"

"No."

He worked to get her lying down with him again. "See if you can get back to sleep."

That won't be happening. She'd just endured the most vivid and detailed dream she'd ever experienced—until the very end. She was cursed with a high-resolution mental image of Erin's broken smile, but the crux of the dream—the man who entered—remained hazy. She remembered awful bloody eyes and a mouth filled with more teeth than could be natural.

Stolen teeth. In her dream, the killer was taking his victim's teeth to fuse them jigsaw fashion into his gums.

Did she know him?

Kathy felt a deep chill at the possibility. Had her subconscious mind found a clue at the crime scenes? Was there something about the Reiki symbols, something about the missing teeth or seeing her old massage table in such a brutal way that told her unconscious mind something she couldn't face?

Greg caressed her back. She closed her eyes. His touch was more tickling than soothing. That was good enough at the moment.

Did she dare tell him her thoughts? She could imagine his reaction, "Dreams, Kathy?" But what if he did believe her—what would happen? Would she be forced through endless batteries of tests designed to jar her memory?

No, she had to keep this to herself. She had to trust her mind to give up the information at the right time.

She just hoped it would hurry the hell up.

She slept again but stress kept it shallow, dreamless, and unsatisfactory. She felt Greg get up a few hours later to take a shower. Kathy joined him. She woke up a little under the water. Yes, she could make it through the weariness. In fact, she was already eager to go to the Academy. She knew exactly how she'd spend her day.

They went downstairs. Kathy thought of the big breakfast she'd seen him eat before. *Time to introduce him to my notion of cooking.* While Greg sat at the table checking his messages and talking on the phone, she took food from the refrigerator. It took only a couple of minutes to present the results to him—a halved banana, grapes, three slices of fresh melon, and a granola bar.

"What do you call this?"

"Breakfast."

"It's not breakfast; it's a fruit cup," he said. He took the granola bar and bit into it. He started tapping on his phone again.

"What are you doing?"

He smiled. "Summoning directions for the nearest Mickey D's. It may not be healthy, but it beats starving to death."

Twenty minutes later, they parted company with a kiss. Kathy drove to the Academy and found Brenda on the phone. She was negotiating with a catering company for Erin's memorial celebration.

"I'm so sorry this has gotten dumped on you," Kathy said. "When I got the idea—"

"Are you kidding? I wish I could spend every day planning a party using the Academy's credit card. It doesn't really feel like work."

She smiled and nodded. "I wanted to know if we've finished digitizing all our past enrollment records?"

Brenda started to laugh. "I've said it before, Kathy. You have the best sense of humor."

I was afraid of that response.

"How far along are we?"

"Twenty-five percent—tops. We're doing the current students first. But slowness is the price we've got to pay for doing it ourselves. It would already be done if we'd outsourced the job."

"Damn," Kathy said.

"Did the ACICS drop a bomb on us or something? Digital record keeping was never a requirement of the accreditation review before."

"No—and don't worry about ACICS. You've done more than your fair share there. But I need you to bring every student file into my office."

"You're serious?"

"What's the matter?"

"I'd rather deal with the ACICS. There must be at least two

crates of student material at this point. Can I at least help you narrow it down by year?"

"No. I want to see all of it. Even the prospects that sent query letters or put in applications but decided not to enroll. We've kept all that stuff, right?"

Brenda nodded. "I never thought we should have, but yes, it's all there."

"Good," Kathy said. She turned to go.

"Kathy, who are you looking for?"

She offered Brenda a wan smile. "Call it the man of my dreams."

30

RENDA AND A CONTRACT CUSTODIAN WERE WHEELING THE
materials into Kathy's office on a dolly when she returned
from a class Wednesday afternoon.

"I thought you said a couple of crates!"

"Sure—of student profiles," Brenda said. "That didn't
include for all the ancillary paperwork too."

Kathy counted six enormous packing boxes stacked atop
each other. The custodian maneuvered it against the window,
pushed in, and extricated the flatbed.

"Anything else, ma'am?"

"No, thanks," Brenda said. The custodian rolled the dolly
away.

"You were right. This makes the ACICS look like cake."

Brenda sat down. "I really want to encourage you to throw
a lot of this stuff away as you go through it. Trust me on this.
No college can keep every scrap of communication it has with
people—and if they don't enroll, why bother?"

Kathy frowned. She wasn't such a hoarder at home. In fact,

she thought it very good to throw things away. She had no idea why her professional personality was so different. Fear of messing up a detail, perhaps.

"Any idea what's in what box?"

"The top three are what I'll politely call the garbage. The next two are the important records."

"The bottom?"

"Employee records."

Kathy frowned in trepidation when she heard that. Her intuition was telling her to go to bottom box. What if the killer once worked— She didn't let herself finish the thought.

"Can I help you sort through any of this?"

"I don't think it will take too long. I'm going to focus mostly on our male students."

"Kathy, is any of this related to the murders?"

Kathy looked up sharply before realizing that Brenda must be burning with curiosity. She'd made no further statements about her role in the investigation, but her name was popping up more often in the press. Worse, camera footage on the news showed her exiting the house where Allison Stockett was murdered. That certainly got some student and faculty tongues wagging. But Greg and the Bureau had helped keep the media off her since Monday. There'd been no calls seeking quotes from her, and she had none to give. She just feared the Academy would suffer by her association with the murders. If the school suffered, so did its students. That wasn't acceptable.

"It might be," Kathy allowed. "But it's more about Erin. I want to make sure the Academy finds a way to keep in touch with its students. If I can't do it myself with every graduate, then at least we can send out a newsletter or something—any contact that reminds them we're still a resource to turn to."

Brenda nodded. "Good idea."

"Right now I want to see how much of the contact information we have on file is still valid. Did you know how many e-mail addresses in my contact list bounced when

I announced Erin's memorial service? Eight. All former students."

Brenda shook her head. "People forget to send updates. People have lives."

"Until they don't," Kathy said.

Brenda looked shocked by the sharpness of this retort. She lingered a moment and then excused herself.

I'm sorry, Brenda. This time you just don't understand.

Sighing, Kathy began to open the boxes. She seldom ignored her intuition when it made suggestions she disliked, but this was an exception. Intuition told her to go for the bottom box first. She started with the top, straining to lower it to the ground. She cut the tape, opened the flaps, and dug in.

After twenty minutes, she thought, *Brenda is right—this stuff is worthless.*

The contents almost entirely consisted of applications that never materialized into enrollments. A lot of the papers were several years old, before the Academy even opened its doors. Back then, Kathy promoted by leaving applications at every area high school career day. These efforts won her a few students, but only years later, after they followed the traditional college route, earned degrees that didn't satisfy them, and remembered massage therapy as an intriguing career.

She examined the names on each paper, had no idea who they were, and started feeding the pages into her office shredder. She thought of it as a private offering to Brenda to atone for her earlier attitude.

Kathy went through the entire contents in just over an hour. She emptied the shredder into an industrial-sized trash can in the janitor's closet down the hall and returned to attack the next box. She moved faster now, confident little to none of the contents needed saving. The applications in the second box were at least more current. Some of the names had a passing familiarity. She thought she remembered conversations with some of them—chats about aspirations and options. She found it harder to shred these documents when she had some memory attached to them.

And what if the killer was someone bitter over being rejected by the Academy, or for being forced to quit because of awful circumstances? She stiffened as the thought occurred to her. Suddenly shredding the contents of the first box felt like an act of criminal negligence. She breathed deeply, trying to center herself. Hands shaking, she went through the second box in silence. She packed the material back up when she finished.

Two down.

Kathy stood and fretted over the third box. She was getting into the meat of the Academy's documentation now. Every student ever enrolled in the Academy had a profile folder that included their photo. Most of her students graduated but a few did not. Sometimes life just presented someone with too many obstacles and distractions. A family member got sick, a husband lost his job. Suddenly the Academy was playing second fiddle due to an awful act of fate.

An awful act of fate.

She dug in. The third box was far better organized. It contained forty thick file folders, each labeled by name and year. She began to separate the men from the women. She opened the first folder and smiled. Al Grossman. He was in the Academy's third class. At forty, he'd been the school's oldest pupil at the time. She flipped through the portfolio until she found his picture. Al was a short but powerfully built man with a fascinating backstory. His father and brother were both excellent jockeys who'd rode in the Kentucky Derby, the Preakness, and the Belmont. "I was cursed with the tall genes," Al had announced at the Academy's Fall Open House. He was five foot six. Kathy touched the picture as she remembered him. She hadn't thought about Al in a couple of years. He'd graduated and gone on to take classes at other schools. He'd wanted to specialize in Equine Massage.

If nothing else comes of this, I'll still be happy I did it. She felt so good remembering these wonderful people.

Somewhere in here, though, might be someone she did not want to remember at all. She could not shake the feeling the man who appeared at the end of her dream, the man with the obscured face, had spent time at the Academy. She was certain that a single photo would spur her memory and make the dream face recognizable. That wouldn't make him a suspect, though. Before the killer entered, everyone present at the end of her nightmare had been a student, except Brad and herself. Kathy sat back, thinking. She'd been so focused on the killer's appearance that the rest of the dream had gone unexamined. If she really started analyzing it, she feared the dream might have no message at all—or perhaps a very different one than she wanted to hear.

Had the Academy gotten too large? Was it inevitably edging closer to the college system she found so distasteful—enormous, crowded classes with a professor who never knew his students' names? Had she added enough staff to compensate? She had a faculty of eight regular instructors and several more guest demonstrators. What was the Academy's average student-teacher ratio? Twelve-to-one?

She remembered when it was five-to-one.

Kathy sat back, pushing the box away. She looked at the remaining crates along the wall. Her intuition sparked again when she glanced at the bottom one.

The faculty records.

She took another deep breath. *It just can't be a staff member.* There'd been little turnover since the Academy opened, and no teacher seemed remotely capable of the butchery she'd witnessed. Maybe her intuition wanted to confirm that the dream really was about her fears that the Academy was getting too big. If it could not provide efficient, intimate instruction, then it failed to prepare its students to succeed.

The way she'd failed Erin.

"Damn it." She pulled the open box back to her and just pulled files at random without regard to gender. She'd spent so much time patting herself on the back about staying in touch with her students. Erin's death had cracked that little fantasy for her. Now it threatened to shatter completely. She read the folder names. Barry Emory, Gayle Thompson, Maggie Carmichael. Without looking, she had no idea what year they enrolled. The names didn't jog her memory at all, though she'd likely taught them all in at least one class. *Sure, you stay in touch with all of your students. You keep telling yourself that.*

There was a knock. She looked up and found Brenda.

"You've been at this for two hours. Would you like a cup of tea?"

"I'm thinking of straight whiskey at this point."

Brenda nodded, smiling shyly. "I wanted to make sure you didn't forget your afternoon class."

"I haven't," she said, lying. In fact she was shocked to find she was going to be late if she didn't run down the hall right now. She shoved the folders back into the box and locked the door behind her.

31

JUDD GARVIS.

The name came to her in the middle of her lecture, causing her to lose her train of thought. She recovered and continued.

When the class ended, she nearly sprinted back to her office.

His file wasn't in the first box of student records. She tore open the second and dug through.

There he is.

She sat down trembling with expectation and laid the file out on her desk.

The mind was an amazing thing in what memories it could willfully suppress—like child sexual abuse trauma. She didn't think she'd ever experienced the mind's ability to forget so dramatically until a name just popped into her head.

Judd Garvis.

His folder was not very thick—a few pages. One was a note from his psychiatrist explaining his erratic behavior. That came after he'd already been dismissed from the Academy. Garvis had delivered it himself, hoping it would get him back in. But his actions had been too irrational, borderline dangerous. The note promised that as long as he stayed on medication, his mood swings were under control. In the end, it was Kathy's decision to make the expulsion permanent.

Blowing up in rage because he couldn't understand a concept, he'd struck a member of her faculty and put her in the hospital for two days.

That was four years ago. Her mind seemed to have scrubbed the whole incident from her conscious memory—until now.

She knew Garvis was the man in her dream without having to seek out his picture. As soon as she found it, though, there remained no doubt.

Should I tell Greg?

She knew she couldn't—not on the basis of a dream. But she had to find Garvis and talk to him. The idea did not appeal to her. He was a hulking man. She remembered thinking him a sort of gentle giant…when he was gentle. As his personality changes started to show, triggered by the stress of school and a change in his medication, Garvis became gruff and clumsy. With his strength, his massages could do more harm than good. Ultimately, no student would be his study partner, and Kathy had to assume the role herself. It was the only time she'd ever felt scared on the table. She was just thankful Garvis had no interest in acupuncture. To think of him putting needles into anyone's back…

And yet, he had been quite normal at the beginning. She'd never questioned his desire to become a healer, to use his massive hands to help others. Mental problems had thwarted him in that as it had probably thwarted him in other ambitions.

An awful act of fate.

But had his afflicted mind spiraled into total darkness?

Kathy looked at the photo. He was not an attractive

man by any means. Pudgy and with unkempt hair, his face just looked crooked. He had a slight harelip and a nose that had been broken at least twice. He was thirty years old in the picture but looked nearer to fifty.

She took the photo from the file and put it in her purse. A quick run down of his contact information proved to be badly outdated. The listed telephone number no longer belonged to him. His apartment no longer existed, having been torn down to make room for a light rail transit station. Garvis might not even live in the state anymore. Considering her suspicions, she hoped that was true. Her last-ditch effort was calling the public library for advice. They repeated her online searches, confirmed no listings, and suggested hiring a detective.

Kathy smiled to herself. She just happened to have one in mind.

Bringing it up to Greg was another matter. She wasn't about to give him a name or even tell him she wanted to research someone.

Later that evening, they went to a restaurant. She waited until they had ordered dinner that night to casually ask about the process of researching someone's background. She was terribly interested in his work. Wasn't there some fantastic computer system where anyone's name could be typed in and all their secrets told? Did the state have something like that? It must be a very delicate thing to access. Surely no one like her could just walk up and use it to satisfy their own curiosity. Right?

Greg was clearly pleased by Kathy's interest. If he realized she was pumping him for information, he betrayed no signs of it.

"But what happens when, say, someone gives you a wrong address? You can verify it's wrong. But how do you find out where a person really lives?"

Greg shrugged. "Most adults at least have one utility bill in their name, right?"

Kathy nodded.

"Well, they're usually paying utilities at the place they live. So that's one simple way to do it. People who claim to live off the grid are just deluding themselves. The basic fact is you can track almost anyone these days. You don't even need to be in law enforcement."

Kathy leaned forward. She hoped she looked astonished. "You don't?"

"God, no. As long as you're willing to shell out a few bucks. Let's say you decide to take a roommate. You want to make sure an applicant hasn't lied about her employment history, right? So there are all kinds of online personal information aggregates you can use to check someone out. Intelius alone will give you just about everything a person could conceivably want on someone. Hell, fifty bucks will get you someone's known addresses, relatives, aliases, bankruptcies—you name it."

"Intelius?"

"That's one of the big ones. There are others."

"How does it work?"

"Anyone's life can be charted on paper as a web of interconnecting data. Someone wants heat and water, they have a utility bill. Someone gets caught running a red light, there's a citation record with the car data. Someone sues someone, there's a court record. A lot of this information is entirely public, but seeking out the individual strands of data discourages most people. Who has time to search in a hundred different places? Services like Intelius act as a clearinghouse and they get paid well to do it. It's not so different from the tools we in law enforcement can access."

"It sounds so amazing," she said.

Greg smiled and reached out to touch her hand. She was glad to see him looking so happy. It must have been a welcome change to show off his own expertise after days of hearing about Reiki. He had given Kathy more information than she thought possible. In fact, when their food came, Kathy already had more than enough to digest.

32

At noon on Thursday, Kathy told Brenda she was going out for lunch and would be gone a few hours. As soon as she got in her car, she pulled the Intelius printout from her purse. The database didn't have a recent phone number for him, but it did have an address. It'd take her about twenty minutes to get there.

She drove despite her dread, which spiked as soon as she pulled up to the curb. *I hope to God no one is actually living here*, she thought, staring. The building seemed to be a small warehouse sitting on a rubble-strewn concrete lot. She stayed in her car. Hers was the only one around.

Calming herself and rechecking to make sure her cell phone was charged, Kathy got out. *See. The air's not toxic. And if Garvis actually lives here, so what? Your house wasn't that hot to look at right away, either.*

But her house had called to her. The building she looked at now screamed—Run for your life!

She stepped toward it, squaring her back. Her heels

crunched gravel and grass, a sound that threatened to unnerve her. *What the hell am I doing? Call Greg, tell him your suspicions and leave it up to the pros.* She realized that if Greg knew what she was doing, he'd put her in a straitjacket.

She remembered how mad she'd been at Erin before learning of her greater fall, just because she thought Erin went to a massage appointment at a motel without telling anyone. It was a serious lapse in ethics and common sense. *And here I am essentially making the same mistake,* she thought, and all on the account of secrecy. She should have been more forthcoming with Brenda, if not entirely truthful. After all, what sort of lunch could possibly justify a warning to call the cops if she didn't return in three hours?

The building had no ground-level windows. The one entrance was a maroon metal door that looked tiny and inadequate when flanked by so much wall. Getting closer, she found the door was actually ajar. Kathy froze, considering her options.

She leaned forward and shouted Judd's name into the opening. Then she waited and listened.

She shouted twice more before deciding he must not be in there. *This place is abandoned. No one could actually live here.* Either Intelius was completely wrong, or else Judd just listed this as his address once, maybe when applying for a credit card. Probably he made it up on the spot having no idea it was a real location, and it worked its way through the databases to become his home address. She swallowed, trying to let her intuition guide her through the fear. She sensed she needed to go inside.

She checked her phone again and reached for the doorknob. The door's hinges made an excruciating whine, as if sobbing for her fate. Kathy shuddered at the sound. She glanced behind her once and stepped through. The door started closing as soon as she did. It was heavy, perhaps steel, and already hot to the touch from absorbed sunlight. Once more, the door did not shut all the way. If she had to run, she could barrel into it with her shoulder and force it wide enough to make an escape. She'd have preferred to brace it open and looked around for something to prop it wider. Nothing seemed adequate for its weight.

Looking around, she realized the building's exterior had fooled her into thinking there were two floors. But it was just one space with windows positioned so high they could only be opened with a twenty-foot ladder. The filthy panes filtered the sunlight into a sad brown. Kathy turned as her eyes adjusted more to the darker environment.

Someone had been here recently. The interior was undergoing some sort of renovation. Kathy had seen pictures of industrial warehouses transformed into astonishingly beautiful living places, but this one wasn't being turned into any home she could imagine. Broken pieces of concrete were strewn along the ground, the rubble thickening toward the far left corner. Someone had started to jackhammer the floor there. She took more steps, certain the vast area contained no hiding spaces. Her fear dwindled when she knew she had the place to herself.

The right wall showed the most attention. A long, narrow table was being constructed there. She touched it and found the structure a little loose and wobbly. A fantastic act of imagination let her see the end result. A bar. This place was being turned into some sort of restaurant.

Looking with a sense of perspective now, her generous creativity repaired and furnished the space in her mind. Her experiences with remodeling made her appreciate the hard, involved labor. And she'd never had to try dancing with a jackhammer.

Did this place really belong to Garvis? Was he doing what he could to create something new—to start his own business? She wondered if she had influenced him at all. It was the overriding message she gave to her students, the importance of establishing their own practice and becoming masters of their fate. But Garvis, in the grips of mental illness, had shown only an interest in tearing down. Building up seemed beyond him. But perhaps with the right medication, and a patient teacher—

The door slammed shut.

Oh God.

"Who the hell are you, lady?"

Garvis.

He was standing at the door twenty feet from her. He seemed huge, larger than she remembered with a body that barricaded the exit. Kathy saw certain details through the shadows his face attracted. The harelip stood out purple and glossy, like a triangle of grafted flesh. The face was much fatter. What passed for a chin sprouted a cactus nest of thick whiskers. He came forward. Kathy backed away. Her heels struck a chunk of concrete and she pivoted, half falling. Her ankle felt gimpy, but it still held her weight.

Garvis got closer. His hairline had receded to a suggestion of fuzz. The added flesh on his face squeezed his eyes closer together and seemed to pinch them around the bridge of his nose. This and his size gave him the permanent effect of an angry bull ready to charge. She thought she was being stared at by a starving predator with no peripheral vision.

"Judd—"

"I know you, lady?"

His voice was remarkable coming from such a body. The tone could not help but be menacing, but she detected uncertainty, even fear—as if she could ever pose a threat to him! It was a loner's voice, used to being the only human sound in its world. He made a sudden lurch forward. Kathy's reflexes were already on a hair trigger. Her feet struck more debris. This time she did stumble. She cried out as the world went upside down and she struck the ground hard on her hip.

Pain shot all the way to her lower back. Kathy clutched herself and tried to roll. She imagined him falling across her like a massive, crumbling tower.

His shadow did just that. It felt almost as heavy.

"Jesus Christ, lady, what the fuck are you doing?"

Sputtering, hands arthritic with fright, she dug into her purse for the cell phone.

He bent down and snatched the purse from her grasp. The strap broke and dangled down before her, swaying like the end of a noose.

I'm dead, she thought.

33

As she tried to sit up, the contents of her purse started dropping to the floor.

"Stop that!"

"Don't like me going through your business? Didn't stop you from going through mine!"

A stab of pain shut her up. *Got to get a handle on that first,* she thought. If she didn't, she'd never be able to make a run for it. She started to summon energy into her hands.

A tube of lipstick click-clacked on the ground, a hollow noise the walls picked up and amplified. Garvis took things from her purse and inspected them as a curious gorilla might before chucking them in boredom.

Kathy brought her hand to her pelvic bones. The pain dropped a notch as she applied the Reiki energy to herself. Her hands directed and channeled energy from areas of her body that had a surfeit of strength to the damaged tissues. The ache here dulled to something manageable. Her lower back and sacrum were still killing her. She winced as she rolled forward a fraction, freeing her hands to move above her buttocks.

"Just the way things are, isn't it? You sneak into my place, then you trip and break your goddamn neck, and I have to pay you a million dollars."

The way he spoke, Kathy thought he described something that had already happened to him.

"Judd," she said, trying to control any fear in her voice, "stop a moment and listen to me. It's Kathy."

"Kathy?" He sounded like he'd never known a Kathy, Katherine, or Katrina in his life.

"From the Academy."

"Academy?"

"The massage school."

He stood motionless. *He's remembering*. It was what he remembered that worried her. A moment of regret, all too fleeting, passed in his gaze. His expression soured further. He threw her whole purse down and vultured over her. She had the distinct feeling of being menaced by King Kong and spared only a second to note where her bag—and her cell phone—lay. In the next instant, Garvis bent down into her face.

"I remember you! You ruined my life!"

"Judd—"

"It's because of you I'm such a failure!"

Kathy flinched as he started kicking pieces of stray cement in random directions. A spray of little pieces struck her cheeks like shrapnel and brought her hands to her face. He kept kicking and swearing for several minutes before the rage left him.

Shivering, she lowered her hands and peeked. Garvis stood with her back to him. He seemed to be just staring at the wall. His heaving, sweating bulk resembled a great mechanical machine that had overheated and couldn't restart until it cooled. The sound of his wheezing respiration rebounded off the walls.

She inched along the ground. Her body made a small scratching sound as it moved through the bits of rubble and dust his kicking had disturbed. She was within arm's reach of her purse if she just stretched.

"Barrister," he said.

He turned and glared at her. Kathy found herself caught reaching for the bag. The damnable thing was she felt guilty for it.

"Go ahead and take it."

She nodded, uncertain. She didn't follow through at first, expecting him to charge as soon as she reached for it. When she had the bag in her hand, she drew it against her chest like the most precious thing in the world. She groped inside and clutched the cell phone. Her fingers rubbed along it like a rosary.

"You hurt?"

Kathy nodded.

"I'd like to say I'm glad."

Kathy swallowed. Her head was pounding.

He walked down to where the bar was being constructed. Kathy was dazed. Was he letting her go? Did he want her to run, to entertain a hope of escape that he knew he could crush?

He went around the bar and came back with three tools in his massive hands—a sledgehammer, a giant hacksaw, and a drill. He returned with it with his mouth open, sort of smiling. He had all his teeth. For a moment, he seemed to have more than that. He looked just like the monster in her nightmare.

"You don't know what real pain is."

"Judd, if we hurt you in any way—"

"If?" He dropped all the tools but the sledgehammer, which he held above his head like it weighed nothing at all. His strength awed her as much as it frightened. "I wanted to help people. You said I was useless."

"I never said that, Judd!"

"You called me a worthless piece of shit. I remember."

He was delusional. He had told himself these stories over the years and stored them someplace in his head. Someplace her presence here had caused him to go again.

"You just needed a little more help, Judd. I'm sorry I didn't know how to give it—"

He brought the hammer down on the floor. It caused a shocking burst of sparks as the head exploded into the concrete. The screaming bang of it caused her to wince. She jammed her fingers into her ears and curled her legs like a refugee under bombardment. He swung it again and again, punishing the floor until it broke apart and powdered.

"Does it look like I need any goddamn help?"

She swallowed, opened her eyes and looked at him.

"I'm building my new dream here."

A dream? What was his dream—recreating hell on earth?

"No," she whispered. "No, you don't need my help."

"I found this place. Or it found me. We found each other. My mom died. I never really knew her. She died, and I got some money."

"I'm sorry she died, Judd."

"Why? Because that way I wouldn't have the money to buy this place? To buy my tools?"

She shook her head fast, terrified. He wasn't rational. The nicest thing she could say to him would sound cynical and suspicious. *Speak when spoken to. Don't volunteer anything.*

"When this place gets finished, everyone will come here. Everyone will ask how I did it. They'll want to know my secret. You want to know what my secret is, Kathy?"

She nodded.

"The secret of my success is a dead mother and getting kicked out of a fucking massage school!"

He laughed then, a rabid, trumpeting sound and crashed down with the hammer.

Garvis dropped it and held up his hands, staring. What? What did he see in the lines of his callused palms? Did he imagine them around her throat? Did he see them forcing open her mouth and plucking out her teeth by their roots? She had no doubt he could do it. But had he already been doing it?

"I wanted to help people," he said.

She risked an opportunity. "You had—have a gift, Judd."

He kept his palms up. His stare deepened as if absorbed by a fascinating movie.

Finally, he said, "Girls were afraid of them."

"Of your hands?"

Garvis muttered something that was neither agreement nor disagreement.

"Everyone was afraid of them. They said I pressed too hard. They said I hurt them."

Kathy just nodded. She surprised herself with tears. Here was a man whose problems neither massage nor Reiki nor any other art she practiced could heal. She would never know the horrors of his life. Despite the pain he'd caused her, Kathy saw only a brooding, tragic figure. She felt almost as if she were seeing how an abused child alone in his room might act, free at last to release the rage and pain in private. She tried to imagine his mother and could not.

Had he never been normal? Her intuition said yes. She thought his troubles had developed late, in adolescence perhaps. They only started to seriously manifest themselves during his time at the Academy. And in the interim years, his condition—what was it? a personality disorder? a brain injury?—had worsened. She sat up, finding strength in her compassion. He had bought and made this isolated warehouse into his world. He slept here, somewhere, and dreamed of transformation. His dreams might be someone else's nightmares but they were his, and even if he did own this building the dreams were his only true possessions.

He isn't a killer He probably matched the killer's psychological profile in every conceivable way. But her sense of the man bluntly rejected the match.

He lowered his hands and shuffled around. His expression looked lost and vacant. He looked down at his tools, toeing them with his worn, massive sneakers. He no longer seemed like an adult, just an impossibly large, petulant child.

"Why are you here?"

"I—I try to follow up with all my students, Judd."

He picked up the saw. She had no idea what type of saw. Its teeth were like the teeth of the killer in her nightmare.

"But you kicked me out."

"I wanted to say I was sorry for that. I didn't explain myself the way I should have."

Garvis stared. Kathy swallowed and continued.

"I knew you had a gift—I just didn't understand it exactly. I do now. It's here. It's right here all around us, in the place you're building."

He followed her gesture and looked around the broken room. Then he smiled. His smile was almost as broken. "I still remember what you said about having a practice. This is going to be my practice."

Kathy nodded vigorously. Her muscles were in bad shape now, constricting and stiffening across her body. She felt a few drops of blood on her face from the spray of concrete. She tried not to think of the filth in those cuts.

Would he react if she stood up? She had to try sometime. He watched her. Seeing her move, he charged over. She gasped, about to scream. He took her arm to help her up. His grip was far too hard, a vise, but she felt no aggression there. He was simply incapable of being delicate.

"You're going to have a terrific success here, Judd. I can feel it."

"What was that thing you talked about all of us having? That sense?"

"Intuition," Kathy said.

Garvis stared down at the floor but he did not lose his smile. "I thought I had it. A voice in my head. I'd always heard it, but I didn't know what it was. When you described it, I thought it must be intuition. My voice didn't always say good things."

Kathy tensed again. *Leave now. Promise you'll come back and then get the hell out of here.*

"What does it tell you, Judd?"

He shrugged.

Kathy edged toward the door. He could stop her at any time. She'd never win a foot race with him with her body half beaten. She kept one hand in the bag, holding the phone. *I can call 911 at any time. I'm not alone.*

"It never told you to hurt anyone, did it, Judd?"

Nearer to the door now.

"I don't remember."

"That's okay," Kathy said.

So close. She remembered the heaviness of the door. Could she even open it?

Judd said, "Where are you going, Kathy?"

She closed her eyes and waited for a terror that never materialized. When she looked over at him, he hadn't moved. Judd Garvis stood content again in his kingdom.

"I have to go now, Judd."

"Where?"

She swallowed, thinking. "Home."

"I thought you were going to say back to school."

She gave him her best smile. "You wouldn't have liked that, would you?"

He smiled back. This time his smiled lacked humor and humanity. "No," he said. "I don't think I would."

<h1 style="text-align:center">34</h1>

"My goodness, Kathy!"

She looked at Sharon's expression and knew the answer to her next question.

"Does it look bad?"

"Bad? I thought bruises like these only showed up in movies."

She'd gone to Sharon's spa immediately after the encounter with Garvis to seek her assessment about the tissue damage. Kathy inadvertently found her to be a sounding board on what possible excuse she could tell Greg.

Sharon eased her onto the massage table, on her stomach, in the spa's only unoccupied suite. Then she went to a cabinet and started to work in silence. Kathy watched her make a poultice of healing herbs for a compress.

After a moment, she said, "You sure as hell didn't just fall down."

"It was on the stairs," Kathy said.

"Thirty flights worth?" Sharon looked up from her preparations. "C'mon, Kathy. You're too smart for this."

Shocked, Kathy realized right away what her friend was implying. *Does she think I'm in an abusive relationship?*

"You couldn't be more wrong."

In a disapproving tone, Sharon said, "I hope so."

She heated the compress and brought it against the small of Kathy's back. Kathy winced at the touch but the herbs had an immediate effect. She felt a tingle on her skin that quickly seeped into her muscles.

"Can you hold that one in place? I want to get another one ready for your thigh."

Gingerly, Kathy reached around and grabbed onto it.

"I'll work around the bruises with a light Thai treatment to drain the lymph and remove toxins. Meanwhile, you want to tell me what really happened?"

"Me falling down thirty flights of stairs would actually be more believable than the truth. I couldn't convince you if I told you ten times."

"Start by telling me once, and we'll go from there."

She went through the key events, editing out her relationship with Greg. This felt wrong to her, as if she concealed their relationship to avoid reigniting Sharon's initial suspicions. Sharon as it turned out knew shockingly little about the murders. In a way, the spa was the equivalent of Garvis's warehouse for her. Between business and devotion to her children, she seldom read the paper, watched the news, or surfed the web. She'd heard rumblings, of course, but did not see how it related to massage aside from political ploys from people like Bernard Morrison. Kathy realized she'd told her friend almost nothing about her own involvement. Sharon didn't even know who Erin was.

When Kathy finished with the basics, Sharon said, "You know what you did was beyond stupid, right?"

She blushed. She wasn't used to any criticism from Sharon. It hurt more because it was so correct. "Guess I'm not cut out to be Nancy Drew."

"Nancy Drew doesn't have to worry about being raped or murdered, Kathy. You should have just given his name to the police as a lead and left the rest alone."

"I don't think I was in real danger."

"You thought that while he was swinging a sledgehammer around?"

"I know, I know." Kathy closed her eyes—thinking about the scene made her remember the sound of its splintering blows. In her imagination, her forehead was directly under it and the hammer was dropping, dropping…

"He sounds like a nutcase."

"When I wasn't terrified of him, I just wanted to cry for him."

Sharon applied a second and third compress.

"Do you think he could be this killer?"

Kathy had been asking herself this question the moment she returned to her car. Her intuition kept telling her no. She almost always got into trouble for not listening to her intuition when she trusted it. Now was one of the few times she wasn't sure she did trust it.

"I don't know."

35

KATHY HAD BEEN ON THE TABLE FOR HALF AN HOUR when one of Sharon's young staff members opened the door, leaned in, and with an exaggerated panic said, "They're attacking again!' He began to laugh.

Sharon sighed. "Go ahead and call the police."

The staffer nodded and ran out.

Kathy tried to turn and look at her. "What's that all about?"

Sharon went to the sink and washed her hands. "Have you ever seen that Alfred Hitchcock movie, *The Birds*? It's a line from the movie—said when the birds gather en masse to attack the town. I don't know how it became a joke for us. Someone says it whenever they appear."

Kathy went up on her elbows. Her body felt far better than it had before—almost normal. "When who appear?"

"Oh, those silly protestors."

"The mob from before?" Kathy made it onto her elbows. "They're still coming around?"

Sharon dried her hands. "Like flocks of birds. This will be the fourth time."

Now Kathy sat up and swung her legs over the side as she closed the front of her robe. "I had no idea you were having to put up with this nonsense all the time!"

"I actually don't mind a good fight. It gets the blood pumping. But these jokers will start hurting my business if they keep it up. I'm done sparring with them. An expensive trespassing ticket from the cops is a better argument than I can make. Sit tight and relax. I've got to go tend shop."

Kathy obeyed her directive for ten minutes. When Sharon didn't return, she got nervous and decided to just go take a peek at the crowd. She was still in her robe as she padded down the hall. She heard the commotion thundering outside as she reached the arboretum. When she entered the lobby, she found several spa patrons standing about looking perplexed and anxious.

Through the spa's glass doors, Kathy saw a great wave of people shouting and waving signs that said incredible things. She heard one of Sharon's customers, an elderly woman who looked particularly scared, say, "I just come here to ease my arthritis. But if everyone's thinks this is some sort of brothel, maybe I shouldn't. What will they say at church?"

Kathy frowned. Sharon was right: those idiots outside would drive her customers away if they kept at it long enough. She moved past them to the door. Sharon and five of her staff had formed a line between the building and the crowd. Sharon wasn't saying a word. Kathy wondered if the crowd's sheer size had overwhelmed her. There were at least a hundred people jammed into her parking lot.

On the left periphery of the mob, looking satisfied with himself as he spoke to a reporter, was Bernard Morrison.

Kathy pushed on the doors and stepped toward Sharon. It amazed her how much the glass muted the decibel level of the crowd. She found herself cringing with echoes of Garvis's sledgehammer in her head. The crowd's chanting had an identical explosiveness.

"Sharon!"

Sharon turned, saw Kathy, and came to her.

"You should really get back inside until the police come. I don't know what the hell these people are up to."

She pointed to Morrison. "There's the cause of your problems."

"That nasty-looking old man? Never seen him before. Who is he?"

She told her. Sharon grimaced.

"Well, politician or no, I'm a taxpayer and he's on my property. Excuse me while I go kick him off of it."

Kathy followed, increasingly awed by Sharon's fortitude. *Would I be as tough if the Academy came under siege—if these people mocked and ridiculed the character of my students?*

They reached Morrison, who was now egging on a large subset of protestors while the media filmed. Kathy saw it wasn't a news crew covering him at all. The cameraman did not have the typical identifying markings. Morrison had hired a private cameraman. He was like a director who put himself into his own movies. "They call themselves 'bodyworkers' now," he brayed with the most derisive laugh Kathy ever heard. "Well, we know exactly what and how they work, don't we?"

His audience thundered in righteous agreement.

"I want to cite some statistics," Morrison declared. The crowd quieted down. *Clever bastard,* Kathy thought. The entire mob had now turned toward him. Those who'd been in the front of the crowd now found themselves near the end. Almost everyone had their back to the very spa they were protesting.

"Do you know how many so-called legitimate spas and massage parlors have been busted by the police as prostitution fronts in this state just in the last month? Six! And two of those were right here in our city limits. I've talked with people across this state, and I've talked with law enforcement officials from across the nation. The situation is getting worse. And now we have Internet sites promoting this massage filth to our children!"

Kathy stirred, and not just from a lingering pain in her back. Morrison's figures were accurate—the police had closed two massage parlors in the city in the last month. Kathy applauded both actions. But Morrison wasn't telling them everything. Those spas were never legitimate. There were no licensed massage therapists working there—of course not! She and Morrison had actually discussed this problem in detail through her work on the state board. He knew damn well he was shaping a lie.

"Mr. Morrison," Sharon said, approaching.

"Yes?"

"Kindly get your butt out of my parking lot and take your fan club with you."

Kathy watched them. Morrison's lips twitched into a little smile. "And you would be…Madam…"

Some in the crowd caught the joke. So did Sharon.

"It's Miss, actually. As in I won't be missing you. The police are on their way. Are you stupid enough to sit around and wait?"

Morrison shook his head, still playing to both the camera and the crowd. "When the police protect the right of perverts over the concerns of the community, I can guarantee you I won't wait. I'll take action, and I see now that I must take action. We're going to shut every spa down until we can determine just how widespread their criminal activities are. Look at what they've brought to this city and our state! There's a direct correlation between the sex industry and the sex crimes industry. You've seen the news. These 'massage therapists' are being murdered—and it's truly a horrible thing. We must protect these young women from the perverts who seek to harm them. It's time to shut these places down!"

Kathy shook her head. Sharon looked stunned. She'd

obviously never run into someone as conniving as Morrison. His followers showed no trace of reason as they whooped and chanted.

A rage built inside Kathy as she thought about the crowd. How could any of them think Sharon's spa harbored even a trace of corruption? They were damn fools, led by a bully. She doubted any of them had ever experienced a massage personally. They were acting on perverted stereotypes. Now their prejudice threatened to destroy her best friend's joy and pride. She couldn't let that happen.

Sharon took her aside several feet and whispered, "Damn politician. What does he want with me?"

"Just a soapbox," Kathy said.

"To get himself elected mayor?"

"Mayor? Morrison's more ambitious than that. It's the governorship at this point."

"And there's nothing we can do about it."

Kathy looked over the crowd with their signs waving in triumph. She followed them all the way back to Morrison's smarmy face.

"Yes, there is."

She marched toward his position just as the faint call of police sirens asserted itself over the din.

"Kathy!"

"It's okay," she called back. "I'm going to confront Morrison head-on."

"But Kathy," Sharon said, waving her hands, "you're only wearing a robe!"

36

"Congratulations, Kathy! The boys here tell me you've caused the largest riot in the city's history."

She looked up to find Greg standing in the doorway of the interrogation room. Two cops flanked him. One of them had booked her three hours ago. Mortified, Kathy pulled at edges of her spa robe and made a complaint about the air conditioning.

Greg motioned at the two officers and they left. He stepped closer, hands in his pocket.

"Quit looking so self-satisfied."

"I'm not," he said, grinning. "I'm just completely in awe."

"Of what?"

"Your right hook, apparently."

"I didn't hit anyone, Greg."

"That's not what Morrison is saying."

"Well, Bernard Morrison is a liar."

"I know," Greg said. "His cameraman made a nice record

of the whole event, which we gladly confiscated. Sorry you've had to wait so long."

"You could have came and told me this sooner."

"Kathy, I'm not with the feds. I don't come and go as I please into other police department jurisdictions. I was lucky to get in here at all."

She shifted. "Is something new in the case?"

He shook his head.

Kathy looked down at the floor, feeling glum. Her body ached again—not as bad as before, but much of Sharon's hard work had been undone. It really was a riot in the end. She'd almost been trampled. So had Sharon. So had Morrison, for that matter. This made her smile a little. The police sirens blaring in everyone's ears stopped some of it. The horrendous crash of shattered glass ended all of it. The spa's beautiful front doors lay in ruins. Kathy's last memory, before being led away in handcuffs, was of Sharon holding back sobs as her staff swept up a thousand shards.

"I didn't cause the riot. Morrison had a little something to do with it too."

Greg pulled up a chair and turned it around so that he sat facing its back, legs straddling. She blinked. What's he about to do, interrogate me?

"Morrison's film footage may say otherwise on that point," he said.

"He did start it."

"Well, he's a politician."

"So?"

"So think about it, Kathy. How many politicians ever get called for the bullshit they pull? Not too many."

Her anxiety spiked. She'd never dreamed she could be held culpable for the mess. Would she go to jail? Who'd run the Academy?

"You're saying I'm going to be prosecuted?"

"I'm not sure what the city wants to do."

"Greg," she said, leaning forward. She desperately wanted to rest her forehead against his chest or shoulder. He shifted his weight, more than willing to oblige. Then her lower back twinged again and she gasped, her left hand shooting to the sore spot.

"What's wrong?"

She laughed. "What's wrong? I'm sitting here wearing underwear and a spa robe in a room with a temperature that must be regulated by Eskimos—"

"But you're hurt."

She twisted right and left at the base of her back. "I fell down, Greg, that's all."

"Can you stand?"

"After sitting in this chair?"

"Quit messing with me, Kathy."

He got up and squatted down beside her, his hand on her arm. He eased her up. She could only make it halfway before the pain locked her muscles in place. His eyes widened. He went and closed the door before returning to her.

"Here—turn around and let me see."

"Greg! I'm practically naked under the robe."

"I've seen you fully naked, Kathy."

She grabbed his insistent hand and nodded toward the mirror wall. "Is anyone watching?"

"No. Sometimes a mirror is just a mirror. This station has two interrogation rooms. One has an adjoining room separated by a two-way mirror. The other room, this room, has a one-way mirror. If you took it down, all you'd find is a wall."

She nodded, relenting. He released the right flap and pulled it back. She'd already seen the big purple blotches covering her skin. Greg stared a moment in silence.

"I want to kick someone's ass," he said.

Kathy swallowed, starting to shake. "I've got no one to blame but myself."

When Greg helped her into her living room ninety minutes later, she felt ten years had passed in the space of ten hours. Greg turned on the television and then went to change his clothes, leaving Kathy to get an objective look at the "largest riot in the city's history." It didn't seem too impressive to her. But it had always been a tame city. She smiled at that. She didn't smile at the footage of her stepping toward Morrison in the embarrassing white robe. The picture was dark and frenetic, taken by someone using a cell phone. She'd intended to walk up to Morrison, call him an old pal, and make a statement on how completely wrong he was. How that could be enough to spark a riot mystified her.

The piece finished with an on-scene interview with Bernard Morrison, his hair nobly tussled from the experience. He straightened his tie as he spoke.

Greg came in with a stack of letters in his hand, having collected her mail from the floor.

"We're living in a culture of violence that doesn't like it when someone stands strong for our traditional values. It's the type of society that breeds these sex massage parlors and incites the passions of weak-minded men to murder."

"God, turn it off," Kathy said.

Greg changed the channel to ESPN instead. "SportsCenter," he said. "Nice and safe and not a political ideologue in sight since Keith Olbermann quit. Can't promise you we won't see a brawl, though."

He set the remote control aside and reached for her hand.

"What are you doing?"

"You gave me a massage. I want to return the favor."

"No," she said quickly. "That's really not necessary."

He grinned. "Not so confident when the tables are turned, are you?"

"You're not a trained massage therapist—you could do more harm than good."

"It's just a back rub—"

"It's not just a back rub, Greg!"

He stared at her a moment and looked away. "Sorry," he said, his voice low, and walked toward the kitchen.

37

"Hi, Andrew."

"Are you ready for me?"

"I'm always ready for my favorite client. Isn't it a beautiful Friday?"

Gayle Thompson led the young man into her living room, where the massage table was set up for the appointment. Heavy drapes hung over the windows, darkening the room to dusk. Lit candles flickered, creating a peaceful ambience.

Massaging clients in her living room didn't make for the most glamorous business, but it sufficed. At her age and with the nest egg she'd established, she could afford a more leisurely practice. Gayle had become a massage therapist after spending twenty years in real estate. That cutthroat life cost her dearly in terms of family. She had two adult children, a son named Tim and a daughter, Gwen. She seldom saw them. Tim lived in Colorado with his wife. Gwen was finishing up a college degree in Ohio and would not return after graduating. Divorced early, circumstances had forced Gayle to be an absentee mother much of the time. Now her children seemed determined to return the favor.

She was fifty-five now. She had her first massage at the age of fifty-three. The experience even now couldn't be captured in words. She still counted it as the most serene hour of her life and one of the most clarifying. Gayle had spent two decades selling houses to others, but it was the one-hour massage that at last made her feel at home in her own skin. Two months to the day after that massage, she enrolled at the Academy of Healing Touch.

Andrew had been one of her first clients when she started her practice last year and had since been a massage therapist's dream. He often got a massage every week, saying he played a lot of sports and needed to keep his muscles energized. Gayle believed him. He was one of the fittest young men she had ever met. She wanted to introduce him to Gwen. A picture of Andrew might be enough to entice her daughter back home for a visit.

But she considered Andrew as more than a customer. He was only a few years younger than Tim, and in his absence she'd started to think of Andrew as a replacement. She would never tell him, of course, though she suspected he knew. There was nothing wrong with a harmless, innocent fantasy. Somewhat shy at the beginning of each session, Andrew became amazingly frank and talkative on the table. Most clients just wanted to close their eyes, listen to music, and enjoy Gayle's work in silence. Andrew, however, talked about girlfriends, breakups, hassles at school. Even his hatred of dentists was a topic for him—the two of them had certainly bonded there.

No aspect of his life seemed off-limits. At first, Gayle found this deeply unsettling; later it became intoxicating. She'd always considered her realtor work rewarding, but she seldom felt like she knew much about her clients. She never would have imagined such openness from a man thirty years her junior. She found herself responding to it, revealing herself to him, struggling to match his honesty. In many ways, Andrew knew more about her than either of her children. There was nothing sexual between them—not even a thought. Her ethics class in massage school remained one of the most powerful seminars she ever took. She knew the intimacy of the work could develop into inappropriate feelings. She knew there were boundaries between the therapist and the patient.

And between teachers and students. She sighed, thinking of her boyfriend, Lou.

Lou had been her main instructor at the Academy. He was a man of vigorous middle age only a year older than her. Their attraction was immediate and too powerful for any talk of ethics. She still felt guilty about the relationship—she supposed any student who ever dated a teacher did. She'd been a competent but not great student, and Lou never once showed favoritism because of the affair. When she graduated from the Academy a year ago, their relationship had not stopped.

But the seed of their relationship became the seed of her doubt. Lou had done nothing so far to earn her distrust. But if he would date—sleep with—her while she was a student, would he have qualms about going after another? Their work lives were quite different—he was so dedicated to the Academy that he taught at an irregular schedule to accommodate all students—that she sometimes wondered if his dedication was really to being surrounded by prettier, younger women.

I shouldn't have told Andrew those things. She opened her mouth about it five months ago. It was just so hard to hear his frankness and feel like she had nothing to give in return. But telling him about Lou revealed too much. She had spoken as if she sought absolution for both their affair and her suspicions. Perhaps her unease came from believing that a mother would never tell her son such things. Andrew had fixated on the details in an obsessive way, asking her about it in separate sessions. It was how a son might react if his mother told him she suspected his father of being unfaithful. If he brought it up today, she would have to find a way to redraw their boundary about what was appropriate in their conversations.

"Have you been doing okay, Andrew?"

"Pretty good," he said. He had removed his shirt and dropped his pants, appearing before her in just boxers. He lowered these too.

Caught off guard by how readily he stripped, Gayle had him get onto the table and quickly draped his lower body with a sheet.

She started to gently knead his shoulders.

"Do you want the regular treatment, Andrew?"

"Do you know trigger point?"

She smiled. "Yes, I do."

"I'd like that this time."

She ran her fingertips along his back, searching for muscle knots. These knots were actually contractions in the muscle tissue that caused an area of radiating discomfort. Each area was called a trigger point because it could also cause pain in other parts of the body that seemed completely unrelated. For instance, a trigger point in the calf muscle could actually send pain to the jaw. A person might think they had TMJ when they really needed to be massaging their legs. The concept was called referred pain. Gayle had been fascinated when Lou explained its complexities. She'd always loved the idea of hidden connections.

"I'm not finding any muscle knots in your back," she said. "Where are you having pain, Andrew?"

"My teeth," he said.

She smiled, thinking of his hatred of dentists. The trigger points that referred pain to the teeth were mostly located in the masseter, the powerful jaw muscles. Gayle moved to the top of the table by his head.

"What are you doing?"

"Seeking trigger points along your jaw."

"But it's my back that's the cause, right?"

"No," she said. "Not if you're having trouble with your teeth. There's no trigger point in the back muscles that refer pain to the teeth."

Andrew was unusually quiet as she worked, which made sense to Gayle as her fingers were probing close to the mouth. She smiled as she worked, thinking about his interest in various massage types. He often talked about the therapies she was using and usually revealed a complete misunderstanding about how they worked. Regardless, his interest seemed so intent that she wondered if he was thinking about it as a career. She liked the idea—the son following in his mother's footsteps.

She took her hands away from his face.

"Are you still dating that one girl, Andrew?"

"No."

She smiled. "Moved on to someone else, huh?"

"No."

Gayle bit her lower lip. Perhaps he just wasn't in the mood for conversation today.

Something's wrong.

"You'll meet someone nice soon enough."

"Like the way you met Lou?"

He said this with surprising sharpness.

"I'd rather not talk about Lou," she said. "Let's focus on your needs today."

"I've never tried to date one of my teachers."

Gayle tried to laugh. "That's probably a good idea."

"Why," he said in the same edgier tone. "It's working for you, right?"

"Please, let's not talk about Lou. That's sort of private with me at the moment."

"Oh," he said. She thought he sounded glum. *I'm such a hypocrite. I'm the one who started it.*

She returned to looking for muscle knots and found none. His body in fact seemed completely relaxed, as if it had been massaged no more than an hour ago.

"Do you have any plans for the weekend?"

"Oh, a few things," she said with a touch of nervousness, thinking of tomorrow. She'd be meeting Lou at his place and then the two of them would drive for a special celebration at the Academy. She didn't know the student being remembered, though Lou did. Both of them were still a little anxious about showing up as a couple.

"What about you, Andrew?"

"None."

She doubted this. How could such a good-looking young man have no plans on a Saturday night? Gayle smiled to herself, feeling old.

She withdrew her hands. "I don't think you have any muscle knots, Andrew. If you're teeth hurt, it's probably something else. I can't find any trigger points."

"Girls make my teeth hurt," he said.

The comment was so weird and unexpected that Gayle laughed automatically.

"Is that because they're so sweet, or because girls just make you grind your teeth sometimes?"

She was looking at the back of Andrew's head, her hands still on his face. Suddenly his body turned beneath her hands. She pulled away as he shifted onto his back. He pulled the sheet away to reveal a strong, large erection.

"Andrew," Gayle murmured, too shocked and embarrassed to get angry immediately.

"This is my trigger point."

She stepped back, dazed, shaking her head.

"Turn...turn back over, Andrew, and I'll try something besides trigger point. Okay?"

He rubbed the tip of his penis with his thumb while squeezing his eyes shut—an expression of pain rather than ecstasy. When he opened them again, they were wet with tears.

"It's not supposed to do that, is it?"

"Andrew, honey, I don't know what you—"

"When I touch down here, it triggers pain here," he said, indicating his head.

"That's not…that's not a real trigger point. I don't—Why don't you turn over and let me look at your back again? I bet I missed a knot and that's what's causing your headache."

"I have to give you my headache and my toothache now."

He started to laugh, getting off the table.

"Andrew, don't," Gayle said, backing away, confused and trembling. What had happened to him? Where was the nice boy she'd massaged so many times? Where was her son?

"Do you know what they say? They say there are trigger points between people."

"What, Andrew? I don't understand."

"They say when your teeth hurt, it makes my head hurt."

"Who says? Andrew, pain gets moved within the body; it can't be transferred outside of it. Someone's been telling you ridiculous stuff."

Andrew came closer. "I want to make your teeth stop hurting."

She backed up a step. "It's your teeth that were hurting, Andrew. Remember? I'm not in any pain."

"Because you're sending all of your pain to me!"

Gayle turned to run. Andrew caught her in a moment. Something came around her neck. The sheet! Andrew had twisted it into a tight braid. She cried out once against the tightening of her noose. It came out a mere frothy, gargling sound.

Lou. She imagined his large, powerful hands throwing Andrew across the room. *Lou, please save me.*

Her sight was almost gone when Andrew spun her around to face him one more time. Delirious, she tried to smile at him.

He was always such a sweet boy.

38

For Kathy, Saturday night came after spending Friday in prolonged agony at home applying ointments and taking hot baths.

She pulled up to a curb half a block away, the only place she could find after circling the Academy's parking lot and immediate area. It was six o'clock. Erin's memorial service was scheduled for seven thirty, with appetizers and drinks beforehand.

Thank God for Brenda. She'd never meant to foist every aspect of the event planning on her and felt guilty—even cheap—for being so uninvolved in her own idea. In certain ways, this fact only seemed to highlight rather than end the lingering estrangement she felt for Erin.

As she reached the parking lot, Kathy just felt like a hobbling old woman. Her body remained stiff and sensitive to the touch. She stopped and stared at the cars. It appeared that at least three-quarters of the Academy's former students had returned for the memorial. *I'll have to be careful with my body language.* She didn't think she could survive too many hearty, uninvited hugs.

At the door she heard the combined noise of several overlapping and animated conversations. She entered quietly and just looked around in awe. Brenda had outdone herself with the decorating and the setup. Amanda and Jim were manning a registration table and as she walked over to them, both smiled.

"Hi, guys," she said.

"Hi, Kathy," Amanda said. She cast a glance at Jim, who caught it and hurried to shove a welcome packet her way. Kathy took up the nametag and pinned it to her blouse. She looked at the next items in Jim's handout.

"This is incredibly touching."

Brenda had designed a short history of Erin's life with a reproduction of her student picture. A small tremor ran through Kathy as she read the biography. She glanced up from the story of her past student to the faces of her current ones. Amanda smiled so much like Erin. Had they met, they would have become the best of friends. Kathy was going to make sure Amanda didn't make the same mistake Erin had made. She'd never fail her students again.

"Do we know how many people came?"

"I think a bit over a hundred," Amanda said.

Kathy nodded. "Don't stay too long at the table—both of you make sure to enjoy yourselves. I really appreciate your willingness to pitch in."

She walked away from them but went left, away from the most crowded spaces. The classroom doors were all open and she saw separate groups in there, taking every available space. She had a momentary, unsettling flashback to her dream. *No— none of that! Not tonight!*

Kathy smiled and calmed herself. She felt only gratitude that so many students had returned. Many journeyed in from other states. Few of them ever even knew Erin. Yet they came. Why? The answers seemed suddenly beyond her comprehension. Was it just a chance to catch up with the people they did know? Was it just an excuse to travel a bit? She supposed the reasons were as diverse as the people.

They were here. That was all that mattered.

As she watched the people mingle, she saw something that fascinated her. The younger, current students were chatting with the older ones. She watched Amada leave the table and go talk to Stephanie Atkins, a forty-year-old massage therapist who had graduated from the Academy three years ago. Stephanie had a practice in Washington, DC. She appeared to be demonstrating a new technique to Amanda, who watched avidly. Stephanie's hands moved and swept in a combination of strokes. It was like viewing a particularly beautiful type of sign language.

She listened, wishing she could be invisible and just eavesdrop. Other graduates were sharing anecdotes with the current class and listening to stories in turn. Kathy heard her name mentioned several times and blushed. "Kathy's just a wonderful mentor," she heard. "I wouldn't have had the courage to start a practice without her. I thought I was going to have to spend my whole life working for some chain and barely scraping by. Kathy taught me how to be independent."

There were so many conversations like this that Kathy began to feel she was the one dead, a ghost attending her own memorial. Of course people would say only nice things. No one mentioned the times she failed: the times she forgot to mention something important in class, the times she got too busy and overlooked someone's needs or forgot to follow up with them. No, only the nice things could be said tonight. She shook herself out of her imagination and moved on.

Skirting the edge of the gathering, Kathy found not everyone was smiling. She came to a group who stood apart from the rest. *In more ways than one*, she thought with a special ache. They were the members of Kathy's first class.

Erin's class.

Stacy, Peyton, Michael, Lisa. Three more joined them—Elizabeth, Claire and Marta. The entire first class. *They all came.* Their identical solemn looks stood out as easily as gold badges among the general merriment.

She could no longer content herself to wander the periphery and observe. She came to them. "Hi, guys," she said. She froze, hearing herself. "Hi, guys" were the first words she had ever said to them as a group, the first day she stood before them and felt a rush of stage fright that left her mind momentarily blank. They were her very first words as a teacher.

"Kathy." They seemed to say it aloud in unison. They came forward and embraced her. She steeled herself through the pain, which was not as great as the emotional loss she shared with these people. She found herself crying. They all cried and somehow, quite unforced and unplanned, they gathered into a ring. They held hands in a chain and talked about the old times. They talked about "Thomas Preston Miller" and this made Kathy laugh.

"The new class just calls him Herbert," she said.

At last, they talked about Erin. Kathy found it even harder to take than she'd imagined. They were guarded in their memories, careful to steer away from the recent past. Who last saw her, who last spoke to her? None of them could seem to recall. They now knew that Erin's murder was not a single incident. She was the victim of a serial killer—one who preyed on sex workers. The media had taken to bracketing the women together as Craigslist Call Girls. It was almost impossible to think of Erin without that awful association in mind.

As more and more people noticed Kathy's presence, they started to move toward her. The ring was broken as one student after another came to hug her. The pain jolted her each time. She did her best to hide it knowing she wouldn't be able to mask it for long—not in a room full of empathic massage therapists.

Just then, a warm, gentler arm snuck its way around her waist. She turned to find Greg holding her. He looked amazing, freshly shaved and in a sports coat. They'd hardly seen each other the last two days. After she snapped at him about the massage he wanted to give her, both had distanced themselves. It was necessary space for the separate pressures each felt.

Kathy smiled, turned and kissed him. When she finished, it seemed like half the room had watched it happen. She blushed.

"I wasn't sure if you'd…be able to come."

He grinned. "I couldn't let you down. Are you ready to show me off?"

"Right this way, Mr. Modesty."

She moved through the crowd greeting old students, meeting spouses, reminiscing. She found Brenda supervising four young men—they appeared to be in high school—assigned to carry trays of hors d'oeuvres among the masses. She seemed to be managing six different things at once and in a total zone. She looked up just once, saw Kathy standing near, and grinned.

"This service was a great idea, Kathy."

She touched Brenda's wrist. "Thank you for what you've done to make today happen."

Brenda looked past her at Greg. "Who's the hunk?"

"Just someone she met in jail," he said.

Brenda's smile broadened. "Remind me to start my own riot sometime soon!"

"Oh," Kathy started with a touch of embarrassment. But her mirth was too great, and in the next moment Brenda was gone off supervising again.

"So, this is your school?"

She nodded.

"I'm extremely impressed. I can't imagine how much effort it took to start. And look at all these students. You can see how special this place is to them."

"They just came back to honor Erin," she said, her voice lowering.

"They came back to honor you."

She took his hand, leading him from the main body of people. "Where are we going?"

"Principal's office," she said.

His own pace quickened.

Inside her office with the door shut, Kathy drew the blinds.

"How are you feeling?"

"Like it's been a hundred years since I saw you," she said, moving into his careful arms. She put her right cheek against his chest and sighed.

"We should talk."

"About anything," she said. She felt herself melting against his body.

"I want to know how you really got your bruises."

She pulled away, shocked. "But I told you—"

"I was allowed to look a little more at Morrison's film footage."

"Then you saw me fall."

"Once."

"The camera didn't capture everything, Greg!"

Greg looked at his feet. There's something else he doesn't want to tell me.

"Why were you at the spa?"

Kathy just looked at him. Her intuition struck. "Did you interview Sharon?"

"I did not; I have nothing to do with the investigation."

"But you've been looking into it on the side," Kathy said, her voice rising.

"I've taken an interest in the reports. I've gotten to know a few of the guys on the City PD and they've told me some things. You were at the spa to have your bruises looked at. That's a fact. You didn't have any bruises on your body when you left for work that morning, unless I'm going blind."

Kathy turned from him with a grimace. "Do you know how important this night is?"

"Yes."

"Then why the hell are you trying to interrogate me right now?"

"Because I never really clock out of my job, I guess. But more because I love you—and the question is too big for me to keep inside, even for a few more hours. You'd stall and be angry with me no matter when I asked. You'd say it if I asked in bed, in the shower, or at the breakfast table. So why am I asking you right now? Because it is better to know as soon as possible, and now is as good a time as any, Kathy."

His answer overwhelmed her. She shook her head, fighting tears. "Some things aren't your business, Greg."

"You were trying to track someone down earlier in the day."

"No, I wasn't."

"Who was the person?"

"No one!"

"And here I thought you were really interested in my work," he said with a faint smile. "Did Intelius give you any leads?"

She began to sense that Greg knew everything. But why this game if that was true?

"I guess you'll never know."

"I can find out, Kathy."

"Is this how you'd be in a relationship, Greg? Threatening me with your authority any time I decided to keep something a secret?"

"That's not fair," he said.

"Seems pretty accurate to me."

"Then I don't know what else to say. We should both walk away before one of us really gets hurt."

He went past her to the door.

Kathy stood in her office alone for ten minutes. She sat at her desk and cried without a sound for ten more.

Why am I trying to protect Judd Garvis?

"I don't know what to do," she said. Her own voice haunted her against the muted sounds of the celebration. She'd be expected to address them all soon. The idea was appalling in her present condition. If she broke down in front of them, they'd think it was for Erin. They'd never know her greater sorrow was the possibility of losing Greg.

She got up, steadying herself, and thought she looked presentable. She opened the door and stepped into the hallway.

She heard a quiet conversation nearby. Two people were in one of the small demonstration rooms.

"I'm sorry, Jim, it's just not working out."

Amanda.

"I don't understand."

"I don't either. In so many ways, I think you're exactly what any girl would look for in a guy. You're nice and sweet and really cute. I guess the problem must be with me."

"What's wrong with you? Do you have any pain?"

Kathy frowned. She'd never gotten the chance to speak with Jim alone like she wanted. She didn't want to eavesdrop further but her intuition told her to stay.

Amanda laughed. "I'm in pain if I think you are. That's what makes this so hard. I think I'm causing you to hurt. When it comes to the two of us, being together like you want…I just don't think it can work. You know what I mean?"

There was silence. If Jim answered her, it was through a nod. Kathy heard footsteps nearing from inside the room. She ducked back into her office and waited. At the door, Amanda said very clearly, "I'll see you in class on Monday, okay, Jim?" Then she walked down the hallway toward the party.

Kathy waited several long moments, pondering. The door did not open again.

Is Jim just going to sit in there? She wondered if she should go in.

What if he's crying? Give him his space.

In certain ways, these thoughts felt more like what she wanted for herself from others just now. She listened a few moments longer and decided she had to act. She opened the door a little and peaked in. Jim was sitting at a table, just staring. Kathy walked over to him.

"Jim?"

He looked up. "Hi, Kathy."

"You okay?"

"No."

His voice quivered. He spoke like a man who wanted to cry but couldn't. The dry hurt was there but not the tears to water it.

"Do you want to talk about it?"

"I need Amanda," he said.

His answer startled her. Need. So much different than love but also so similar.

"Love doesn't always work, Jim. You know that, right?"

"I know."

"So we find someone else who loves us—who needs us back, who gives to us what we give to them. And that's so hard sometimes. I can't tell you how often I've been rejected."

"You have?"

"Everyone has, Jim. It's okay. It's hell, but you get through it. And it's incredibly worthwhile, especially in the end when you do find that person who wants your love and returns it."

Jim began to smile. Kathy's uncertainty lessened to see it.

"It is worthwhile," he said, and got up.

"Where are you going?"

"They said there was cake."

Kathy smiled. "There is! Got get yourself a piece. Get three or four, in fact."

She sat in the empty room a few minutes, musing. She

thought about Greg and wondered if half of what she'd just said to Jim was also self-directed. Shaking her head, Kathy knew she had to rejoin the crowd. She walked down the hallway to the central reception area. If anything, there seemed to be more people than before. Kathy moved toward the front of the crowd as best she could, the crush of their bodies sometimes excruciating to her. Brenda had put a lectern beside a gorgeous picture of Erin that was mounted to a tripod. *I have to find the words. I have to find the words to honor her.*

She smiled at the large, almost overwhelming audience. The room started to hush in expectation. Just before Kathy started to speak, she saw Amanda come stand in the very back. She looked as happy as Kathy had ever seen her, whispering back and forth with a handsome young man. Kathy recognized him at once—she had practice seeing him from a distance.

Amanda was with Brad.

39

THERE WAS A NOTE ON HER DOOR WHEN SHE GOT HOME.
Kathy—I'm sorry. I did what I had to do. I'm returning to Edgerton now. The Bureau's done with me. Thought you might be too.

She swallowed hard as she read and looked immediately at her house. The windows and the beveled glass frame around her door showed an inner dark. The idea of Greg being gone caused Kathy to turn around and sit on her front step despite the pain of stooping. She felt old. Like Betty, she thought, turning to glance toward her neighbor's house. It was a little past nine and her lights were still on. Kathy felt so lonely she almost considered paying her a visit.

I did what I had to do. What exactly did that mean? Just confronting her about the bruises? Or had he gone further? She dreaded to think just how far he could go.

The Bureau's done with me. She found tones of both relief and disappointment in that sentence. It must be awful to contribute to something and then be dismissed as unnecessary.

At the same time, she sensed Greg's fundamental decency had been injured by the events of the last few weeks. A little distance would heal his psyche. Kathy closed her eyes and wished she could send him to someplace as good as himself. She'd very much like to join him there.

Thought you might be too.

"Not on your life, Greg," she said toward the night sky.

At the moment, though, another couple concerned Kathy the most. Amanda and Brad had left together before the memorial ended. This surprised and troubled Kathy. Maybe he couldn't bear the scenery anymore—the pictures of Erin, the papers that printed her life story. But Kathy assumed he'd at least want to talk with her first. They'd not spoken about Erin or the investigation in many days. She did not even know what he'd been doing all this time.

When the ceremony finished, only a few remained to help clean up. Brenda and her young servers took care of a lot of it. Jim was there, too, but he did very little. His expression throughout seemed shell-shocked and distant. Kathy sensed pain and confusion coming off him, and her intuition told her this was his first breakup. As with the reception table duty, he'd obviously volunteered for cleaning because Amanda also signed up. In her rush to be with Brad, she must have forgotten her commitment.

Kathy had tried to talk to him, to thank him for staying and helping—treating him as if he'd managed the whole thing himself. Jim said little. Rather than bringing him out of his shell, her words seemed to reinforce it. He left twenty minutes later in utter dejection. It took another thirty for the rest of them to finish with the mess and lock up. She worried about him—about all three of them. They were all so young and inexperienced. In the end, though, Kathy knew she could do little about a love triangle. It was just easier to fret about them than stew over her own troubled relationship.

Sighing, she went inside. The living room seemed a lot

larger without Greg's tall, solid figure taking up space. She realized from the note that he must have come straight home and packed after confronting her. Her spare house key was on the coffee table.

Fighting off tears, Kathy made her way up the stairs and started a hot bath. Entering her bedroom, she disrobed. It was a painful process, and she did it away from the room's full-length mirror. She'd been shocked to see the full detail of her bruises and needed no reminders. One side of her looked seemed a painter's palette for a particularly bleak artist.

She found a white cloth on the bed. One of Greg's T-shirts. She snatched it up to her face. Traces of his scent electrified her. There was no aromatherapy to compare with the sweet, recognizable odor of someone you desired, someone you loved. Kathy placed it back onto the bed, already knowing she would go to sleep wearing it—and nothing else.

40

KATHY WOKE EARLY AND FORLORN ON SUNDAY MORNING. She wore Greg's T-shirt downstairs. The fabric engulfed her petite frame and wearing it reminded her of how she felt in his arms. Despite her uncertainty about the relationship, Kathy told herself it would be okay. By tomorrow she would be able to call him and explain her actions.

Tomorrow was a long way off, though, and Kathy desperately wanted human interaction. She thought first of Sharon but decided against calling her. She'd be getting the boys ready for church and after that she had insurance matters to settle. Besides, Kathy had already burdened her twice.

There were any number of possibilities, but the one person who kept coming to mind was Linda Jennings.

Linda was Kathy's own mentor—a second mother, one vastly more sympathetic and supportive. Their communication had never dwindled the way it had with Erin, but Kathy now felt like she'd let it slip for far too long. Even as late as a year ago, she and Linda used to talk at least twice a week. Now it was twice a month. Linda was seventy years old and harder to contact quickly because she had no use for computers. Kathy blushed to think how a simple phone call felt like a hassle in the age of Facebook and e-mail. Not that Linda had any great love for phones, either. She was an old-fashioned letter writer through and through.

Kathy did call her, and they ended up talking for an hour. At about the forty-five minute mark, Kathy realized she had been doing almost all the talking and began to feel very selfish and vain. But Linda anticipated these feelings and dismissed them. "When someone needs to talk, dear, you listen closely. The ear is the most remarkable part of the body, particularly on a friend."

Kathy smiled. Tears welled up in her eyes at Linda's gentleness. Then Linda surprised her with an invitation to visit—today. She lived four hours away, in a little valley outside of Sugarloaf Township. The distance had always seemed like such a huge hassle.

"I'll be there by two," Kathy said.

She got into her car. Her muscles felt much less tender now than they did yesterday, though a long drive would do them no favors. She got onto I-80 W and found only light traffic. She bore down on the accelerator. She rarely sped but the temptation to reach Linda faster compelled her.

After two hours, she found herself without radio reception. She'd brought no music with her as she rarely drove for stretches longer than fifteen minutes. Kathy frowned at the idea of two more hours without music. After scouring the FM band five more times, she switched over to AM on a lark.

She dialed through several religious programs obscured by static before reaching a station with a very strong and clear signal. What she heard depressed and captivated her. It was some state political talk show. Under most circumstances,

Kathy would have screamed and ran from these pugnacious broadcasts. This time was different. The host was in the middle of an interview—

—with Bernard Morrison.

He was spouting the same repetitive nonsense, purposely confusing massage therapy and prostitution. The argument clearly was now his bread and butter, but Kathy was stunned by his change in tone. In front of Sharon's spa, he'd acted indignant in a calculated way. Now he simply seemed unhinged. He sounded shrill. His more careful arguments, bolstered by a selection of statistics, were replaced with sheer fantasy. He made no distinction between legitimate massage and prostitution at all. Did massage therapists touch your bare flesh? Yes. Did massage therapists get paid to do it? Yes. Did their clients get a "little relaxation" from it?

Yes.

Therefore, massage therapists were sinning whores.

Kathy found Morrison's argument's illogic so blatant that she felt more embarrassed for him than anything else. Her feelings soon turned to outrage as the callers kept chiming in with their support. Who were these people? She knew very well the prejudice and hang-ups massage practitioners had to fight with segments of the public, but she had difficulty believing these callers weren't paid actors.

When the station went to break, the host read off the show's call-in number. Kathy quickly shot a hand into her purse and rummaged for her cell phone. She programmed the digits in. The phone rang.

It was Sunday. Chances were the show had been taped days before. But she had to challenge him if she could. Ignorance would always triumph if intelligent people did nothing but scoff at it.

The show's screener answered.

"Am I on the air?"

The screener laughed. "No, ma'am. Do you have a question for our guest this morning?"

"I've got quite a few things to say, actually."

The screener evidently liked her tone of voice and sensed a gold strike of confrontation in the works. She would be on as soon as the show returned.

Less than a minute.

Kathy waited. She didn't even need to summarize her thoughts. She'd fought this battle in person and on paper so many times her points were ingrained.

"We're live in just a few more seconds."

Kathy nodded and looked at the speedometer. "Hell!" She mashed on the brake and checked automatically for a policeman behind her. The highway had few cars on it just then. That was good. She'd been going almost ninety in a sixty-five mile per hour zone.

The show had returned during her brief distraction, and she heard the host introducing her. She turned the radio down to eliminate feedback.

The host's name was Chuck. "Hi, Chuck," she said. He assured her they were about to engage in a serious, adult debate.

But when the show went live again and Chuck said, "Ladies and gentlemen, it looks like we've got the Riot Queen herself on the phone," Kathy knew she had troubles.

She'd fought political battles for massage before, but never in the arena of talk radio. The host began berating her at once, carrying Morrison's water for him.

"Chuck, this is the woman who assaulted me," Morrison said at last. "Everyone's seen the news footage of the riot she caused. I'm assuming you're calling from jail, Ms. Barrister?"

"No, I'm not calling from jail."

"Well, I hope you're not at the spa my people will be protesting this afternoon. One surprise assault by a crazy woman in a white bathrobe is more than enough for a single lifetime!"

"Bernie," she said, "you know damn well that I didn't—"

"The two of you are on a first name basis?" Chuck asked.

"Yes," Kathy said, "we worked together on crafting the regulations—"

"Ms. Barrister is among the many bureaucrats responsible for the completely inadequate rules that govern the massage industry in this state. She's the worst sort of government official. A so-called expert who—"

"You're a government official, Bernie. I'm a business woman and teacher."

"Oh, we know what sort of business you're in. I'm an elected representative who answers to the people. Who do you answer to?"

Kathy laughed. "Thankfully my conscience."

"Your conscience?" Morrison repeated with scorn. "It must be taking quite a beating these days. You run the Academy for Healing Touch, don't you?"

Marvin Gaye's voice suddenly interjected itself—When I get that feeling, I need sexual healing.

The song snippet ended as quickly as it began. Chuck was laughing and congratulating someone in the sound booth.

"Yes," Kathy said, her annoyance spiking. She had to keep an eye on the speedometer. The needle suddenly looked like a measurement of her blood pressure.

"The first dead prostitute, Erin Haley, attended your—"

"Erin made bad choices but she was not trained by me to be a prostitute!"

"Oh, of course not," Morrison mocked. "She was trained as a 'massage therapist.' Funny, that's just what she advertised herself on Craigslist."

"Now let me ask," Chuck interjected, "how does one get a license to specialize in sex massage? And does it cost much? I'm thinking my wife could use a new degree."

Kathy dropped the phone away from her ear a moment. Good God.

Finally, she said, "There is, of course, no such thing as that."

"Now," Morrison said, "let's talk about your second student."

Kathy glanced at the speedometer again. She was creeping up to eighty-five.

Wait a minute—second student?

"Bernie, what are you talking about?"

"I'm talking about the 'massage therapist' the police found murdered in her home late last night—right in the city, like the last one!"

Kathy slammed the brakes so hard she almost lost control of the car.

"What?"

"Don't tell me you're not aware of this, Ms. Barrister. I believe her name has already been released."

"The name was Gayle Thompson," Chuck said, adopting a very serious tone.

That's familiar, Kathy thought, repeating it to herself. The car was just barely creeping along now. Suddenly a blaring horn shook her out of her stupor, and she looked in the rearview mirror just in time to see a car barreling toward her. It swerved into the passing lane and blasted past so fiercely her car shook. A middle finger greeted her from the passenger side.

She steered to the shoulder and parked.

"If—if she was a graduate of my Academy, then all I can say is—"

"Oh, she was. Funny connection, isn't there? Two of your students murdered. You as a consultant on the case. Sort of makes me wonder what else you're involved in regarding these crimes, Ms. Barrister."

Kathy's hand trembled so badly she could barely hold the phone. "You're an awful man, Bernie," she managed to say, snapping her phone off. Gayle Thompson.

What in the hell was happening?

41

STILL PARKED ON THE HIGHWAY'S SHOULDER, KATHY CALLED Linda to apologize. She was not going to be able to make it after all. Then she turned the car around and sped back to her house. She arrived at one thirty.

Greg sat in his car, parked in her driveway.

She braked to a stop at the curb with a strange sense of disassociation and vertigo. It was as if she'd come to visit his house. They got out simultaneously and nearly ran into each other's embrace. Her body did not hurt when he held her.

"I'm glad you're safe."

She frowned, puzzled. "I was driving to see an old friend, but I had to turn back. I heard the worst news on the radio."

"Gayle Thompson?"

She nodded.

"I got the call about it very late last night. I was already in Edgerton by then."

"Were you told to come back?"

"Yes. But I would have come anyway," he said.

She shook her head in disbelief.

"We have to talk—about a lot of things."

He went to his car and pulled out an armful of file folders. Her eyes widened at the possibility it was all information about the murders.

They went inside. Greg motioned her to sit as he spread the folders unopened across her coffee table.

"Did you know Gayle Thompson?"

Kathy frowned. "The name sounds familiar, but I can't place it. There are always a few nontraditional students who avoid getting me as a teacher. Sometimes I think that makes them better off. Maybe she was one, or maybe I've just forgotten her. I guess it wouldn't be the first time."

"I think it would be easy to forget most of them, based on the number of people I saw there last night. You're fooling yourself to think you can remember every single name and face."

She nodded. *I'm very good at fooling myself.*

Greg said, "We've already confirmed it, Kathy. Both at the victim's home and then with the help of your administrative assistant—"

"Brenda!" Kathy said.

Greg nodded.

Kathy arched her brows. The police had tasked Brenda for evidence and she hadn't said a word about it?

Greg seemed to anticipate her ire. "The school records were only checked this morning. I thought it would be pointless to contact you."

"Thanks."

"But I do need to ask you about someone else."

"Who?"

"Tell me about Lou Nichols."

Kathy's back straightened. She knew she looked caught off guard—she was. She expected him to say Judd Garvis. What could Lou have to do with any of this?

"He's one of my best instructors. He's been with the Academy since we opened. In fact, he was one of my instructors before that."

"He wasn't at the Academy last night."

Kathy turned her head, trying to remember. Hadn't she seen him? There were so many people.

Greg continued. "He wasn't at the Academy because he was busy contacting the police about his girlfriend. They didn't live together—by his choice, I believe. He called and left a message for her on Friday. Guess it didn't bother him too much when she never called back. But when Saturday afternoon came and still no call, he got suspicious."

"Intuition," Kathy said.

"If you like. The police came over. Her car was in the driveway. Everything seemed okay. Turns out things were terribly wrong. Lou Nichols' girlfriend was Gayle Thompson."

A queasiness rose in Kathy's stomach. Lou—with a student? She didn't have long to entertain the thought as Greg opened the top file folder. This one contained a DVD inside a slim jewel case.

"I'm not supposed to have a copy of this."

"What is it?"

"A copy of the police interrogation of Judd Garvis."

She gave him a sharp look. "You already knew about him, didn't you? When we were in my office?"

"No. Mr. Garvis was picked up at nine this morning. The police and the Bureau are naturally curious when two victims of a serial killer happen to have attended your school. When questioned, Brenda said you'd been looking into past student files. I'm sorry to say you're work computer was seized. The Intelius files were still on it."

Kathy shook her head. "Greg, how could you—"

"I had nothing to do with it. I was not there, and I told them nothing about my own suspicions. But I was there when he got questioned. He's a dangerously unstable man, Kathy."

"I did get my bruises from meeting Judd, but he never hit me. You have to believe that. I really did fall. There was so much debris on the floor, I couldn't step anywhere without tripping."

Greg looked doubtful but just nodded. Then he said, "He matches the psychological profile in so many ways. A strange fascination with massage, bitterness about getting kicked out of the Academy, feelings of inferiority around women that leads to the use and abuse of prostitutes. Add in the fact that he's crazy, and we'd have the perfect suspect. On paper."

Kathy looked up. "On paper? You mean he's not the killer?"

"The timeline's okay, but there's no DNA match with any of the evidence we've collected. Garvis also appears to have no understanding of Reiki, though in a schizoid state some other aspect of his mind might express such knowledge."

"There's got to be something else."

"There is," he said. "The killer has done a few things well. He makes up a new e-mail account for every woman he solicits. You need a computer for that and Garvis doesn't have one. That doesn't rule him out right away. The killer is probably using library terminals to create his identities. That's where we get into trouble. Garvis is a man who stands out. We've already ran his photo by staff at libraries in town. Also staff at libraries around Brunz and Edgerton. No one remembers him. He'd be memorable, Kathy—a man like that stepping into a library. It's possible he went to libraries in other states, I suppose."

"I had a feeling it just wasn't him."

"Kathy," Greg said, "I respect your opinion about intuition, but I don't share it. How would you feel if you were wrong about him, and learned that he killed even one more time because you opted not to go to the police?"

She wanted to be flippant in her answer. *Well, I wasn't wrong, so the point is moot.* But she knew Greg was right. Even as she conceded this, however, she sensed that Greg wasn't here just to give her the latest scoop. The tips of his strong fingers were red from pressing into the jewel case. They pulled on it in opposite directions as if it were a piece of paper he wanted to tear in half.

"Judd's been released, hasn't he?"

Greg looked surprised. "Yes."

"Did he say something about me during the interrogation?"

"Nothing to be concerned about."

Kathy glanced away, smiling. He'd said that to her before—a long time ago. She couldn't remember the circumstances. But she knew that whenever he said it was exactly when she should start becoming very concerned indeed.

42

VERY EARLY MONDAY MORNING, KATHY AND GREG KISSED on her porch. They had gotten up to watch the sunrise. Neither said much. To Kathy, the moment seemed elegiac somehow, like it was the last they'd see together. The sky was already a peerless blue. By appearances, the day seemed ready for perfection. *No one will get murdered today*, she thought. The sunshine afforded too much protection. But over the past weeks the sunshine had failed them all one too many times.

Don't think that. One day the fear would be over and the two of them would be standing here again, still in love and very safe.

"It's beautiful," Greg said. "Hard to believe the same sun is rising over Edgerton right now."

"It's rising over Brunz too. We can't let dark times make us forget the light."

He nodded. Kathy sensed great uneasiness in him.

"What's wrong?"

"I'm just worried. One murder close to your house. Two of your students are victims. I just wish I didn't have to go back."

"I'll be okay," she said, affecting a laugh. "If nothing else, I've got Betty to protect me."

He laughed too. "My house feels an awful lot further away when I think of you being here alone, that's all."

Kathy nodded. She didn't want him to leave either. She didn't feel afraid, though. Not in the daylight.

Greg took her into his arms again. She relaxed into his hold, her left cheek against his chest. She became greedy for his heat now that it was about to leave her. When he bent for a kiss, her greed transferred itself to a desire for his mouth. The forcefulness of her kissing caused him to back away, almost stumbling. He had a big grin on his face.

"You know, I don't mind a long daily commute."

She laughed, partly because she'd been entertaining the idea herself. But four hours worth of driving every day?

"I'll call tonight," he said.

"Or I'll call you."

He kissed her one more time. "There's always the weekends."

"All the more reason to look forward to them," she said.

At last the moment could be delayed no further. Greg stepped off the porch and walked to his car. She stood staring off in the direction of Edgerton several minutes after his car was out of view.

The house did not seem at all safe or inviting with him gone. Kathy showered and readied for work fast, taking none of the time she usually enjoyed in the morning. Less than forty-five minutes after Greg's departure, Kathy drove away as well.

She arrived at the Academy at seven thirty. The earliest weekday classes started at nine and she expected to find only the janitorial crew in the building. Even Brenda wouldn't arrive until eight thirty.

One of the window washers opened the door for her. He looked concerned. "Ms. Barrister, a young woman is waiting by your office. She said she was a student. I told her we weren't open. The girl, she started crying—I didn't know what else to do."

She thanked him and hurried down the corridor to her office. She heard a small sobbing sound and checked around the corner.

"Emily?"

Emily Ryan was just twenty-four but looked far younger, a short, curly-haired redhead with the epitome of a button nose. Kathy never looked at her without failing to think Raggedy Ann at her cheerful expression. The complete lack of cheer she saw now worried her.

Emily was sitting on the floor with her back to the wall, knees bent toward her chest. She didn't seem to realize Kathy was there.

"What is it, Em?"

"Kathy," she said, trying to compose herself. "Sorry."

"Don't be. I'm here for you if you want to talk."

"I just wanted to be someplace safe."

Kathy frowned and tried to remember what she knew about Emily. She came from North Carolina and was living away from home for the first time. Her and her brother had moved here together. Had something happened? Did Emily no longer consider her own apartment safe?

"That's okay," Kathy said. "This school will always be a place of shelter. You'll always be safe here."

I hope that's true.

She got Emily to stand and they went into her office. There was a moment of shock when she saw the empty space where her computer should have been. *God, how soon will I get that back? All the ACICS accreditation renewal forms were on my hard drive.*

She had Emily sit down on one of the chairs at the front of

her desk. Then she went down the hall to the staff kitchen. She returned with two cups of steeping tea.

She gave one to Emily. "This is a calming blend. I rely on it a lot."

Emily sipped at it.

"So tell me what's going on. Can I help?"

Emily tried to talk but was overwhelmed by emotion. It took a few minutes before she settled down enough to be intelligible.

"I saw on the news that another massage therapist was killed. They said she went to this school. And that first girl went here too."

"I see," Kathy said.

"I'm afraid of what will happen to me when I start working."

Kathy swallowed, trying to think. I'm afraid of what will happen to me when I start working. In a less profound way, she'd had this conversation many times before with students about to graduate. There were always doubts and anxieties about their future. Now they feared for their very lives. How much darker the lives of her students had become!

"Now more than ever, Em, it's important that we stick together. Massage therapy isn't a solitary, isolated profession, despite what the media wants you to believe."

But Kathy knew from experience how lonely and intimidating it was to start out with no customers. It was the same feeling any person in business striking out on their own had to endure. She'd always taught from the point of view of a traditionalist. She believed massage therapists thrived best by forming private practices. Many didn't have the fortitude for this. They sought jobs in big national conglomerates like MassageEnvy or similar companies that hired therapists right out of school and paid them pennies. Kathy considered such practices exploitative in the extreme. But she saw how the current environment of fear made the idea of working in a well-lit, busy corporate spa setting seem very safe. Serial killers never seemed to strike in office buildings.

The tea started to work. Emily sat with red but drying eyes. Her breathing stabilized. She looked embarrassed as she stared off into space. Kathy waited with her hand resting on Emily's shoulder, hoping it offered the support she felt her words could not achieve.

"I feel so stupid," Emily said.

"Don't. Please, don't. I think most of the school is thinking exactly the same thing right now, and that's my fault."

"Your fault?"

"I'm your teacher. If I don't address the fears of my students, if I don't recognize it for what it is, then in a sense I'm teaching to your fear. The burden of responsibility is always on the teacher."

Emily's response stunned Kathy. She shook her head as if trying to ward off a break down. She didn't succeed. She cried harder than she had before. Kathy patted her shoulder, bewildered, and leaned in trying to understand. Emily's reaction so confounded her that she worried either of them might have gone crazy. A figure appeared in her window— Brenda. She looked nervous and pale, wearied down to her bones. It was a stunning switch from the energetic woman Kathy remembered from Saturday night. But there was no time now. She shook her head and bent to Emily again.

Emily was trying to talk. She said…

…she knew it was wrong…

…she felt so guilty…

…she didn't even know he was seeing someone else

Emily Ryan was having a relationship with Lou Nichols.

43

LOU LOOKED LIKE A WRECK WHEN HE PRESENTED HIMSELF at Kathy's office door three hours later. Kathy studied him, sickened in so many ways. She was sickened also that her outrage dampened any compassion she had for him. His girlfriend had just been murdered. Kathy almost despised herself for doing what she knew she must.

"Sit down, Lou."

He entered and slumped into the very chair Emily Ryan had warmed.

"Guess you heard."

"I heard, Lou. I'm surprised you came in."

"Is that why you posted a note about my noon class being canceled? Did you think I wouldn't show?"

"Partly," Kathy said.

"I'm like you, Kathy," he said. "You know that. Teaching focuses my energy. I think I'd go crazy if I had to sit at home grieving."

He wasn't entirely lying. With the bags under his eyes, sallow complexion, and mussed hair, Lou looked like someone who'd been shattered and was trying to get himself together. He also looked like someone caught in a desperate act.

"I see."

He looked at her, head shaking. "Gayle was my favorite student; we had a connection."

"Not to be indelicate, Lou, but you started dating her after she graduated, right?"

"Of course—of course, Kathy."

Now he was entirely lying.

"You know, I think I understand you a lot better now," Lou said. "We're really in the same boat now."

"Oh?"

"We've both lost students that we cherished. Maybe we've even lost them to the same guy."

You bastard, she thought, wondering if the fullness of her rage showed on her face. How dare Lou try to work her feelings like that, comparing her relationship to Erin with his unethical seduction? Even if he and Gayle had engaged in the affair mutually, Lou knew better. He knew it was against the rules. Still, Gayle was dead and the relationship had continued beyond her graduation. Kathy could have overlooked it, considering the circumstances. But he had crossed the line with Emily, a girl thirty years his junior. He was cheating on a former student with a current one. Kathy couldn't help wondering how many others there had been. Thinking about Lou propositioning her students poisoned every idea and image she'd ever had about him.

"I know about your relationship with Emily Ryan, Lou."

She got up and came around her desk before he could react.

"What the hell is the matter with you?"

"Kathy—"

"No. Don't say anything. I'm sorry for your loss, Lou. I

really am. But there are some other things you've lost as well—like perspective and ethics. Your actions could ruin us, Lou! It might even hurt our accreditation renewal. I can't even imagine our fate if the media got wind of this. With Bernard Morrison out fanning the flames of prostitution, a story about one unethical teacher could go quite a long way toward shutting us down by default. What student would want to come here? Did you think about anything other than yourself?"

Lou shook his head. Anger showed in his eyes like a live wire. "I can't believe you'd bring this up now! I've made some mistakes—"

"Spare me. Better yet, spare yourself. Go home. You can't stay here. I don't want you near my students."

"They're my students too, Kathy. I spend more time with them than you do. I teach a hell of a lot more classes than you!"

"Not anymore."

His eyes widened. "You're letting me go? You, who I trained myself, are questioning my abilities as a teacher?"

"Not your skills," Kathy said. "Just your morals. You're gone, Lou."

Lou stood up. Kathy tensed with the same fear she had confronting Judd Garvis. Though she and Lou were the same height, he resembled a small tank with his compact, muscular frame. His fingers looked like they could massage a piece of hammered steel into liquid metal.

"You're going to really regret this. That's all I've got to say. All you'll have for doing this is a lot of regret."

Kathy returned to her chair. "I've got plenty of that already. A little more won't mean a thing at this point."

44

Kathy barely got through the day's ethics lecture. Emily Ryan was in that class and wouldn't meet her gaze the entire time. That was fine because whenever Kathy looked at her, she thought of Lou and her temperature and her volume went up a notch. Gradually she realized she was shouting at them, as if yelling substituted for conviction. She stopped. Most of her students stared at her with expressions of nervous confusion. A few even looked afraid.

But everyone showed some degree of fright now. A general sense of dread permeated the Academy. Kathy walked the hallways noting a drop in the usual level of conversation. She stopped by lecture rooms, peeking in on classes that didn't seem as full as they normally were. Attendance was dropping. The students who did show up had forlorn, weary faces.

She headed toward her office hoping Brenda had made headway with the police on getting her computer returned. Before she arrived, the one person Kathy actually wanted to see intercepted her. Amanda's cheer was obvious and seemed profoundly out of place next to the gloom of her fellow students. *We're all creatures of our own little worlds*, she told herself, thinking of how happy she could be with Greg even with all this madness occurring. Recognizing the joy on her face, it was obvious Amanda had found her Greg—in Brad.

"Come inside."

Kathy pointed Amanda to what she now thought of as the hardest working chair in the Academy, and took her own seat beside it. Amanda had some papers in her hand. Kathy recognized them as Academy application forms.

"What's put such a big smile on your face today, Amanda?"

She grinned even larger. She waved the application papers giddily before thrusting them at Kathy. She accepted them in bewilderment.

"I'm so glad you introduced me to Brad. Well, I guess you really didn't introduce me. But he came to see you and I was there—"

"Slow down," Kathy said, looking. Could this be right? The application papers had Brad Haley's name and signature all over them.

"He wants to enroll!"

She put the papers on her desk and leaned closer to Amanda. "Slow down, Er—Amanda."

She couldn't do it. Amanda began to gush like she and Kathy were two teen girls having a sleepover. "I was interested in him the moment I saw him. Not just the cuteness part—it was the sensitivity. A boy who cries."

"Because his sister was murdered," Kathy said with a bluntness that killed Amanda's schoolgirl enthusiasm right away.

"I realized that; we've talked a lot about it," she said, speaking in a lower tone.

"How did you get to know him better?"

"He came back here looking for you. We started talking."

"About his sister?"

Amanda nodded. "About everything, really. He told me what you did for him."

Kathy's eyebrows arched higher.

"The Reiki," Amanda said. "He told me how the cop hurt him and you healed the injury. He came back here to talk to you about it."

Kathy considered this. It seemed plausible enough, but why hadn't he called? She realized he would always be in her thoughts after she saw him breakdown at The Johns. He was her only link to Erin and she had perhaps considered herself his last link to Erin as well. Kathy blushed at the possibility of such presumption.

"I'm glad he found you," Kathy said, touching Amanda's hand and smiling. "You'll be good for him, and he damn well better be good to you. But I want you to be careful. He may not be the most emotionally…stable. He's grieving deeply."

"I know," she said. "I hold him every night and sometimes he cries. I do everything I can to comfort him. I wish I knew Reiki, too. It must be so powerful."

End this conversation. Amanda's freedom with intimate details brought an unwelcome acidic sting to her stomach. Amanda had either found the love of her life or was making the biggest mistake in it up to now. Maybe they were flip sides of the same coin: heads she married him and won, tails the relationship broke apart after Brad sponged the last of his grief into Amanda.

It was so powerful.

Cho ku rei.

She looked at the application. "Does Brad seem to have a real interest in Reiki?"

"It's all he talks about sometimes. I've been getting a little jealous of you, Kathy, because he originally thought all massage therapists could do it. He wants to learn. Does the Academy teach it?"

"We never have, though I'm certified to do it. Learning it

requires significant meditation skills, Amanda. I'm not sure he's ready for it."

"But he meets the school's entry criteria—"

Kathy smiled again. "I'm sure he does. I'll put his application on file for consideration next term. That will give him some time to think about what he really wants to do."

Amada's sudden fidgeting told Kathy she didn't care for this answer. It was as if she'd expected Kathy to rubberstamp the application and let him start tomorrow. Was there something else to the urgency? Was Brad pressuring Amanda to pitch his case? She knew Amanda to be self-assured, mature, and capable. But he clearly infatuated her. Whether the feeling was actually love did not matter. Amanda wanted to please a man who had a powerful attraction for her.

Cho ku rei.

Power—to heal the body and make it whole. What greater power could there be?

Kathy knew the killer's answer. She had read it many times already in bloodstains on fabric and plaster.

45

GREG CALLED HER MONDAY NIGHT. KATHY LAY ACROSS her bed and listened. His voice was as relaxing as touch to her, and even the occasional silence between them had its own soothing charm.

"I don't want to get off the phone with you," he said.

"We used to talk like this on school nights, didn't we?"

"Not exactly like this."

Kathy laughed. "I suppose not."

They talked until eleven, when fatigue started to crowd out her thoughts.

"I'll call you in the morning," he said.

They chatted for a few more minutes. Then Kathy closed her cell phone and just lay in bed, wishing she'd dimmed the lights beforehand. If lights could be considered loud, these bulbs were screaming at her right now.

She massaged her eyes and considered, despite the length of their conversation, how much she'd hidden from Greg. She'd said nothing about Lou. She'd said nothing about Brad's

Academy application or his interest in Amanda—and Reiki. Amanda's eagerness to please him still bothered Kathy. What if Brad—

But I must be wrong. She wasn't walking in the world of intuition anymore. She was in the world of DNA testing and fingerprinting, either of which would have implicated Brad by now. She was in Greg's world.

I love being there.

I love Greg.

She'd not stated it to herself in such frank terms. Even now she was aware of a sweet trace odor of him on the sheets, and she turned over and touched the fabric with the back of her fingers, as if it might summon forth his body. It felt strange and foolish, perhaps even dangerous, to obsess over anything that reminded her of him. Yet she felt greedy to satisfy her desire.

Kathy would have been content to lie there awake thinking of him all night despite how tired she felt. The damn ceiling lights seemed to assume an angry type of brightness, a challenging glare. She wanted darkness but was too lazy to turn off the lights.

She turned onto her back, put both hands over her eyes and sighed.

If I only had a slingshot…

At last, fatigue bowed to annoyance and she stood and went to the light switch. There were no other lights on in the house. She stared into the darkness beyond her bedroom and felt nervous. *The front door's locked.* Her nightly habits had been the same since her first apartment. She always checked the lock before going to bed.

Checking again would make Greg happy.

She turned on the hallway light and walked past her office and private practice area. Her massage table in that room's corner looked like some big pet enjoying a deep sleep. She smiled and headed downstairs, flipping the few switches available to her as she went. If the house had a significant flaw, it was a puzzling lack of overhead fixtures. The house was only forty years old yet most of the rooms seemed built on the assumption their occupants would carry around candles. Table and corner lamps provided most of the light, even in the living room.

She reached the bottom step and found the light from upstairs a weak suggestion at her feet. She'd have to wander in darkness to reach the switch in the foyer. This had never bothered her before, and she scolded herself for being afraid. It wasn't as if Judd Garvis was going to leap out of the kitchen at her.

He won't.

She tiptoed toward the foyer. She felt ridiculous in her caution. Under any other circumstance, she could have checked the door and been back upstairs in the time this was taking.

Confident, she reached the foyer and turned on the light.

She screamed.

There was a man on her doorstep. She saw part of him distorted through the beveled glass frame. The light had clearly startled him, for he had pushed the mail slot open and his fingers were poking through. She watched two small objects drop onto the floor. They made the slightest patter sound on the wood. In the next moment, the hand retracted and began to pound the door. Kathy screamed again, backing away, running to the dark living room. *Goddamnit, I left the phone upstairs!*

She huddled in the darkness, shivering.

Suddenly she heard the mail slot hinges whine. The man outside screamed at her through the opening. No words—just an inhuman scream. Kathy screamed back, kicking her legs on the floor. Her terror reached fever pitch. She imagined his eyes gazing through the slot. She thought she heard breathing— terrible, asthmatic breathing. *Oh God, oh Jesus oh God!*

The foyer went silent. What if he was still there, his face pressed to the glass frame, leering in at her? Kathy saw it in her mind's eye all too well. She was drenched in sweat. The floor beneath her seat was soaked, and she realized with complete disgust that she'd peed herself. She began to cry as her thoughts went wild. He could be anywhere now. In the front yard, in the back. At the side. She looked to the window on her left. He could be standing there trying to see in.

She screamed again and scrambled upstairs, falling and banging her knees on the steps. She crawled her way like a scampering dog, dragging herself by her hands at the end as her legs went numb. She clawed into the bedroom and slumped against the door with the phone at her side. Her fingers took over a minute before they stopped shaking long enough to steady the phone and dial 911.

46

They say refer all pain to elsewhere. They say take off the shirt.

"The shirt," I say, and it comes off her. They said it would.

Things are here that look familiar. Maybe that's wrong. They say go far away from the familiar. They say refer the pain far away. Refer the pain to another body.

"What's wrong?" she says.

"Nothing," I say. "I just wanted to—memorize you. Smile for me."

They say lift the hands, take the picture. I do. It develops inside me, and I shake to make it happen and when I'm done her face appears, captured. Captured. They say it is time to capture her.

"Let's just get this massage started," she says.

They say take out your penis and blind her. I do.

They say strap her down.

"Oh please don't! Please don't do this to me, Andy!"

I do do this to her though.

They say refer the pain. My teeth hurt. My front teeth hurt. Last time one bottom tooth hurt and they said refer the pain and I took her tooth out where mine hurt and that stopped it. Now two teeth hurt.

They say put the pain in her teeth and then remove the teeth. I ask about the head and they say not yet. They always say that. They know they cause the pain in my head, and they will not be referred. But they do not know that I know. I am biding my time.

She wakes before I get the second tooth out. They say kill her now, and I do. Then I take the tooth.

For a long time I argue with them about the table. They say take it; I say no. They say take it. I take the table.

Later I scrub the table.

I've noticed things.

They go away when I see her. When I don't see her, they come back.

They don't like her.

In my apartment, I tell them I like her a good deal. They scoff.

Is love a pain?

Sometimes, I say.

Then refer the pain.

Once I tried to trick them. I said I prefer the pain.

Then have some, they said, and punished me in the head.

When I finally overcome it, I say, "Take off the panties." It is a different girl this time and the familiar is gone. Not her but a herclosenenough.

"I said I don't do full nudity," she says. "Just a tit job. You want to put your cock between my tits and I'll jerk you off with them."

Do this they say. My penis gets so hard it hurts, and it is a pain. Down there on her it is already missing like after the tooth. Someone has already used her to refer their pain. She must want to cut mine off. I kill her before she can.

They say make the magic figures so you won't get caught.

I do.

In my apartment, I lay on the table and think of her. They don't like this.

Aren't you glad you listened to us and took the table?

Yes, I am glad I listened to you and took the table.

Then listen to us now.

You are hurt, they say.

You are your own god, they say.

You have your own altar, they say.

Yes, I say.

They point me to the book again. It has been a while since they went to the book. The book says: He shall then slaughter the goat for the sin offering. They say just as sin is referred, so too is pain. They say you have your own altar now. You are your own god.

You are hurt, they say.

I take the table where they tell me to. The first girl does not come. My penis hurt, and I said I would try a boy. The boy did not come.

The third girl said she would come and she did. My fourth tooth hurt. I referred the pain.

On my dresser is referred pain. Many teeth.

Why don't my teeth hurt when I'm with her?

Because you are referring the pain.

To her?

Yes, they say.

I want to refer all my pains to her, I say.

You will, they say.

I want to sleep with her here tonight, I say. I want to love her on the table.

But the table is gone now. You left your altar. Remember?

I do. It was a close call. I had to leave the altar.

I am a god who sleeps on the floor, I say.

We will sleep there with you!

She is the sun and the stars and the moon and the falling stars. She lets me touch her. They go far away when this happen. They go into her head to tell her she is a goddess. My goddess.

I understand how we will be together. Her lips will hurt, and she will kiss me and refer the pain to me. Then my lips will hurt, and I will kiss her and refer the pain back. Day and night our love will be pain eternal in its give and take.

She does not love you, they say.

"I do not love you," she says.

She will refer pain but she will not receive, they say.

They are always saying.

My teeth hurt again.

47

"Detective Beacon?"

Kathy heard the question but barely looked up from the sofa where she sat shivering with an emergency blanket draped over her. Her legs were pulled against her chest, feet tucked up under her. She was so compact and drawn in that she felt like an egg.

An egg with a crack in its shell.

She watched Greg flash his credentials. Then he stepped around a designated perimeter that made most of the foyer impassable. Behind him, other investigators were examining the door and mail slot. They reminded her too much of Allison Stockett's crime scene. Kathy felt like she'd been murdered and didn't know it.

"Greg," Kathy said with a small sob as he put his arm around her. She was on the verge of losing it again.

The embrace she had longed for most of the evening now came under circumstances so perverse that she found little comfort. She rocked in his arms. She had called him after dialing 911. She did not remember what she said. Maybe she didn't say anything except scream and cry into the phone.

He kissed her on the temple and said, "Don't move." He got up. As he did, she caught a glimpse of his watch. It was one in the morning. *I must have called him around eleven forty-five.* Greg had made a two-hour drive in about eighty minutes.

"Greg," she said, "how did you get here so—"

He bent down, smiling gently in anticipation. "Traffic was light."

Kathy watched him go talk with three officers in the foyer. Something wrapped in a plastic bag was passed into Greg's hands. He looked at it and said, "Jesus." Kathy shivered.

"Should we put out a hunt for Garvis again?"

"I doubt it was him, but it couldn't hurt. Do you all have a handle on the media yet?"

"Got it silent so far. All but him."

Kathy strained her head to see whom they were referring to but could not. Woozily, she tossed the blanket off her and rose, supporting herself against the sofa as she came toward the foyer.

"Who is it, Greg?"

Greg came back to her at once.

"That goddamn kid who was at the Stockett murder."

"The blogger?"

From outside her door, in the yard, she heard Carson's voice declaring his right to know what was happening. Greg looked murderous but surprised Kathy with a smile. "Do you think Betty has a sniper rifle? Maybe she can put a scope on him."

"That's awful, Greg."

"No, he's awful. Little bastard with a police scanner and nothing to do but play *Halo* online until some action breaks. He sure got here quick."

Kathy noticed a moment of doubt in his expression. "You don't think—"

"No, not really. About the only thing in the profile he'd fit is the need to solicit a prostitute for sex. And I'm sure he does."

He took her arm and guided her back to the sofa. They sat down.

"You're going to have to sit through some more questions. I'm sorry you're going to have to relive whatever happened."

"I'll relive it every night in my dreams, I'm afraid. He was putting s-something through the mail slot. I saw them fall."

Greg nodded.

"They were a pair of teeth, weren't they?"

After a moment's hesitation, he nodded again. "They appear to be."

"I want to see them."

"That wouldn't be a good idea. Maybe tomorrow—"

"Now!"

A short silence ensued. Kathy realized all the police in the foyer and on the porch were staring at her.

Greg got up. He was gone a few minutes. He returned with the plastic bag.

"You're sure about this?"

"Yes."

But as she took the bag from him, Kathy didn't feel sure at all. She couldn't explain the compulsion to see the teeth, except that she felt violated by them and needed to see what had invaded her home. Looking at them through the plastic, she found them smaller than she imagined, dull and dry. She detected no blood. The teeth had been…extracted…some time ago.

She swallowed against a wave of nausea and handed the bag to Greg without looking at him.

"Is that enough, Kathy?"

She shook her head, thinking. "Are they…Erin's?"

"There's no way we can know that yet."

"They look like front teeth to me."

Her hands trembled.

"Well, I'm not a dentist," he said. He got up to return the bag. She looked after him, watching him move into the foyer and out the door. The investigators continued to stand around talking. The entire porch and the steps beyond had become their territory. After that she couldn't see. There was only the purple dark and a quiet like the world gone mute.

And mad.

48

Kathy woke up alone and bit back a scream. She heard the television on downstairs. *Greg's still here.* Her fear ebbed away.

She got up, put on a robe, and went downstairs. She found him sitting on the sofa, hunched forward with another collection of open file folders spread across her coffee table. Greg was so absorbed by the information he didn't seem to see her. Kathy stared. The arrangement of data looked like the messy outline to an unfinished novel. Greg's right index finger swept across photographs and maps. He muttered something.

"What is it?"

He looked up, a little startled. Then he smiled. "Sorry."

"It's okay. What is all this?"

"All the information I've collected, along with data from the Bureau. I woke up early this morning feeling like I'd have a breakthrough if I looked at it right away."

She smiled. "Intuition?"

He shook his head in frustration. "I wish to hell mine was as good as yours."

He was not telling the truth; he'd found something.

She sat down beside him. "You had these folders here the last time but you wouldn't open them. Was there something you wanted me to know?"

He shifted, looking uncomfortable at first. Then his expression relaxed. "Maybe there's something to your intuition after all. Yes, there was something I wanted you to know. And then I decided against it."

"Why?"

"Because it would make you very upset, and because the Bureau thinks I'm nuts. More to the point, they think my involvement with you has clouded my perspective and makes me want to put you at the heart of everything."

Kathy cocked her head. "The heart?"

"You see," Greg said, his voice lowering, "I think it is possible you're a target for this maniac. Maybe you're his goal."

Kathy swallowed against a piece of steel in her throat.

Greg indicated the folders. "It begins with the Haley murder, though she wasn't the first victim. That happened in Patterson, remember?"

"So they found the symbol drawn there too?"

"Yes," Greg said.

"But I'd never met the woman who was killed in Patterson. She certainly wasn't a student of mine."

"No, she was prostitute who advertised her services on Craigslist as 'erotic massage.' Like Erin."

I didn't even flinch when he said that. Am I just numb to it now?

Greg shuffled through more papers and continued.

"Edgerton, Brunz—the other murders take place much closer to you. It's almost like a dart thrower trying to zero in on the city. And then, at last, he hits it—Allison Stockett. With your old massage table left at the scene."

"I was hoping it would just be coincidence."

"The Bureau thought so. Stubborn bastards. The death of Gayle Thompson turned a few heads. But instead of seeing you as a target, some of the people there theorized you could be the killer."

Kathy stood up, gaping at him. "You're serious? That's unbelievable!"

"Not as unbelievable as you'd like to think," he said, continuing even as she challenged him. "Police work is about eliminating probabilities and possibilities. You knew two of the victims, and you know a hell of a lot about Reiki. It's almost scary in some ways how well you fit the psych profile on this case."

"Great," Kathy said.

"Only a couple of people took the idea seriously, but you can't blame them. It's their job to entertain ideas. I proposed that far from being the killer, you could be his main target. That too was shot down—until this morning. Everyone's taking the idea a bit more seriously now. If you look outside, you'll see a policeman parked at the curb. You're going to be protected, Kathy, I can assure you."

"I'd rather just have you," she said.

"You do," Greg said, breaking into a big smile. "I'm on loan to the Bureau until this is solved."

She bent toward him, into his arms, and rocked in his embrace.

"I'm grateful. Very grateful to have you here."

"We'll solve this. The Bureau and the City PD are putting men on stakeout at the spas as well."

She grimaced. "Are you looking for the killer, the mob… or prostitution?"

"We know damn well most spas are legitimate businesses. The police are on your side. No, it's the mobs we're interested in. If the psych profile has any legitimacy at all, then protests like that are likely to draw the killer to them."

"I thought you said most of the profile was useless."

Greg nodded. "But not all of it. Would you like to see the profile?"

Kathy nodded and Greg pulled out another handful of pages from his mess of folders. "These are my notes on it, not the whole thing," he said. He handed them over and she read. The profile said the suspect despised prostitutes and likely had significant body image problems. Was likely obese or with a distinguishing visible deformity. Despised the idea of human touch. Probably wore layers of clothes even in summer as a way of hiding his body. Could be drawn to like-minded people as another way to release his demons. Likely to agree with conservative Christian ideals not for religious reasons but for how their beliefs squared with his particular psychosis. Might necessarily share their notions that any nontraditional, non-Western idea constitutes "the occult" themes and adopt such symbols for cover.

Kathy saw that Greg had written "Reiki = bullshit" in the margins. She found it only mildly offensive at this point and just rolled her eyes. Greg didn't notice.

"I had the profile in mind the moment I saw Garvis," Greg said. "The point, though, is that Morrison's rallies can fill the psychological needs for cover the killer needs. He's likely to be attracted to them so he doesn't feel alone. Doesn't feel like a freak. That's why we're keeping tabs, Kathy. We want to see who shows up. If there are a few similar faces, maybe one of them is our man."

"But why would I become his target?"

Greg shrugged. "It's possible he saw you at the spa and just liked your look—so to speak. It's more probable that the way I dragged you into this mess as a 'consultant,' combined with your affiliation with two of the victims and Morrison's rantings have created a fusion in the killer's mind. Delusional already, always desperate for a pattern to explain his actions to himself, he suddenly finds it in you. You become the crux of his existence."

"My God," she said.

"Maybe that's why he broke his routine. There's been no evidence that the killer ever harassed or took any blatant act against his victims prior to setting up a 'massage' appointment with them. Certainly nothing as graphic as what happened here last night."

"He could have killed me then and there."

Now she felt Greg's muscles twitch as if he shivered. It made her want to cling to him more tightly, as if she were protecting him.

"Yes," Greg said. "He could have."

"Why didn't he?"

They stared at each other.

Kathy's cell phone rang.

49

KATHY'S BRAKES SQUEALED AS SHE ENTERED THE ACADEMY parking lot. There was a police car and an ambulance already on the scene, its bay doors flung wide open. The doors looked like open jaws rather than nurturing arms.

Brenda came running toward Kathy as she and Greg got out.

"What happened?"

"I was in your office, getting your computer set up, when I heard this commotion. It sounded like screaming," Brenda said.

She stopped to breathe.

"When I reached the front door, there were students sort of slumped there looking terrified. Then I heard this sharp bang against the door and more screaming. It was Amanda. I looked out and found her on the ground, halfway between here and the door, with her arms over her face. There were these three guys in the parking lot throwing rocks at her."

Kathy and Greg exchanged glances.

"Did you recognize them?"

"No," Brenda said. "They looked crazed. They were shouting stuff—calling Amanda a whore. Awful things. The rocks just keep pounding down on us. It was like something out of Iran. I yell at the students to call 911 if they have a cell phone. They do. Then I start trying to open the door to get Amanda inside. That's when Jim—"

"Jim?"

"Yeah, Jim. He runs past me out the door and just charges at these guys. He took a rock to the face, Kathy, and didn't even slow down. It bought me enough time to get the door open and drag Amanda inside. She had some cuts and bruises, but I don't think anything was broken. An ambulance took her away."

Kathy was confused. "What about the one that's out there?"

"That's for Jim."

As she said this, the doors opened and Jim was being wheeled toward the ambulance bay on a gurney. Kathy and Brenda started toward them while Greg went to speak with the police officer.

Jim had a bandage on his face. His eyes were shut. His shirt had been removed to place heavy gauze over his ribs. Kathy's eyebrows shot up in surprise at his physique. Jim seemed to have such a slight build that his wiry, muscular frame impressed her. But he wasn't made of marble.

"They kicked him," Brenda said. "Two on one, the bastards kicked him."

"I thought you said there were three—"

Now Brenda smiled with admiration and satisfaction. "There were. Jim knocked the first one down. Knocked him stone unconscious. The other two beat on Jim and then ran away. They didn't even try to help the third guy—he's sitting in the back of a squad car now."

Kathy spun around to look. She saw the back of someone's head. It looked like it belonged to a caveman.

The paramedics started to lift Jim into the ambulance.

"I'm the school administrator," Kathy said to them. "I'm coming with you. Is there room in the back or should I drive behind?"

The paramedics looked at each other. One shrugged. "We've got room. You'll have to get your own transportation back here, though."

"Done."

"Kathy," Brenda began, but let her objections drop.

Greg came back. "They got one of the guys."

"I know. What about him? One of Morrison's thugs?"

"A Morrison-inspired thug, at least. The nuts are starting to come out of the woodwork."

"I want to sue him," Kathy said. "Bernard Morrison is instigating this crap. My kids are getting attacked because of him. Is there anything you can do?"

Greg shook his head. "First Amendment."

Kathy started to climb into the ambulance bay. "I guess Betty was right after all."

Greg gave her a grin.

50

THE AMBULANCE ROCKED ALONG AS IT SPED TO THE NEAREST hospital. Kathy kept her gaze on the floor, her knees bunched tight to keep the narrow aisle free. Her concerns for Jim eased only when she looked at the attending paramedic's face. He looked bored.

Bored is a good sign. Right?

"They hurt me," Jim said.

The words came out so low that she barely heard them over the ambulance's other noises. At first, Kathy thought the EMT had mumbled something. When she realized Jim had spoken, she leaned over and took his hand.

"Can you hear me, Jim?"

His head lolled back and forth as gently as a paper boat on a pond. The left side of his face was normal. But Kathy cringed every time the right came into view. Jim looked like he'd been struck by a baseball bat. He must have taken both a rock and a boot to the head.

She thought of the man Jim had knocked out. The police had him in custody. He'd pay. Thanks to Jim.

All three of them would.

Jim moaned again. "Said they'd hurt me if I got in their way."

The urge to help him overwhelmed her. Kathy leaned over and brushed the hair from his eyes. In her peripheral vision she noted the paramedic's watchful, disapproving gaze.

Jim's exact state had not been explained to her but she knew he was medicated. He seemed to drift in and out of consciousness. Kathy kept her hold on his hand and glanced at the paramedic. She offered a conciliatory smile.

"Thanks for helping him. He's one of my favorite students."

"You're a teacher there?"

"Yes. I also founded it."

"And you're proud of that?"

His tone and bluntness shocked her. "Why wouldn't I be?"

The paramedic shrugged. "I think you do more harm than good. Telling people to light some incense and sniff it to cure a headache isn't my idea of medicine."

"I think you mean aromatherapy. There's more to it than your description," she said. She kept her voice calm, but she felt like exploding. Her nerves had been taxed too much to maintain the inner peace she normally possessed when confronting skeptics. The paramedic's attitude was toughest to take. They were both healers who took different approaches. Knowing that he saw her as an enemy made Kathy grind her teeth.

With evident amusement, the paramedic ran the tip of his tongue across the inside of his lower lip. Kathy followed the progress of the bulge from left to right.

"I've got a pack of matches. You want to light them, blow them out, and hold them under his nose? You think that would heal him? Or would you give him glue to sniff?"

She laughed at his ignorance. "Actually, I think I would make a compress of lemongrass and clove bud essential oils to help numb his pain. Or perhaps a liniment featuring a combination of birch and cayenne, both of which inhibit neurotransmitters. Birch contains several compounds similar to aspirin, after all. But I suppose neither of those solutions are as exciting as jabbing someone with a needle."

She smiled.

"Bunch of bullshit," he muttered.

"If you say so."

"Lady, I know so. See, I went to a real school with real training. Anatomy and all that. Science."

"Science," Kathy repeated, nodding. She was quiet a moment, and then looked over at Jim. "How deep is the bruising, do you think, along his zygomaticus minor? The swelling seems more centered at the levator labii superioris—you'll notice how the puffiness doesn't quite reach to the connective tissue around the eye."

The EMT crossed his arms and looked away.

"Of course, I wouldn't use aromatherapy to treat deep tissue injuries, as you seem to think," Kathy said. "Here's what I'd do."

She leaned forward and moved her right hand toward the injured portion of Jim's face. The EMT's eyes widened and he sort of snarled, reaching forward to seize her wrist.

"Take your hand off me," Kathy said, barely calm.

"Don't touch him!"

"You'll find that I don't need to."

The EMT looked confused but Kathy sensed curiosity overcoming his unease and distrust as he let go. She turned her attention to Jim, placing her hand less than an inch above his right cheek. It hovered there, perfectly still, as Kathy closed her eyes.

Her hand began to go through a series of positions as she

sensed the complexity of Jim's pain and drew upon the energy inside her, the energy she needed to give to him.

"What are you doing?"

The EMT's voice was not welcome, though she noted with satisfaction the absence of condescension in his tone.

"It's called Reiki," she said, continuing to channel the energy.

"What the hell is that?"

"A way to relieve pain and induce healing that doesn't require touch."

She continued a minute more in silence. Her energy was building. She felt it move through her arm and into her hand and flow into Jim's face.

"Holy shit," the EMT whispered.

She opened her eyes. The muscles in Jim's face were twitching. Kathy gave a sideways glance to the EMT and saw him leaning forward, his attention fascinated.

"What's going on?"

"The injuries have depleted his energy. Reiki is a technique that allows his body to siphon off my energy in order to start healing itself. It isn't magic or witchcraft."

She finished and withdrew her hand.

Jim's eyes opened. "Where am I?"

Before either of them could speak, he noticed the strap across his chest and began to struggle.

"Jim, you're in the ambulance; you were attacked."

He stared at Kathy as if he could not see. "Amanda?"

"No, it's me. Kathy."

"Amanda?"

Kathy and the EMT exchanged glances.

"They were angry," Jim said.

Now Kathy did reach and push a few strands of hair from his eyes. His gaze followed her fingertips like his life depended upon it.

"I'm really proud of the way you stood up to them, Jim. The way you defended Amanda is an inspiration to all of us."

"Amanda."

His eyes weren't focused. Kathy doubted he was even half-conscious. *Poor Jim.* He loved Amanda so much but there was nothing he could do to win her. The pain of rejection must still be overwhelming him. Now he had the physical ache to accompany it. She wished she could extend her hand to take the unrequited love out of his head.

Only time can do that, she thought, and the EMT gave her a questioning look. At that moment, Kathy realized she had spoken the thought out loud.

51

The doctors wanted to keep Jim overnight for observation, and Kathy spent two hours dealing with hospital bureaucracy on his behalf. *No wonder people were turning to alternative medicine more and more.* She didn't know of any massage therapist, Reiki practitioner, or acupuncturist who spent more time worrying about a patient's insurance coverage than they did the patient. Jim had no discernible medical coverage at all. That unfortunately wasn't atypical for her students, but she distinctly remembered Jim telling her once that his parents were wealthy. Brenda had been unable to contact them at the emergency numbers in his student file.

Kathy was stepping out to wait for a cab when she caught sight of a familiar, if unwelcome, face. Scott Carson, the blogger, sat in a junker car in the hospital parking lot with the window rolled down. As ever, he was tapping notes into his iPhone.

"You," she said, walking over.

Carson looked up and smiled. "Ms. Barrister—a pleasure."

"What are you doing here?"

"Heard about what happened at the Academy. I was seeing what I could find on your injured student."

"Jim?" she said automatically, without thinking. As soon as she saw Carson's expression, though, she knew she'd erred. Big time.

"Whoa, was there someone else? I heard it was a girl—Amanda. What's her last name, by the way?"

"Sorry, I can't tell you."

"Can't, or won't?"

"Won't."

He nodded and smiled. His smile seemed permanently adversarial, as if molded by a lifetime of dealing with uncooperative people.

"So, another student got hurt as well? What's his name? First will do."

"Look, sorry, but I just can't say."

Carson sighed. "Well, at least I know what hospital he's in. That's more than I know on Amanda…what was her last name again?"

Kathy almost answered him before catching herself. *I'll be damned.*

"So you've gone to other hospitals trying to track down people you don't know?"

"I'm dedicated," Carson said.

"How did you hear about the fight?"

"Police band radio," he said.

"You listen to police scanners all day, and you show up anytime a crime scene sounds promising?"

He smiled. "Like a bad penny. I always turn up."

Kathy nodded. His occupation was weird, but she begrudgingly admired his dedication. She had no idea how he could do this all day and make money. To judge from his car, a battered Toyota Celica, he didn't make any money at all. But who was she to judge? Smart people followed their bliss even if the road did lead to poverty.

"Well, it was good to see you again," she said.

This was a lie, but a polite one. She started walking away. She heard his car door open and close.

"Ms. Barrister."

She turned. "Yes?"

"Is there any more information you can share about…last night."

Her eyes narrowed. "You know about that too?"

"I've heard things."

"Are you posting things on your blog about me? Because if you are, you could be inciting violence—"

"I'm not posting anything too indiscreet."

"The media hasn't reported anything that happened to me last night. And if you—"

"It's not about me," he said. "It's about my blog. I'll advertise it anyway I can. One mention on Fox or CNN and my web traffic will soar. The Drudge Report started off exactly the same way. These murders have become huge news. If I can scoop the big boys in any way, I will. I might even win myself a John Jay Excellence in Criminal Justice Reporting Award. Maybe even a Dart Award too. Do either and I can make my way in life as a professional writer. I won't have to drive that piece-of-shit Celica around anymore, either."

Kathy backed away from him in disgust. Carson smiled.

"If you're so eager to read what I'm writing about you, why don't you go to my site? Badpenny.com. I can always use the traffic."

The cab pulled into the lot. Kathy raised her hand at it. She turned back to him.

"The only traffic I'm interested in is what I can put between you and me. Goodbye."

52

SHE THOUGHT ABOUT JIM ON THE RIDE BACK TO THE ACADEMY. What if he'd never had rich parents? She began to think he'd made it up—after all, people fabricated their backgrounds all the time for reasons that had nothing to do with illegality. Some were ashamed of poverty while others were ashamed of wealth. Ethnicity, religion—any number of reasons.

But if Jim didn't really have money to burn trying out different careers, as past conversations had intimated, then Kathy's sense of ethics began to gnaw at her. The Academy was expensive, and he would rack up several thousands of dollars in debt before graduating. For most people, this was a fair trade because it allowed them to enter a profession they loved and could make a living doing.

That was not Jim's case. Shouldn't she, for his sake, suggest he pursue something else? How could she simply take his money knowing he really had no future as a massage therapist? There are certain messages one should never hear from a mentor, and yet these are the messages only mentors are uniquely qualified to deliver. Kathy knew she'd never master the art of telling any student that a particular subject exceeded their grasp.

Almost every aspect of massage therapy exceeded Jim's grasp.

Amanda's earlier assessment of him had been spot-on, and Kathy knew it. He simply lacked something. He'd attended the Academy through one semester already and none of his instructors' comments were fun reading. He was not an industrious student, but he got by. He was never incompetent; he seldom outright failed a test, but successful massage therapy went beyond learning terminology and concepts. Ultimately it was a profession most uniquely suited to the lucky few whose mind and hands were able to hold an independent conversation with each other. Amanda was a perfect example of this gift, as Erin had been before. The inner self's intuition about a patient's need, and the hands' ability to accept its instruction and guidance, were the hallmarks of the true healer. Jim's hands sometimes acted like each finger was shouting at the others.

The cab pulled up at the Academy. Kathy got out, paid, and started toward her office still thinking about Jim.

If only he wanted to learn massage therapy on a lark, as something to broaden his mind. He certainly seemed to approach the subject with that attitude, yet when questioned he expressed such a selfless desire to heal that Kathy felt moved. She felt her determination as a teacher rise. *I can mould him. I can make him understand and turn him into a great therapist.*

She'd asked Amanda to pair up with him at the start of the term, thinking an association with such a superior student might work wonders for him. The strategy had worked before. But with Jim, it seemed to have backfired entirely. He had simply added Amanda to his list of hopeless desires.

When Kathy got to her office, Brenda was already waiting.

"Do you have Jim's file?"

"On your desk. Ironic that we've got his and the current crop of students digitized and still had to dig out the hardcopy. I'm hoping we can get your computer back soon."

She sat down and looked. "Is there still no answer?"

"The emergency contact number Jim has listed comes up disconnected. I haven't been able to track down any relatives."

Kathy looked over the file. Nothing else out of the ordinary there, though students were supposed to keep their files updated at all times. Recent experience told her this wasn't happening. The world just moved too fast.

She looked up from the file at the sound of a hurried knock. Brenda turned aside to reveal Amanda standing in the doorway.

"Kathy, is Jim—"

Kathy rose. "Never mind about Jim for the moment. Are you okay?"

She had a small bandage over her face and light bruising. She told them she had a few smaller cuts on her torso from the rocks but otherwise felt fine. The hospital had released her, and Brad drove her back.

Kathy asked Brenda to leave. When they were alone, Kathy said, "Jim's okay. He got it a little worse than you, I'm afraid. His cheekbone is fractured. They thought his ribs might be too, but thankfully it's just bruising."

Amanda cupped her hands over her mouth. "He—he saved me. Those guys just showed up out of nowhere. I thought they were going to stone me to death."

Kathy smiled. "He cares a lot for you."

She studied Amanda's reaction to this carefully. Amanda seemed pained by the fact. At last she said, "If only it could have been anyone else besides him."

"Why?"

"Because now that he's hurt, I feel like it's my fault!"

"Do you feel guilty, or do you feel like you now owe him your love?"

Amanda stared at her. She shook her head. "Maybe both. I didn't even know he was here. He really shouldn't have been—I know he doesn't have a morning class."

Kathy gave a small smile. "I suppose he's not the type to come in early to use the library, either."

Amanda's laugh was not without warmth. "Definitely not," she said. "I guess I should go visit him?"

"No. And once he's back, the three of us will work out a new study partner arrangement. We'll separate the two of you in a way that's respectful and doesn't hurt his feelings."

Amanda's relief showed on her face. "Thanks, Kathy."

Her phone started ringing. Kathy's gaze riveted on the caller ID. Greg.

"Amanda—could you excuse me?"

Amanda left.

She picked up the phone. "Greg?"

"Kathy," he said, talking fast, "you've got to come to the Bureau right now."

She sat straight. "Is it about the men at my school this morning?"

"What? No," he said. "It's about the teeth."

She listened to him rush out an explanation.

The teeth weren't Erin's.

They weren't even real.

53

KATHY MET GREG AT THE BUREAU HQ, WHICH WAS SITUATED on three separate floors of a downtown skyscraper. She rode the elevator up thinking it an odd place to locate their organization. It seemed impossible to think that serial killers, child molesters, and tax cheats were being pursued on floors seventeen through twenty while on twenty-one an advertising company struggled to find new ways to market vacuum cleaners to single fathers. She'd picture the Bureau existing in some underground bunker a mile beneath the city.

He met her on the twentieth floor. Once more she took her cues from his formal bearing. "We're just down this hall," he said, and she followed him into a small computer lab. It seemed no larger than an examination room for vision checkups. The room's lights had been dimmed, giving prominence to a monitor that flashed images she could not interpret. They appeared to be extreme close-ups—of something.

A technician came to meet them. "Hello, Greg."

Greg made introductions.

"So you're the one who got the visit from the Tooth Fairy last night," the tech said. Kathy stiffened at his tone.

"I'm the lucky lady."

Greg pointed to the monitor. "Tell her about the teeth."

The tech laughed. "I think she already knows all she needs to know. These pearly whites aren't real." He went to a scanning device on the right side of the room. Kathy realized the images belong to the object being scanned. Suddenly the monitor went dark, and the tech came back with his gloved right palm outstretched.

She shivered when she saw his offering. The teeth looked terribly jaundiced and dry. How could someone think them not real?

Suddenly the hand closed and shook back and forth. The teeth made a little rattle in the hollow of his fist, as if he were rolling dice. Kathy flinched.

"Cut it out," Greg said.

The tech relented. "I'm sorry. No, they aren't real. Not that a trained eye would need all this technology to confirm it."

"Sorry I inconvenienced everyone by not getting out my orthodontics textbook before calling 911!"

"No need to be sorry. These," he said, opening his palm again, "are dental bridges. Old dental bridges at that."

Kathy looked between Greg and the technician. "Where could someone get old dental bridges?"

"Who knows? Maybe someone's grandpa sneezed them out twenty years ago and this joker's been keeping them in a dresser drawer. Maybe they were found on the side of the road. The most important thing is they're not real teeth."

"The important thing," Greg said, in a rage, "is some bastard knows Kathy's address and is sick enough to play a joke like this!"

"Take it easy, Greg," she said in a quiet voice.

"I feel like we're back to square one. Instead of a taunting message from the killer, we've probably got ourselves some dumbass kid looking to play a joke. Don't you understand, Kathy?"

She shook her head.

"My theory's back in the Bureau's garbage can. They no longer think you're a target at all."

"That's a good thing."

"Not if you're really still a target it's not."

The tech said, quite casually, "I hardly think we're back to square one, Detective Beacon. The actual murder that happened—"

"Shut up!" Greg said, eyes wide with realization.

"—on Sunday night still—"

"Greg?"

"—suggests a connection—"

"Shut the fuck up!"

The tech stared at both of them, dumbfounded. Kathy returned it with equal intensity.

"Actual murder?"

Greg cast one withering glance at the tech, who promptly scurried off. He took Kathy by the shoulder and led her out of the room.

"What did he say about an actual murder? I haven't heard anything."

"Very few people know. I'm sorry."

"But when was it? Did it happen in the city?"

"I can't say."

She shook herself free from him. "The hell you can't! I'm not connected to it in any way, am I?"

Greg put his arm across her shoulder and guided her into an adjacent room. He shut the door. For a moment he just looked at it, his back to her. Kathy's intuition almost blared inside her head. She did know the murder victim. But who was it? She knew so many massage therapists in the state.

Greg turned around to face her. She'd never seen his face look so grim. "Kathy, I have terrible news."

5 4

Two days later, on Wednesday, Kathy sat by herself at the end of a crowded funeral home. In her numb state she had no awareness of the people around her. There were at least a hundred. Recorded choir music played in the background. *That isn't right or fair.* The thought sounded distant in her head, as if she wanted to flee her body. She did. The last funeral service she'd attended was her father's over twenty years ago, and she remembered fixating on the recorded music. It seemed cheap. She remembered surprising her mother by being outraged and demanding live musicians. It had been the perfect storm of naïveté, grief, and teen angst. Her mom had simply said, "Funerals usually aren't like weddings, Katherine. The dead don't get live entertainment." She'd hated her mom so much for that response.

Kathy wiped tears from her cheeks and shivered.

Two rows ahead, on the other side of the aisle, Sharon's twin boys, Jacob and Ryan, grieved against the separate sides of two identical uncles. Kathy had met Sharon's younger brothers a couple of times in the distant past and remembered them as being real hell-raisers at the time. Dressed in suits and solemn-eyed, they looked both respectable and mature. One uncle appeared to have a wife and kids of his own; the other sat alone. They were a strong family and that gave Kathy hope. Sharon's poor boys would need the support to endure the sorrows facing them.

Kathy took a deep breath. Her inhale betrayed a soft, whimpering sob. She had already cried so much this morning alone that her body felt dry and empty, but the tears were waiting just behind her eyes as her sorrow rebuilt itself in the pit of her stomach. Almost anything might set them off now, and so she stared at her feet and tried to block out all sensation.

Her cell phone vibrated in her purse. She reached in and looked. The caller ID told her it was Greg. Kathy stared at his name a moment before turning the phone off.

He didn't know, she thought, trying hard to get past her suspicions. On Sunday night, while Kathy was being made the victim of an elaborate joke that drew Greg and the police to her doorstep, Sharon was working late at her spa. She was alone in the building—foolishly, Kathy wanted to say, but she clamped down the urge—and the killer either broke in or was already hiding inside after it closed. No one was sure yet. There was no video footage. Ironically, Sharon was working late because she was evaluating bids on installing a security camera system on the premises following the riot damage.

He did know. She was sure that Greg already knew Sharon had been murdered when he'd arrived at Kathy's house. Therefore he knew as he talked to Kathy on the couch, and he sure as hell knew when he calmly talked to her over breakfast. She had no proof, just a feeling. Greg denied having any knowledge of the murder until late Monday morning. Kathy remembered how he'd said there would be times when he'd have to keep her in the dark. He had a job to do. She knew her cold-shoulder routine was making that job harder for him. Regardless, just then, a part of Kathy began to hate him.

She could barely stand to think about him right now. Doing so just reminded her of how she took comfort in his arms while Sharon bled to death on the floor of her office. She felt as if her calling 911 had betrayed Sharon in some way or condemned her to death by drawing the police to her house when they could have been at the spa. The roles should have been switched. It should have been Sharon who got the fake teeth. *I'm the one who should have died.*

Greg had already left one message for her, saying he wished he could be there for her. She was glad he was at the Bureau. She didn't know how she'd react when she saw him again.

If he did know, what was he supposed to do? And you kept secrets from him!

God, she hoped her common sense and reason would win out and keep her from hating Greg. She saw the two of them on her couch going over the case files, while Greg knew the entire time that her best friend had been murdered hours earlier. If she entertained the scenario for much longer, there'd be no going back on her feelings. Her rage and grief needed a victim. Greg threatened to become the primary target regardless of guilt or innocence.

Crying silently now, Kathy raised her head and looked toward the casket. The lid was shut. Kathy knew why. They all knew why. The papers had given just enough detail in their own luridly discreet fashion. Kathy refused to imagine what the killer had done to Sharon, knowing it would give the killer too much satisfaction. Worse, it may have been giving him credit where none was due. As Greg had tried to explain, Sharon's murder was not necessarily related to the others. The symbol had yet to be found, and her teeth were intact. Just as lunatics stirred up by Morrison's antics had attacked the Academy, a similar lone nut might have assaulted Sharon. Greg seemed to insinuate this but would say no more when pressed. Thinking about it made her angrier with him.

It didn't matter as far as the public was concerned. The killer was all anyone talked about. Even here whispers began to penetrate her numb senses. Some idiot, talking too loudly in the back row, even made some innuendo about what Sharon was doing when she died.

Kathy stood, marched back to where he was, and told him to shut up.

She couldn't return to her seat after that. She made her way to the lobby, crying in earnest and hoping to find a bathroom. She felt hate sitting on her chest like a cold, dead weight. It had been there since she learned of Erin's death, hiding, building its strength. Now it was ready to seize her and never let go. Hate. It was the most horrible thing a person could be possessed by, yet Kathy made no attempt to drive it away. She became calm and studied it, as a scientist might crouch in the bushes and watch a deadly animal at rest. She thought of it in terms of ownership. *My hate.*

She felt an irresistible urge to feed it.

"Kathy?"

She looked to see Amanda and Brad stepping through the front doors. Kathy looked around for a hiding place. They were making a beeline toward her. Kathy managed a glance at Brad, who seemed downcast and sheepish. She could not remember the last time they'd spoken.

There was no awkwardness from him as they exchanged hugs.

"How are you, Brad?"

"Better than the last time you saw me," he said, very quiet. He did look better. There was color to his face, a vitality that had been lacking in all their previous encounters. It wasn't hard for Kathy to realize Amanda was its source.

"Brad insisted we pay our respects. I hope this is okay, since we don't really know Sharon."

"She's my sister too, now, as far as I'm concerned," Brad said, his tone changing to one of determination. "I feel related to every person this bastard gets."

Amanda reached for his hand. It seemed to calm him.

"Did you know her very well, Kathy?"

"Yes," she said, and there was so much emotion in the syllable that neither Brad nor Amanda said anything else.

55

Scott Carson, the blogger, was sitting in his battered Toyota Celica with a laptop lodged between his lap and the steering wheel. Kathy saw him right away and stared at him through the driver's side window.

He didn't notice her approach. She rapped on the glass.

"Gah!" he said, falling toward the passenger's side. The laptop went to the floor, and he started to curse and reach for it as he rolled down the window with his other hand. Kathy leaned into the opening.

"Hanging around like a bad penny again?"

Nothing about her tone should have thrilled him, yet Kathy found him grinning. She wondered if he had any awareness of decorum or respect.

"I'm writing a blog entry now," he said. "I have to write it in Word and save it for posting later, though. This place doesn't seem to have Wi-Fi."

"You're a real piece of work, you know that? Do you think this is a Starbucks? You're outside a wake!"

"I know, I know. It's just things are happening so fast I'm having trouble keeping up. Can I interview you?"

"Why?"

"Surely you know you're at the center of all this. If you aren't, you're as dumb as the police."

"The police aren't dumb."

"Well, I sure as hell hope they're smart enough to be watching your back. Two of your former students are dead, another victim gets killed pretty much in your neighborhood, and your school gets assaulted—"

"Your point?"

He looked ready to laugh at her. "The woman that died in there. She was one of your best friends, right?"

"How did you know that?"

"I remember when the crowd was protesting her spa. You were there. I saw you hug each other later and go inside. And you were obviously there for the second protest. I figured you might be lovers or—"

She slapped him. He stared at her a second with no expression on his chubby face. He looked best blank, almost human. It was when he flexed into a slight grin that he assumed an animal cunning.

"Touched a nerve?"

"No," she said. "I have no problem with homosexuality, either. I'm just sick of all the sexual angles these stories have taken."

He was typing again on his laptop. She realized he was transcribing her speech and shut up. No way in hell she was going to be part of his quest for journalistic glory.

"It's all about you, isn't it?"

"I care about the city, and I care about my blog. One day, I hope when people think of one, they'll automatically think of the other."

Kathy looked around. A few people were starting to come outside now. The funeral service would be tomorrow at Sharon's church. There would be no graveside ceremony. Sharon's body was to be taken to a family plot in Ohio.

She looked back at Carson.

"You think the killer is after me?"

"I think he's closing in. Hell, he even taunted you!"

Kathy's eyes narrowed. Her intuition sparked. "What taunt?"

"The fake teeth," he said.

"How do you know about that?"

"I heard it over the police bandwidth."

Not the fake part. They stared at each other. For the first time in her brief meetings with him, Kathy thought Carson looked flustered, as if he knew he'd slipped up. His lower lip showed a slight tremor. His eyes, predatory when he thought he had an advantage, displayed a rabbit-like timidity, liquid and dark. She looked at his fingers and imagined how they'd look poking through her mail slot. You, she thought, bringing her hands against her legs to hide a growing tremor. The hate pressed on her chest again. You're the sick bastard who tried to terrify me!

"What else have you heard? Please tell me. I—the police won't say much."

"What? Even your boyfriend—Beacon?"

"He's not really my boyfriend."

The blogger smiled knowingly. His eyes returned to their stalking demeanor, exactly as Kathy hoped.

"I can tell you things," she said, "but I expect to learn everything you know in return."

His fingertips were poised over the keyboard. "Start talking."

She played her ace card right away to lure him in.

"I gave Erin her first massage table. The killer took it from her in Edgerton. It was found at the Allison Stockett crime scene. Her body was lashed to it."

Carson's face seemed paralyzed, as were his fingers. He

looked like a hungry child who'd just been presented with all the ice cream in the world. It seemed like he would cry, overwhelmed by bounty.

"Are you okay?"

"Wh-what else do you have?"

"I'll need to show you. It can't be told."

"Show me?"

She leaned in. "I'll show the table—it hasn't been touched. I'll show you the room where Allison was killed."

"Right now?"

"Now," Kathy said.

Gasping at this, he turned and pawed at the passenger side door, begging her to get in.

She laughed cruelly. "I'm not risking my life in that! Come with me. I'll drive."

56

CARSON WAS SO BUSY STARING AT HIS COMPUTER SCREEN, typing as he talked about his imminent greatness, that he didn't realize thirty minutes had passed on what should have been a fifteen-minute drive, and that they were leaving the city.

At last he looked up, puzzled.

"How much longer is it?"

"Ninety minutes."

"What? Where the hell are we going?"

"Edgerton, of course."

Carson pivoted on her in the passenger seat. "Like hell! I don't have time to go there, I've got a serial killer to cover!"

"But you had time to sneak up to my porch and shove a pair of phony teeth through my mail slot."

The blogger's stunned silence was answer enough.

"It was you," she said.

"That's crazy. You're insane!"

"That's how you got to my house so quick. You were already in the neighborhood, weren't you?"

She looked over at him. "Greg—that's Detective Beacon's first name, by the way, and yes, I hope like hell he's my boyfriend—will be very interested to know what you did."

"Christ," he said. She heard a clicking sound and glanced over to find he was trying to open the door. What's he going to do—throw himself into the road? By instinct, she started to brake. She caught herself surrendering and forced her foot down on the accelerator.

Be careful. Then she smiled, suddenly very self-assured. This wasn't a mistake like confronting Judd Garvis alone. She could handle a greedy, self-serving pipsqueak like Carson.

"I just want to show you something."

"Jesus Christ, what? The Edgerton City Jail?"

"Oh no. I won't say a word about your stunt. I just want you to admit doing it."

"Why in hell would I do that?"

"Guilty conscience?"

He laughed at her.

"You slipped up, pal. Only a few people know the teeth were fake—"

"I told you, I listen to a police scanner—"

"You wanted to stir the soup even more by trying to scare me, didn't you? Was the killer being too lazy for you? You didn't count on the fact maybe he was murdering Sharon at the same time, and while I was frantically calling the police to rescue me, she was bleeding to death."

"You act like I killed her—"

"You little bastard," she said. The vehemence in her voice almost frightened her, but she took it and owned it. She felt herself merging with her car and with the road. She became Carson's fate.

The blogger seemed to sense this too. He sat back, the muscles about his throat flexing as he swallowed. "Are we really going to Edgerton?"

"Oh yes."

He raked his fingers along his laptop. Suddenly he turned to her.

"What if I told you I knew who did do it, but it wasn't me?"

"Not buying that for a second."

He laughed again, with scorn. "Well, there's not a chance in hell I'd admit to doing something like that. Because I didn't," he seemed to add as an afterthought.

"You already have."

He flinched. "How?"

"Your muscles. The tension in your face. Your change in posture."

"You going to start playing the violin next, Sherlock Holmes? Tell me I must have taken an early morning walk because I've got dog shit on my shoes?"

She shook her head. "Have you ever placed a personal ad online before?"

He smirked. "So now you think I'm the killer too? You're out of your mind. I'm in a car with a crazy person."

Kathy jerked the steering wheel, sending him against the passenger door. He winced and rubbed his shoulder.

"When the crazy person is driving, you answer the questions."

"Fine," he said. "Sure, who hasn't?"

"What happens when someone answers an ad?"

"It's done by e-mail. Usually pictures are exchanged. If not that, then at least stats."

"Stats?"

"You know. Age, height, weight. Tit size," he said, giving Kathy a bold look. "Or penis size, depending. Most of the time both parties are lying."

Carson's mouth, once activated, would not shut up. Kathy had never even been on a legitimate dating website before and found herself admittedly fascinated by the process Carson described. He spoke the rest of the way into Edgerton, boasting of his hookups. "Yeah, I've paid for a massage before. I like it when they say they're professionals. You know, I think even some of them have said they graduated from your school. I'm sure they didn't; it's just an easily identifiable name. Adds a touch of realism."

"To cover for what's really happening, right?"

He smiled, as if even now he were reminiscing about an encounter. "You know it."

Kathy endured his descriptions until they pulled into The Johns. She wondered if Erin's room was back in circulation yet. She shuddered to think of it. But for her purposes, it didn't really matter.

Carson bolted from the car as soon as it was stopped. There was a moment's exultation in his freedom, then just a confused complacency. As he looked around, Kathy leaned over and slammed the passenger door shut again. Carson turned, lunging for the very car he'd just escaped.

She rolled down the window a fraction. He tried to jam his fingers through the opening. It reminded her too much of his fingers wriggling about in her mail slot. She mashed on the button. Carson rescued his hands in the last second.

"What are you going to do?"

"Nothing," Kathy said. "I wanted to show you something. See that door? My student Erin was murdered in that room."

"Aren't you getting out?"

"No. But ask the old woman in the manager's office if she'll give you the key. Her name's Glenda. Heart of gold, that woman."

She started to pull away. Carson went alongside, hammering at the glass. "My computer's still in your car! I need it!"

She glanced down. So it was.

She put the car in reverse and aimed for the exit.

"This isn't funny!"

"Neither was scaring me by shoving phony teeth through my mail slot, you sick bastard!"

She accelerated a little. Carson ran faster, beating at the trunk.

"I'm sorry! I'm really sorry; I know I shouldn't have! Sometimes a reporter has to make a story more interesting; I didn't mean any harm!"

Kathy stopped the car and cracked the passenger window half an inch. "If you want computer, it will be on my porch when you make it back from here. At least I won't have to give you directions."

She mashed the gas pedal down and peeled out, leaving him jumping up and down and gesturing wildly in her rearview mirror.

Kathy thought of all the women who had been killed. She thought of Erin and Sharon.

That one was for both of you.

57

All the way home, Kathy worked at pushing back her anger. Leaving Carson stranded was satisfying but not satisfactory. *Maybe I really am going nuts.*

Erin. Sharon. Gayle Thompson. Allison Stockett. Other names she did not even know. Their deaths weren't fair. They weren't right.

There had to be justice.

She may have bested Greg's time in reaching home. She went past her house and parked in Betty's driveway. Her old neighbor was sitting on the porch drinking tea. She stood up as Kathy climbed the steps.

"Tell me a little bit about firearms."

Betty smiled and took her by the arm. "For you, dear? I think a 9mm. It was my first gun after my husband died," she said, and took Kathy inside to show her.

On Wednesday night, with the gun from Betty resting nearby atop her massage table, Kathy sat at her computer. Her cell phone rang twice. Both calls were from Greg and both went unanswered.

Kathy navigated the Internet and went to Craigslist. As far as she knew, all of the murder victims except Sharon and Gayle had posted there in a section called Erotic Services. There was a Craigslist page specific to each city, and she went to hers, expecting to find it empty. What sane person would post ads there, knowing a serial killer was prowling them? To her shock, though, she found over eighty listings posted just today. Some even made jokes about the killer. The headline of one post read, "Risking My Life to Give You the Best Time of Yours." Kathy shook her head as she clicked through the links. Almost all of them were women with ads remarkably similar to Erin's. *Trained LMT here to relieve all of your tension.* Kathy's disgust spiked. Knowing that some of these people might really be licensed massage therapists like Erin just made the whole idea even more insulting.

He's here looking right now. She shivered. She felt like she was ankle-deep in the ocean and a shark was circling in the depths ahead. Knowing they were looking at the same ads at the same time sent a nervous, creepy thrill through her—as if they were standing in the same crowded room, trying to figure each other out.

Deep body rub by licensed LMT. Great beginning, happier ending.

She scanned and scanned, reading through her intensifying nausea. She got the gist of the language very fast. As with any bait, not all the lures were the same. None of the ads showed subtlety, but some clearly enticed more than others. Pictures helped, but not all of the better ads included them. She tried to think like a man. She tried to imagine Greg reading them and getting aroused. The idea made her so sick she had to push away with a deep inhale, her eyes shut, certain she would vomit. The urge passed after a minute.

Pulling herself back, Kathy went through the procedures

of setting up her own account to make a post. The process took less than five minutes. Staring now at a blank screen, she started to type. Her own ad was going to have a bit more flavor. She composed it to fit in among the others before seasoning it with her particular bait. Reiki. She described it in orgasmic terms that would have been comedic and absurd in other circumstances. She called it healing Tantric power, the fusion of bodily energy. If the circumstances weren't so sad, she might have laughed.

Last, she attached a picture—a digital scan of Erin's student photo. This upset her the most but it had to be done. Kathy did not know how much Erin had changed in the year since she last saw her. Would the killer recognize her right away and understand the ad for the ruse it was? She did not think so. But he would respond to some memory of her face, the recollection of her hair, the trace of her profile. He'd gone for Erin before. Attracted once and surely a slave to impulses, the killer would go for her again.

And I'll be waiting for him. She glanced at the gun on her massage table.

Her respiration coming heavy now, laboring against nerves, Kathy moused her cursor over to the submit button.

What if Brad is reading this site, obsessed with his sister's death? What if he sees this photo?

She squeezed her eyes shut a moment. Every aspect of her plan was unethical. Unethical, improbable, impossible.

To use this photo—it's like Erin's being killed again.

Kathy frowned and dabbed a bit of sweat off her forehead. *I'm sorry about this, Erin.*

She clicked the Submit button. On the monitor, the website changed to confirm the ad. It would go live in five minutes. Then it would be time to start checking the fake e-mail account she set up just for her ad.

It was 9:05 p.m. Kathy stared at the screen.

Hope you're biting tonight, you son of a bitch.

58

THE FIRST RESPONSE CAME AT NINE FIFTEEN. THE SUBJECT line read Work Out a Kink. Kathy stared at it half a minute before proceeding. The message inside consisted of three sentences with no capitalization or grammar and apparently composed by an illiterate. He'd attached a photo. Naively expecting it to be a face shot, she discovered too late it was a picture of a penis.

"God," she said, deleting the e-mail without a thought. That one wasn't the killer. She just knew.

The second and third e-mails arrived minutes later. She deleted the second just as fast as the first. The third was more promising. She exchanged three messages with him, most involving a fuller description of her "services." When it got to talk of meeting, though, the correspondence ceased. *Must have got cold feet.* She understood. Most of her body was a block of ice from dread and awful anticipation.

For the next thirty minutes nothing happened. She

returned to the Erotic Services page and found just four new postings above hers. The cyber street corner was crowded tonight. She wondered if her ad was already doomed.

Sighing, Kathy got up and walked over to the gun. She looked at it, thought about picking it up, and decided not to. How strange it had felt in her hand, not too heavy and curved to meet her palm. It was like a handshake. Staring at the 9 mm, she still could not believe she had it in her house. She'd never been antigun; she just felt like they weren't for her. Seeing those fingers in her mail slot had changed what was and was not for her. Even knowing it was all a sick joke did not matter. She could see those fingers wiggling at her as she shot them off one by one. The fantasy thrilled her as much as it stunned. Kathy knew she'd lost more than her loved ones to the killer. She would never quite be the person she was in the sunny seconds before Brad Haley snuck into the back of her classroom.

The last thing Betty said after giving her the 9 mm was asking after Greg. Kathy said he was fine but very busy. Betty simply told her he was too good a man to let get away.

Am I?

She turned from the gun to her cell phone. It wasn't right not to answer his calls. It wasn't right to pretend she was mad at him now. The earlier anger was over. Even if he had concealed Sharon's death from her, she knew it was unavoidable. He had a job to do.

Let me check the e-mails one ore time, and then I'll call him.

Four new messages.

The first and second e-mails were readily dismissed. She never even got to the fourth. Her intuition rang like a siren on the third.

She studied the message and then looked at the e-mail address. Tuchlvr69@yahoo.com. Was that supposed to be touch or tush? The message had the same perverted quality as all the others, but there was something different about it.

Maybe the good grammar and punctuation alone set it apart, made it seem businesslike and professional in its solicitation. It had a sureness to it, as if she'd already agreed to meet him.

Him.

Kathy took a long, deep breath and leaned forward to face her enemy.

She wouldn't be able to explain the insistence of her intuition even if she wanted. The sense had always guided her, usually without fail, and she trusted it. There was no reason to it. In fact, more often than not it seemed to fly in the face of logic. But she had never had to trust it in a situation like this. She tingled with energy from head to toe.

She hit the Reply button and punched out a response. The keyboard suddenly felt cold and awkward. She reread the one sentence message, corrected five typos, and sent it.

I'm writing to the man who killed Erin. The man who might have killed Sharon.

She saw Brad's crying face. She saw Sharon's twin boys crying in the church pew at their uncles' sides. So much sadness. So many damn tears.

She glanced over at the gun again.

She refreshed her in-box over and over. More messages. But not from him. She deleted these without even opening them.

Come on. Write back.

She leaned closer to the monitor in anticipation. Her lower back made the barest twinge of complaint. She rubbed at with her left hand as her right hand hit the refresh button one more time.

A new message. *Him!*

She sat back in astonishment, panting as her pulse sped up. She listened to her shallow breathing and stared at the screen. *Open it.* The e-mail had a photo attached.

It will be a monster's face. Sharp teeth. Red eyes. Long, reptilian tongue. The photo will lunge at me through the screen.

I'll turn around and he'll be in the corner, standing at the massage table. He'll be a shadow motioning for me to come. Silent. I'll go to him though I won't want to. I won't be able to resist. He'll have the knife in one hand. He'll have pliers in another. He'll—

Her cell phone rang, and she screamed out loud in surprise. She was still staring at her inbox, the new message unopened. Her hands perched bloodless in front of her on the keyboard. The cell phone. She reached for it, looked at the screen. Greg. It felt like a reminder from God telling her she was not as alone as she felt, here with the Valley of the Shadow of Death opening itself to her through the monitor. She wanted to talk to him so badly, so very badly. But not now—not yet. She did not answer the phone. She pressed the volume control to mute the ringer. The phone rested silent, blinking and flashing like some urgent, living thing. Then it went dead and dark.

Kathy waited another minute, her head lowered, collecting herself. Then she looked up and pressed the subject line. The e-mail opened.

An address. A motel name.

The door will be unlocked.

She opened the attachment. It was just a drawing—a yellow happy face. Had any of the others received such a thing?

Kathy stood up and reached for her purse. Then she went to her massage table. The gun sat on top of it. There was a time when such an image would offend her. Now she opened her purse and put the 9mm inside. It was easily the largest item. *Will I be able to use it when the time comes?*

She closed the purse and eased the strap over her shoulder.

Only one way to find out.

She stopped to compose a three-word response and headed out the door.

I'm leaving now.

<h1 style="text-align:center">59</h1>

Out of the way. Dark. She had trouble locating the motel's exact address and stumbled upon it after what she thought were several wrong turns. They were not. She wondered what dark fortune was guiding her tonight.

She parked at the far end of the lot and gripped the steering wheel, breathing deep and methodical. *Call Greg. Call him now!*

She got out her phone and dialed. No answer.

She texted him her location and the word urgent. God, what would he think when he finally saw it?

Kathy put the phone away and looked at the motel. It was not unlike The Johns. Just his style.

She got out and stared. The motel was situated about a mile off the highway. There were just four cars in the parking lot but three hundred yards north was a very busy diner. She could almost hear the warm sounds of chatter and of utensils striking plates. *I can run there if I have to.* The thought bolstered her courage.

The motel consisted of one long, single-story facility offering fifteen rooms. All the doors faced east. Kathy went west, walking through darkness into the building's blacker shadow. The back offered her the noise of the highway. She watched headlights speed along. Time was wasting.

She swallowed once and looked in her purse to check the gun. Should she walk in with it in her hand? Should she wait until she was in the door and then take it out? The debate was so absurd to her she felt like laughing. She thought that if she gave into the compulsion to laugh, she would go insane on the spot, though she wondered if her sanity wasn't already in tatters.

And what if her intuition was wrong? What if there was just some poor slob waiting in there, a creep to be sure but not a killer? The idea of aiming a gun at anyone but the killer horrified her. Did she dare trust herself enough to weigh the man's innocence or guilt based on a feeling?

Kathy completed her surveillance of the building. She had no idea why she checked the back of the motel other than it seemed right and clever to do so. Now it was time to go to room nine and turn the doorknob.

She took baby steps, aware that her walking was transitioning to something more feminine, the type of hip swing and stride she normally reserved for high heels and business meetings. It was a walk and posture that presented professionalism and confidence and left her alert, far different from the unguarded, carefree stroll she normally assumed. She thought her subconscious must have picked up on a desperate need to present authority and control.

She came to the door. The window was lit. Windows in the adjacent rooms were dark.

Unoccupied.

Kathy reached for the knob and paused. She was right-handed. Her purse was on her right shoulder. Suddenly the logistics of reaching for the gun quickly obsessed her. She brought the purse to her other shoulder and unzipped it. *I'll pretend to be left-handed. That way he'll be surprised.* She reached for the knob with her left hand. She stopped, frozen by the sight of her fingertips on the brass.

Swallowing, she turned the knob.

It'll all be a joke, she told herself. There's a family in there. Some thirteen-year-old boy snuck onto his father's laptop and played this joke on all of them while no one was watching. Wasn't there a sound now on the other side, just audible, a parental snore?

The door swung inward, but Kathy went no further. The room seemed normal—even clean. She'd so expected a reproduction of Erin's crime scene that she had to blink when it did not appear. She stood there peaking in. The room had two beds covered in floral spreads. Pale blue wallpaper was peeling in places and the ceiling had a dark yellow water stain in the center of the room. The light itself was maddeningly hushed, as if the overhead light fixture had a missing bulb.

She saw no one. She considered calling out but kept her mouth shut. After taking one step forward, she froze, suspicious of the door. She pushed it all the way to the wall until she knew no one could be hiding behind it. Then she scanned the room again. Her right hand strayed across her chest so that her fingertips were closer to the purse.

She stepped in.

The carpet had a pretentious red wine color that contrasted badly with the walls. Kathy now detected an underlying musty odor, the scent of things hidden, things waiting. Steeling herself, she penetrated deeper into the room, stopping once to look back and make sure the door was wide-open. She reached the edge of the first bed and dipped at the knees as she pulled up on the dangling spread. She did not drop far enough to see under the whole of the bed. Both had box frames very low to the floor. Only a child could successfully hide in such narrow confines.

Or perhaps the monster from a child's dream.

Gaining confidence, Kathy passed the second bed. There was a closet to the left. Kathy made another glance at the open front door. She saw the parked cars. *You're surrounded by people. You're safe.*

She opened the closet, running away from the knob even as she pulled it. The sudden rush of air made metal coat hangers jostle and tinkle like country wind chimes. It sounded like a light chuckle. Kathy sighed and closed the door.

Only the bathroom remained.

She eased toward it. The room veered right into an alcove with a small mirror and vanity with a sink. The toilet and shower were behind a door. The door was closed.

He's waiting for me in there.

Almost gasping in her certainty, Kathy now reached for the gun and drew it. The 9mm had felt comfortable but also huge in her hand when Betty had given it to her. Now it seemed small and inadequate. Her finger felt enormous against the trigger. She doubted she could properly squeeze it. How many bullets were there? She knew it was loaded. Betty had loaded it for her and handed it to her as if Kathy could figure out the rest by osmosis. *There are six bullets. All guns have six bullets. It's the rule.*

She held the gun out. For a second, she considered just firing into the door.

Kathy reached out her left hand, turned the knob, and gave a small push. The bathroom was dark but the light behind her penetrated into it. Nothing—no one—there. She tapped the door open wider with her foot, until it struck the back wall. The shower curtain was not drawn. She leaned forward just enough to see no one was hiding in the tub.

She laughed a little, turning to catch sight of her red, sweating face in the mirror. She stepped toward the vanity and leaned over it, drooping her head, trying to catch her breath.

The door to the main room banged shut.

60

KATHY TURNED BACK AND STEPPED INTO THE LITTLE bathroom, gun clutched to her chest.

She found it impossible to control her breathing and cupped her left hand over her nose and mouth to stifle a wheezing sound. She couldn't hear anything else over it. She looked at the gun for calm. *Just run out with the gun aimed. You'll have the advantage. You can force him to the ground.*

In her imagination, she saw the killer reacting to this bold play with a smirk as he crossed his arms and just dared her to shoot. When she didn't, he started toward her, knowing she was too scared. His intuition was as powerful as hers. He intended to just reach out and take the weapon right out of her hand, snatching it as easily as a parent strips a toddler of his toy. She imagined the gun trembling, her grip weakening. In the next instant, both of their hands were on the gun. Then—

Erin. Sharon. Did he think he could take the gun as easily as he took their lives? Kathy closed her eyes and sought her familiar friend. There it was, the cold weight returning to her chest. Hate. She shivered to think of it in such cordial terms. But she did hate, and she needed hate now. Hate was her gun's true trigger finger. Her breathing slowed.

The mattress squeaked. Kathy opened her eyes and stared at the showerhead. The tension concentrated her gaze. There were twenty-five water holes on the head, each traced with hints of lime. Each hole looked dry as bone, as if water hadn't been run in months. Parched as her throat felt. In the bedroom, the noise of springs increased, the sound of the killer's lazy confidence. *He's testing the mattress, imagining how it will sound when I'm beneath him.* She heard his belt unbuckle and slide from around his waist, a lisp of friction on each loop. Kathy shivered. This was too much goading, too much smirking. Did he already consider her his? She looked at the gun. Six bullets. She'd never fired it. Who did she think she was? Sharon. Erin. Could she? She heard Betty telling her, *Aim and let the gun do the rest. Trust your hands.*

She always had.

Kathy gripped the knob and pulled the bathroom door toward her a few agonizing centimeters. She stared at the hinges as if daring them to squeak. They bore the weight fluidly. She stepped forward into the alcove with its mirror and sink.

Hearing him still on the bed, Kathy's hate went even colder. She reached out and turned on the tap. Time to let him hear she was not quivering.

The reaction was immediate. The bed springs stopped squeaking, and she heard two feet landing on the floor.

A man's voice said, "I'm glad you came. I watched you come in from a distance. I had to be careful."

Kathy stared at the gun.

"I loved your picture."

That voice. Even in her fear, so familiar.

"I'm ready for my massage."

She'd still not spoken or made a sound.

"Are you getting yourself pretty for me? I don't think you need to do much work. I'm going to lie on the bed now. I've got an ache that needs to be rubbed out. I think you'll see where it's at."

The bedsprings sounded out his returning weight.

Raise the gun and step forward as calm as you can. He's on the bed. It'll be hard for him to get to his feet.

She turned off the faucet. Half a minute of silence followed, ended by his sudden chuckle. Somehow, beyond all his crass words, this little noise triggered her final outrage. Kathy squeezed on the handle, extended her arm, and stepped out ready to put a bullet through the killer's head.

"Jesus Christ, don't shoot me!"

The man lay pale and sweating on the bed. His shirt was rolled up almost to his nipples. His legs were splayed; his pants and underwear bunched around his ankles. Kathy saw things she had no interest in seeing but at least his right hand concealed most of the horror. The gun wavered before her out of recognition and surprise rather than fear.

"Kathy? Kathy Barrister?"

She was aiming at Bernard Morrison's head.

61

For the next minute, they faced each other, speechless. The only thing going through Kathy's mind was: Morrison's the killer. It made sense. The mob scenes, the strange religious mania that now seemed to consume him. She imagined how he'd killed Sharon. He'd knocked on the spa door, probably pretending to apologize. Of course she let him in. The lambs always seem too eager to welcome in the wolves.

Morrison tried to talk. "Don't—don't—" he stuttered. His hair was slicked back, soaked with the same sweat that popped up like blisters across his face. His feet made little spasms like the legs of a dog twitching as it dreamed. His black dress socks seemed radiant and darker with sweat.

The door opened.

"Drop the gun," an authoritative voice said. Kathy blinked. An officer stood there, his own gun out. He stood in an approximation of Kathy's pose. But unlike her amateur-hour act, she saw right away he knew how to use his weapon.

She cast the gun aside like it had slime on it. She even scraped her palms against her pants in disgust.

"That's a smart decision," the policeman said. "Let's hope it's the first among many."

Morrison was now getting up, his confidence visibly returning. "Thank you, Officer. You have no idea—"

"Did I ask you to say anything, or tell you to move?"

"You do know I'm Bernard Morrison, right? I've been on a crusade against this type of trash. Tonight I decided the best way I could help was to get in the muck myself."

Kathy noticed the cop's doubtful expression. She prayed it grew.

"My car's outside. You'll find bibles and—"

"The Bureau will be impounding that car right now," a new voice said. Kathy gasped as Greg came through the door with two other men. She didn't dare run to him, though she sure as hell wanted to. As for surprise, he showed none at all. "Tomorrow we'll be searching both your home and government office computers, Mr. Morrison."

Greg's companions seized Morrison off the bed. The politician began to hyperventilate. He looked wildly at her. "Kathy, tell them! We've known each other a long time. She knows I'm only interested in the good of the people. I'm a public servant."

"Now you're getting served," one of the Bureau men said, and even Greg smirked. Morrison was escorted out ranting and ducking his head like there would be hundreds of journalists outside. Kathy saw only the night.

"What about her?"

Greg looked at the first officer. "She's been helping us with the case from the very beginning. I need to speak with Ms. Barrister alone. It's Bureau stuff."

The officer never lost his doubtful expression but he retreated and shut the door behind him.

"Greg—"

He walked past her, shaking his head.

"Kathy, what the hell are you doing? Do you have any idea how stupid your plan was?"

"How do you know what my plans are?"

Greg picked up the 9 mm. After a quick, appreciative look at it, he smiled. "Did you get this from my favorite arm's dealer?"

"Yes."

He nodded, putting it in the pocket of his sports coat. "That's mine."

"You'll get your toy back when the adults are done with it."

Kathy frowned. "Don't treat me like I'm a child, Greg!"

"Then don't act like one." He sat down on the bed and motioned for her to join him. She did.

"I sent you a text of where I was."

"Which wasn't entirely a relief, believe me. When I found out you were offering yourself up as bait—"

"How did you know that?"

"Kathy, the Bureau is monitoring the Internet traffic as best we can, posting fake ads so we can track IP addresses and e-mails. I was helping with that when your post came up. We all did a double take when we saw Erin Haley's picture. We thought the son of a bitch had changed his style. Like maybe he was starting to impersonate massage therapists in order to kill his victims. Your text message a little later helped me put two and two together. But it took a little intuition."

She smiled, then nodded, grateful to him. Her own intuition had been so strong. She was certain the killer had written to her. Being wrong when her intuition seemed so sure shook her deeply.

"Do you think Morrison might be the killer?"

"At this point, anything is possible," Greg said. "It fits key aspects of the profile. Of course by now there's a small village worth of people who do as well."

She looked away, embarrassed.

"You scared the hell out of me, Kathy. I felt sick the entire drive up here, worried I wouldn't reach you in time."

She reached out for his hand and squeezed it. "Now I know I was never alone."

Greg cocked his head. "What?"

"The entire time, I felt so lonely and overwhelmed. I felt like I was tackling something so immense it would crush me and that I had to do it alone. I did it because I hated him—the killer. Hated. It's been growing. Maybe that's an easier thing for you to handle, I don't know. Maybe you get exposed to hate every day. But my job is to create peace. Hate—it feels like a cancer inside me."

She ended with a sob that felt ready to tap into a much deeper well of tears.

"All I felt was the hate and that I was alone with it, but in a way you were watching over me the entire time."

He put his right arm over her. She leaned into him right away.

"Don't ever do anything like that again, Kathy. You have to promise me."

She nodded. His embrace tightened.

"Because I don't think I can stomach the idea of you meeting up with the real killer in a room like this."

"Or Bernard Morrison naked," she said, and was surprised to discover she still had the ability to laugh.

62

THANK GOD FOR MY CLASSROOM. SHE HAD A BROAD, ALMOST goofy grin as she welcomed her students into the Friday-morning Anatomy class. The students, if anything, looked cheerier than her. They had all received a bright bit of news in the morning paper pronouncing the fall of Bernard Morrison. The only thing missing was a photo of the man literally being hoisted by his own petard.

The media gleefully spread the word of Morrison's arrest and news of it electrified the whole school. Kathy felt waves of relief coming off her pupils, as if both their major problems were solved. She did not squelch their optimism. The media was talking up Morrison's potential as the killer, treating it almost as a foregone conclusion. She did not have the heart to tell them the darkness was still out there. But today was a day of sunshine, even for her. She thought of Sharon and promised to make every day left to her count. Right now nothing counted to her more than her students.

So she basked in their joy and began to feel pride in their happiness. She wanted to tell them all of her inadvertent involvement in Morrison's humiliation. For now she was anonymous in the press, part of an undercover sting. No matter. Morrison's threat to the Academy and the profession had been eliminated, and now Kathy had another happy task this morning: welcoming Jim back to school.

She straightened her posture as soon as he came in. He appeared shyer and more tentative than usual. He had always seemed liked by his peers, but the attention he received now, pats on the back and careful hugs and high fives, approached hero worship. Kathy could tell it was too much. Jim looked dazed and a little vacant, despite his smile. He was probably on some kind of pain medication. His face had a big purple bruise that looked like it should be covered in gauze. As the classroom gathered around him now, Kathy winced, fearing they'd hurt him.

Jim walked toward his seat, slowly and deliberately. Amanda was in her usual spot, and as he approached she stood up with a big smile on her face. Kathy thought the smile genuine, but she knew this moment held a lot of uncertainty and discomfort for Amanda. Soon Jim was beside her and she leaned over and hugged him. This was more than Kathy expected and she wondered if Amanda was overplaying her affection. Jim stood motionless with her arms around him. He looked like he would have preferred to stand still for a hundred years if she just kept hugging him. When she released him and everyone started to sit, an awkward moment passed where he and Kathy were the only people standing in the room. He looked at her and gave his shy smile. She nodded back at him and moved to the front of her classroom as he slowly realized he needed to sit too.

"Welcome back, Jim," Kathy said. "Everyone here appreciates the way you defended this school and your classmate."

A round of applause came. Jim smiled at Amanda, who reached over and gave his shoulder a small squeeze. *Bad move.*

She quickly drew the class's attention to the anatomy posters. She took up a dry-erase marker and made a circle on the diagram's face, approximating the location of Jim's injury.

"Now, I talked a little bit to Jim beforehand, to make sure he was okay with what we're going to do today. If you'll look at Herbert here, you'll get a better idea of Jim's own injury. Besides lacerations, he's received deep bruising to the muscle tissue here, as well as a minor fracture to his cheekbone."

Paul, the class's oldest student, whistled with good-natured appreciation and said, "That dude belted the hell out of you, Jim! Wish I'd been there for the tag team."

Jim's face blushed around his big bruise as the class shared a good-natured laugh.

"As massage therapists," Kathy said, steering the conversation, "what sort of modality would we use to help heal this sort of damage?"

The class stared at her as if they'd been told they wouldn't have to think today. Kathy smiled a little, looking at all of them. She noticed Jim's attention was fixed on Herbert.

The silence became embarrassing. She tried another tack.

"Would we necessarily use massage?"

Amanda raised her hand. "His fracture would be a contraindication. Massage should not be used."

"My fracture," Jim muttered, so slow that Kathy barely heard it.

Kathy nodded. "What healing strategies could we use in place of touch therapy?"

Other hands went up. Kathy listened to their ideas, keeping a discreet but careful watch on Jim as they were given. *Come on. Someone besides me say it.*

Then: "Reiki would work too, Kathy."

She smiled. "That's right. Many of you are probably

unfamiliar with Reiki. The Academy has never taught it, though I intend to have a course on it by this time next year."

She looked at Jim. Moment of truth. "Jim, would it be okay if I demonstrated it on you for the class?"

He looked very nervous. The first thing he did was turn to Amanda, as if only she could give permission. Amanda's own tension showed itself for the first time, but she nodded her encouragement at him. Then Jim looked at Kathy. It was not unusual for students to participate in class demonstrations, though nothing about this particular one was usual. He stood and took two steps toward her. Kathy got a chair and placed it toward the front center of the room.

"Have a seat."

Jim looked at the chair, then back at Amanda. Kathy saw many in the class noticing his glances. Their reactions suggested Jim's obsession with Amanda was not as well-known as Kathy supposed.

Kathy patted the chair and he sat down.

"Do you know anything about Reiki, Jim?"

"No."

"That's good. For the purposes of this demonstration, I'm not going to explain anything at all. There are many who argue that it works purely as a placebo—which is ridiculous. Since Jim here doesn't know what Reiki will do, his experience won't be prejudiced by his expectations. We'll just say that Reiki can speed up the healing process and help fractures knit themselves back together where traditional methods fail. And the best part? Your hand never even has to touch your client's body. I don't think Jim would appreciate any of us laying our hands on that bruise!"

The class laughed. Jim looked down at the floor, and Kathy realized right away that she had miscalculated. Situating Jim here made any class reaction seem like a reaction to him. But it was too late now.

"I'm going to stand right behind Jim and raise my hand above the injured area of his face."

As she raised her hand, Jim snagged it by the wrist. His grip bordered on the aggressive, but Kathy managed not to react. She kept her voice pleasant. "What is it, Jim?"

"I want…Amanda…to do it."

"Amanda doesn't know what Reiki is, Jim. She can't do it."

He looked at Amanda. "I want Amanda to do it."

Amanda tried to smile, but when she spoke her voice betrayed the wellspring of tension inside her. "Jim, Kathy's right. I wouldn't be any good."

"Why?"

"Why?" Her tone edged into exasperation. "Because, Jim, I don't know how to do it. You're in the hands of an expert with Kathy."

"But you did it before. In the ambulance."

Kathy felt the class's confusion building and stepped in front of Jim. "You know, what am I thinking? Reiki doesn't have much to do with an Anatomy class anyway. Jim's totally right. Let's break into our study groups. We have a lot to catch up on."

The students reacted quicker than usual, obviously as eager to dispel the awkwardness as she was. Jim got up and went toward Amanda.

"Jim," Kathy said, "we're going to mix it up a little this time."

"What?"

"I'd like you to study with Trish and Lee. Amanda, you're with Paul and Lisa."

"Sure," Amanda said, hurrying past.

Jim stared at Kathy.

"Why?"

"Having different study partners helps keeps us sharp. We get used to the same people."

Jim looked around. "You didn't ask anyone else to switch."

Kathy held her breath. "I know. Everyone's going to starting next session. But I need to get the ball rolling."

"Oh."

He stood there. Kathy saw his eyes weren't focusing. He seemed to be looking at something far away, beyond the surrounding walls.

"Jim, are you okay? Are you on medication?"

"I'm okay," he said. His voice was as distant as his gaze. Then he took his backpack and just walked out of class in a stupor. The class watched him. When the door shut, all stares turned on Kathy.

"Go over the Wednesday lecture," she said, starting to move.

She followed after him and looked up and down the empty hallway. Jim was already gone.

63

Three hours later, when Amanda had just left her office after a thirty-minute talk, Kathy sat stunned behind her desk and considered calling Greg.

What would she tell him? That one of her students had an unhealthy romantic obsession? Greg was a detective, not a relationship counselor.

He would tell her what she'd just told Amanda. Caution and court orders were the traditional solution to overly obsessive people. The way Amanda nodded, Kathy could tell she'd already considered such options. A restraining order was not appealing. Kathy was not even sure how it could work in a classroom environment. Short of Kathy intervening in a direct and unpleasant way, there seemed to be one solution and Amanda had walked into Kathy's office to reveal it.

She was going to transfer to a different massage school.

Kathy thought she'd talked Amanda out of her decision for the moment. She did not want to lose one of her best students because of a situation that challenged her as an administrator. Worse, her intuition was nagging her about Jim. She held back on exploring the feeling all the way. Wednesday night's spectacular failure was still on her mind. That something good happened as a result anyway was pure luck.

Was Jim dangerous? Kathy just couldn't see it. Maybe personal bias was getting in the way—it always seemed to when it came to her students, even ones like Judd Garvis. But she liked Jim. Part of her liked him even more for his unfocused, lazy pursuit of studies. It was not at all characteristic of what she valued in a person, but as Kathy thought about it some more she realized that, in certain ways, Jim reminded her of how Greg had been in high school. Of course, Greg always had some underlying need for order. Did Jim? Kathy supposed he must. Everyone organizes and centers their life around something.

Jim had decided to center his on Amanda.

Kathy glanced at her wall clock. Just then, her cell phone chimed once to indicate a text message. She reached for it expecting a note from Greg. She stared at the unexpected words.

"What is this?"

The unopened message said it was from Erin Haley.

Kathy blinked, shaking her head. Confusion roared through her mind so that she could barely concentrate. How could there be a message from Erin? Who would do something so sick?

The subject line read only: What I Want for Christmas.

Sniffling, lips pressed so tight her face only hinted at a mouth, she opened the message. There was no other text, just a picture.

The image loaded right away, and Kathy jerked back in her chair, dropping the phone onto her desk. She clamped both hands over her mouth, but she puked through her fingers. She raced to bend over her trashcan, sobbing and vomiting.

Brenda heard the noise and came running from her side office. "Kathy? Oh my God, are you okay?"

Kathy dropped to one knee, about to faint. She shook her head and looked up at Brenda in tears. "C-call the state Bureau. Of Investigation. Ask For Greg. Now."

Brenda blinked a moment, looking dumbfounded. Then she nodded and sprinted back into her office.

What I want for Christmas.

The photo showed two bloody front teeth.

64

Kathy sat at her desk staring stonily ahead at the closed blinds while Greg and a technician from the Bureau looked at the message.

"Christ," the tech said.

"I think it's the real thing this time. Here."

Kathy watched Greg slip her phone into the tech's collection bag. "You're taking it?"

"We need to transfer the image and work on figuring out where the message originated from."

"So he has Erin's phone?"

"It appears so."

She and Greg stared at each other as the tech left. Kathy caught a glimpse of students loitering in the hallway trying to look in when the door open and closed again.

"This time it wasn't Carson," she said to herself.

Greg's eyebrows lifted. "Who?"

"That damn blogger—remember?"

"Why would you think he'd have Erin's cell phone? And why would you think he'd send a photo like this?"

Realizing she was stuck, Kathy gave him the short version.

"I will kill that little bastard," Greg said in astonishment. "What he did is terroristic threatening, Kathy. We can put him away!"

"No need. I settled it."

"Like hell!"

"He's a pipsqueak just out for himself. I got my revenge. This time is different. That picture didn't show fake teeth, Greg."

"I still want to have a talk with him."

"You can't! I gave him my word I wouldn't tell you. It just slipped out. I mean it, Greg."

He frowned and said, "Depending on where the evidence leads—no promises."

Kathy nodded, knowing it was the best deal she'd get from him. "What next?"

"We'll see what the techs find."

Someone knocked on the door. Greg opened it. Amanda and Jim were standing there. Kathy tensed.

"Hi, you two."

"Kathy, is this a bad time?"

"Yes, Amanda, I'm afraid it is," she said. She looked at the top of her desk as she listened to herself speak. *Never thought I'd say that to a student.*

"I just wanted you to know…what we were talking about earlier…it's okay."

What's this about? Kathy looked at Jim and smiled. Jim returned it after a moment, like the image in a slow mirror.

"Are you feeling any better, Jim?"

"Yeah," he said. "I feel okay."

She looked at Amanda. The tension was definitely there but she did an amazing job of keeping her expression neutral.

"Jim and I have been talking," Amanda said. Kathy noticed her give Greg a glancing, evaluative look.

"I'm glad."

"About being partners," she said. "We're going to continue to work together. Aren't we, Jim?"

She gave him a playful pat. Kathy's eyes narrowed. It was impossible to tell she had ever shown any trepidation about Jim. That made her nervous. Why the change? Had they really talked and come to some sort of understanding? She imagined how guilty Amanda must have felt after their early discussion. Kathy thought Amanda probably left her office determined to redouble her efforts to clarify her feelings to Jim. Maybe she succeeded.

Greg was starting look impatient with their interruption. Just as he seemed ready to shoo them out, however, Amanda's cell phone rang. She got it right then and there. The call lasted only seconds.

"It's Brad," she said. "I've got to go. We're going out to an early dinner and then a movie."

"Brad Haley?" Greg said. He was finally interested.

"Yes. Do you know him?"

"Detective Beacon is investigating his sister's death," Kathy said. She spoke as bluntly as possible, feeling angry. Amanda in her excitement hadn't seen Jim's reaction when she announced her evening plans. She knew then and there that whatever talk she'd given Jim fell on confused, perhaps deaf ears.

Her expression regained its usual decorum. "I'm sorry. I guess I better go. Will you walk out with me, Jim?"

Jim nodded.

"Sad kid," Greg said when they were gone. Kathy rubbed her forehead.

"I think he'll get a lot sadder before it's over."

"Intuition?"

She shook her head. "Experience."

6 5

ERIN HAD ALWAYS CALLED HIM A CUTE BOY, AND PERHAPS that was why Brad never believed anyone who said the same. He only heard it in his sister's voice, biased and teasing.

"You are such a cute boy," Amanda said when they got home on Friday night.

Brad hadn't seen any similarities between Amanda and Erin at first. He did not think they looked too much alike, but their attitudes toward life were identical. So happy, so positive, so opposite of his own outlook. Sometimes he thought he and Erin were one creature split in half with him receiving its darker disposition. Erin had saved him from complete despair. He realized he might have killed himself without her. The night after he learned of her death, he swallowed pills in an attempt at suicide. It should have worked, but his body forced him to puke them up before any damage was done. He decided then that he would work to avenge her. But vengeance wasn't as easy in real life as in movies. He had no way to get information from the police. All he could do was sit around and stew in his rage and go through some of Erin's old things, hoping to find some lead.

All he remembered about coming to Erin's old massage school was losing control in a classroom full of people. It still humiliated him to think of it. There'd been so many swirling faces staring at him in shock as he cried. The one he remembered most, though, was Amanda's. A face like hers, glimpsed through a window of tears, was not soon forgotten.

He'd been trying to tell himself that she wasn't an emotional substitute for his sister. Amanda had so quickly redirected his energies away from thoughts of revenge that he felt guilty, as if he had abandoned Erin's memory. He could not tell Amanda this, but somehow she seemed to sense it and bring it up. He felt adult when they lay next to each other and talked. He felt like he'd crossed into an age of maturity and manhood, though he'd already gone through more trauma than many people face in a lifetime.

They lay beside each other in Amanda's apartment and stroked each other's bodies. His was still tingling from sex. He'd been with only two other girls in his life and neither of them excited him like Amanda. It was only the second time they had made love, and she smiled and told him to roll into his stomach. He did, nervous. Then she straddled and began to knead his back. It should have been an amazing experience, but it only made him tenser.

"What's wrong, Brad?"

"It's just—my sister. When she first started learning massage, I lived close enough to where I could be her guinea pig. She'd work out new stroke techniques on me. I moved away after a month. Ran away is closer to the truth."

"This reminds you of her, doesn't it?"

He nodded, expecting her to be offended and hit him.

Amanda made a small noise in her throat, and Brad

thought she must be majorly pissed off. Instead she pulled back and moved to lie down beside him, wrapping both arms around his torso.

"I'm so sorry," she said. "I feel like I'm doing everything wrong these days."

"You didn't do anything wrong. The problem is with me."

"Isn't that what a person says when they want to break up?"

He laughed and brought her closer to him, rolling to bring her on top of him, straddling his stomach. Her hands lay flat on his chest, exploring. "I don't want to break up with you. Not ever. It's just that there are things I didn't think about. Erin's still too—"

"Don't apologize for whatever you're feeling," she said. "Not now—not ever. I think I understand. Kathy was even trying to tell me—"

"What? Not to date me?"

"Just about your pain."

"She knows some things about me," Brad said.

"Probably more than you think. She's the most empathic person I've ever met. I wish I had her gift for sensing when someone's hurting. It makes her a brilliant massage therapist. She says I'll be as good too, some day. I can only hope."

Brad looked at the ceiling, thinking. Amanda had talked him into applying to the Academy. He was not sure if he regretted it or not. His experiences with Kathy in Erin's motel room still felt almost mystical to him, the way the pain had simply vanished. And he knew how exuberant Erin had been about her career. But was he just attempting to follow in her footsteps as another way of bringing her back? Often he felt so alienated from people that he doubted he had the ability to sense anything at all from either strangers or friends.

"I hope my application gets accepted."

"Me too." She snuggled up closer to him. "Right now, you give one crummy massage."

The doorbell rang.

"Let it," he said.

They kissed.

The doorbell rang again. They kissed each other with a fiercer passion, as if to force the intruder from their minds.

It rang one more time. They both lay on their backs and scowled at the ceiling. Then there was a long silence—almost. Amanda's apartment had thick walls and floors but that didn't keep out all noise. The couple living to her right were constantly fighting, and the family living below her seemed to be imploding—arguments over money, over children. Their noises were not as intrusive as they were ominous, a constant, droning depression.

They made love again, alternately slow and fast with unflagging intensity. Amanda thought it almost perverse to experience such joy while others fought bitterly around her. She gave herself to Brad, and the orgasm she experienced seemed to have almost visionary qualities to it. She saw them living in their own house, as partners in love and business. It was a brief glimpse of their certain future. As they separated, their right and left hands joined. He raised and brought hers to his mouth, kissing her above the wrist.

The doorbell rang again.

"Goddamn it," Brad said. "Someone just can't take a hint."

"Here," she said, starting to rise.

He shot her an incredulous look.

"What?"

"You're not seriously going to answer the door, are you?"

Amanda slipped on a pale blue sweatshirt. "Maybe it's important."

"It isn't."

"The apartment has a No Soliciting sign on the front doors."

"Like that's ever stopped someone."

She smiled and slipped into the matching sweatpants. She turned, modeling the ensemble.

"You look like the hottest Walmart shopper I've ever seen."

The doorbell rang again.

Amanda rolled her eyes, reached for a pillow, and hit him with it. She went for the door.

"If it's a kid selling chocolate, buy me a bar. I'm starving."

She entered into the living room. Now someone was banging on the door. Amanda frowned, sensing the urgency. Her door had no peephole. She undid the locks, looking back once at the bedroom, thankful for Brad.

She intended to crack the door only. The moment it showed signs of opening, however, an immediate force pushed against her. The door went flying forward, knocking Amanda down with a cry. She struck her head and went bleary-eyed and senseless. She heard the door shut again. What? Who? She didn't know if she spoke the words or not. Her mouth opened and closed. Her legs seemed to be lifting—someone had them. Dragging her. Then they dropped. There were other sounds. A fight? Yelling? The damned neighbors again. But so close this time.

Right over her.

When her eyes finally worked again, she found herself still sprawled on the floor. How long had it been? Her sweat pants had been pulled down to her knees, and she reached for the waistband by instinct. She heard another odd hissing sound and struggled to look. A few feet away, Brad lay naked and writhing with his arms pinned under the knees of a man who was straddling his chest. The man sprayed an uninterrupted jet of *something* from a small canister into Brad's face with the calm certainty of a graffiti artist who knows he can't get caught.

66

KATHY MET GREG AT HER FRONT DOOR ON FRIDAY EVENING. He had company with him—Rierdon and another man Greg introduced as Mark Munson. "Agent Munson is a specialist in cybercrime," he said.

Munson held out his hand and offered Kathy her cell phone. Munson was at least twenty years older than Greg but there were striking similarities between them. Someone might have mistaken them for a father-son pair. Kathy thought it odd that the older man should be the tech specialist. It seemed wrong to her. Munson had the look of an old-time detective, his lean face worn from stress and care, and his lips turned down at the corners in a way that turned his neutral expression into a frown. Kathy made a vow to do everything she could to keep that from happening to Greg.

She took her phone with some hesitation, as if it had been rigged to explode. Then they went inside.

"Were you able to find out where Erin's cell phone was when the message was sent?"

"It wasn't sent from Erin's cell phone," Munson said.

Kathy was startled. "But the subject line said her name."

"A subject line on a text message isn't the same as caller ID, of course. The message you received and the attachment with it were actually sent from a computer."

Kathy looked at them. "You can use a computer to contact a cell phone?"

"Yes. There are actually a number of services that allow you to do this. Whoever sent this knew your cell phone number—no more."

"No more?" Kathy said, eyes widening in disbelief. "You call a picture of bloody front teeth 'no more'?"

"That's not what we mean," Rierdon said. She found even Greg was nodding, and she calmed down.

"Fine," she said. "So do you know what computer the e-mail came from?"

The detectives looked at each other. *They know.*

Greg said, "Kathy, we're going to have to look at the computers in your school."

"What? Which ones?"

"All of them," Munson said.

Kathy drew back. "I was only logged into my office computer at the time. It's all I've got."

Munson glanced at Greg and Kathy saw a subtle nod. Greg said, "How many computers does the school have?"

"I don't know. Mine and Brenda's make two. There must be four more for the teachers. So six."

"There are no computers for student use?"

She thought a moment. "The library, of course. There are six more computers in there. Most of the students bring in laptops."

"So the school offers wireless access as well?"

Kathy nodded.

The detectives seemed to mull this. Greg said, "It won't be easy, but let's at least rule out all the desktops."

Rierdon nodded, then turned and gave a small smile to Kathy. "I take it the school is not open at the moment?"

"No," she said.

"We should move now when it will be the least disruptive," Munson said. "Gather a team. Ms. Barrister, we'll need someone to open the doors for us."

Kathy just stared at them. "If you're implying one of my students pulled a stunt like this, I just can't believe it. This killer has affected us all. He's attacking our very profession—"

Munson said, "What if the killer is in your profession, Ms Barrister. Or learning it?"

She saw they were serious. The idea had never occurred to her. One of the students? The possibility seemed so alien that suggesting the culprit was a real alien in a UFO made more sense. Finally she said, "Let's just check them quickly."

A moment later, she was in the passenger seat of Greg's car. It was the first time she ever wished she didn't have to go to the Academy.

67

KATHY FOUND GREG AND MUNSON AND THREE TECHS were in the school library when she arrived Saturday morning. Their expressions were not kind and both wore the same clothes from last night. She paused, considering. Had they all spent the night here? Greg drove Kathy home after she realized the computers could not be scanned in just a few hours. To her disappointment, he did not stay with her. Imagining them working through the night made her grateful for their dedication. She just hoped dedication was enough against the evil they faced.

"Find anything yet?"

"Your staff lead comfortably boring lives, it seems," Munson said. "We are just in the middle of checking the student computers."

"Is it possible to be done by nine, when the library opens? Our nontraditional students who can only take weekend classes really need the resources."

Greg and Munson both gave weary smiles. "We'll do our best," Greg said.

Munson looked at the ceiling and the corners. "We'll also need access to your security footage during the time the message was sent."

"We don't have any security cameras."

Munson looked appalled. "What is it about massage therapists and their complete lack of concern about security? Is it a privacy fetish? Between this school and the victim at that damn spa—"

Kathy's blood pressure shot up in a flash. "I was real close with the victim 'at that damn spa.' So watch it."

Munson drew back, obviously surprised by her sudden fire. Greg moved to intercede but Munson offered his own apology. "It just makes the job a lot harder. Are there staff assigned to this room? Someone who would remember what students were on the computers yesterday?"

"We have a part-time librarian. She wasn't in yesterday."

Munson nodded. Kathy knew he just cursed to himself.

She watched them work. The Bureau techs had three of the library computers wired into their own laptops, which seemed to be conducting a scan. Telemetry she did not understand scrolled up the screens. If this data was important, nobody's reactions suggested it. They all looked dead on their feet.

Kathy excused herself and went to her office. Her computer was already on, which made her suspicious. Obviously the message hadn't been sent from her own station. Did they suspect she'd sent the photo to herself? Or was Greg looking for something else? She shook her head at the paranoia. She was going to have to learn to trust him in order for their relationship to succeed. Right now she was wondering if she truly could ever trust anything—or anyone—ever again.

She heard a noise and looked up to see Jim standing in the

doorway. His bruise looked a little less purple than yesterday. She sat back in surprise, and then gave a welcoming smile.

"Hello, Jim."

"Hi, Kathy," he said. He sounded tired.

"What brings you in? I didn't know you had a weekend class." *Amanda sure doesn't.*

"I came to use the library computer. They said I shouldn't."

"Oh, them. Hopefully they'll be done very soon. I apologize for the inconvenience."

"What is happening in there?"

Kathy smiled. "Scanning the computers for viruses."

"Oh," he said. He looked ready to leave. Kathy found herself reaching out a hand.

"Jim—don't go. Sit down, will you?"

He sat.

"I was thinking about our conversation at the memorial service for Erin. When we talked about love and…Amanda."

He looked uncomfortable, as if debating in his head whether to run away. He fidgeted so much Kathy found it hard to watch him.

"It seems like the two of you talked yesterday afternoon."

"She told me she was in love."

Kathy became suspicious of his tone. It sounded like Jim thought Amanda had confessed her love for him. "With someone else," she said.

Jim looked at the floor.

"I just don't want you to get hurt. You're too nice a guy, and you have far too much to offer. Is Amanda the first person you've been in love with?"

"The first I ever needed," he said.

That word again. Her intuition sparked. She had to ask him.

"Jim, what does need mean to you? Why do you need her? Would you tell me that?"

He was deliberating faster. Kathy thought she could almost

see the confusion, the war raging behind his eyes. He looked up at her.

"Kathy," Greg said, sounding like he'd run a mile instead of the one hundred feet between her office and the library. "You've got to come see this right away."

She looked between them, flustered. "Greg, can't it—"

"Right now. Please."

"Jim, would you wait here for me? I'd like to continue our talk."

Jim nodded.

Kathy smiled and got up. Greg practically dragged her to the library. He shut the door right away.

"What is it? What have you found?"

Munson and the techs were standing over the far left library computer, pointing excitedly. Greg took her over to them.

"This is it," he said. He sounded like he never believed the investigation would turn up anything.

Kathy looked at the computer, somehow expecting it to be different from the rest. The implications of what she was hearing did not fully register no matter how hard she tried.

"Ms. Barrister, do these computers normally require any type of log-in? A student ID, a password, something like that?"

"We're not that formal," she said.

Munson nodded. "At approximately one fifteen yesterday, someone went to pixdrop.com. It was one of the first services to let people send picture messages from a computer to a cell phone."

Kathy thought of the time frame. "There would have been at least ten students in here at that time on most Fridays."

"We need to round them up."

Greg said, "I want to pursue this, but we should be cautious. It's not impossible a student happened to use the service to send someone else a photo."

"Not impossible, but a damn unlikely coincidence," Munson said.

Kathy found herself in hopeless agreement.

"We're confiscating this computer right now. It's too important."

"I agree," Greg said. He looked at Kathy as if expecting she might object. She just nodded a little and backed away.

"I'm going back to my office," she said. "I need to talk to Jim."

"We're going back to the Bureau." He leaned in and kissed her. Pulling away, he whispered, "I think we're getting closer."

Kathy smiled, though she felt like she had nothing to smile about. The possibility that one of her students might be responsible for all this made the entire Academy feel haunted for her. She hurried down the hall to her office.

"I'm sorry about all that, Jim—"

He was gone.

68

Amanda shrieked into her gag, a stinking rag that was soaked in some awful, bitter fluid and crammed almost into her throat. The fluid that drenched it had an acidic property a little stronger than lemon juice that burned her tongue and lips. She lay on the floor of an abandoned house, bound tight and half-naked.

There was one window without blinds that showed a perversely sunny day. Outside the window she caught a glimpse of tree branches. *I'm on the second story.* She strained against her bindings. The room was stripped bare except for old carpet. The carpet had a disgusting odor that made her whimper whenever her struggles pitched her body face-first into it for a good, nauseating whiff.

Must reach the window. If she could reach it, she could do something. Bang her head against it. Anything to show herself.

She quickly realized she wasn't going anywhere. She'd been tied to a baseboard radiator that gave her just enough room to thrash like a fish trapped on the shoreline. Unrelenting straps pinned her arms together at the elbows, and her wrists were cuffed excruciatingly tight. She could not feel her left hand at all. Her ankles were bullied by shackles with only two chain links between them.

How long had she been here? Hours, at least. Days? *Oh God, not days. Don't let it be days!*

She shrieked and shrieked with only pathetic whines coming from her. At last she tired, raw with thirst and ruined by muscle cramps she could not work out if she tried. She rolled forward—the awful, stinking, scratchy carpet in her nostrils again. She sobbed, head pounding, heart bursting. For a moment her entire body thrashed about, like a dead thing suddenly spasming. Her rage had worked itself out in one last burst, leaving her defeated. She tried counting the seconds, hoping to get a sense of what now constituted a minute or five minutes or a half hour of her fate. She stared at the wall and counted, crying because she could not get past forty-five seconds without losing all focus.

Suddenly there was another whine, similar to hers but masculine and evoking even greater pain. Brad! Amanda raised her head, her senses alert. But she was careless and banged her head with force against the radiator. Wincing at this new stab of agony, she summoned what energy remained to her and worked on calling out to him through the gag, making noises that could roughly approximate his name. She sensed her entire life hung on getting out a single syllable.

He's tied up like me in another room. But where was that other room? She couldn't say how, but she was certain he was close. And if she could somehow get to him, or he to her—

For the first time since she woke, Amanda felt a spark of hope.

69

KATHY HAD A BAD FEELING ALL THROUGH SUNDAY AS SHE waited for Greg to call with an update on the computer. Their telephone calls were short. She could tell how busy he was; busy but not weary. His voice practically rang with energy. When Greg came over that evening, he had nothing else to say about the library computer. But he did outline the Bureau's plan.

She went to the Academy on Monday knowing what to expect and feeling uncertain about her role in it. The Bureau and the local police would be there to interview every single student. They had already received the class schedules of all enrolled students and planned to question the entire student body. She imagined most, perhaps all, would have no problem with it. But the very idea unnerved her, as if she were feeding them all into a bonfire of paranoia.

The police arrived before she did. Greg didn't tell her they'd do that, and she looked at him as they walked through the parking lot. They'd taken separate cars but arrived at the same time.

Her morning Anatomy class was missing half its students, including Amanda. Jim sat alone, sometimes touching his bruise lightly and wincing, as if obsessed with the pain. Then he'd stare at the anatomy posters like they were maps of someplace he didn't want to go. Kathy lectured for the sake of expediency, despite the low attendance. She hoped she didn't sound entirely disheartened and distracted. As she went along, first one and then another student joined the group. By the forty-five-minute mark, the class was missing only one person.

What's taking Amanda so long?

The class ended without Amanda coming in at all. Kathy watched Jim immediately get up and leave. He seemed awkward and jittery. He reminded Kathy of someone addicted to a drug he couldn't find anywhere.

She stepped into the hallway and saw Greg. He had a list in his hand.

"Are one of you interviewing Amanda?"

Greg examined the list. "Amanda Kinsley?"

"Yes."

He shook his head. "We must have missed her."

Her intuition told her to worry. Amanda was a sensible young woman overall and had never missed a class yet. Kathy remembered her expression when she announced she was having dinner and a movie with Brad. Maybe she just hadn't gotten much sleep last night.

Feeling a little guilty for imagining Amanda's sex life, Kathy just nodded and headed toward her office and called up her profile on the computer. She dialed Amanda's cell phone number. Voice mail answered.

Kathy hung up immediately. It wasn't her practice to badger a student for not calling in sick. Her considered her students adults and treated them as such.

She's not sick. She's in trouble.

Her urgency and discomfort rising, Kathy summoned Brenda into her office and expressed her fears.

"She's not obligated to call in," Brenda said.

"No. The point is she would."

Kathy read Amanda's file again. She had three emergency contact names listed—her mother, father, and an uncle.

Brenda looked over her shoulder. "You're not seriously going to call them, are you?"

Kathy swallowed. Brenda's tone of disbelief annoyed her. "Why not?"

"She's probably just gotten food poisoning or something. She said she was going out to eat."

Kathy considered this.

"Last time I had food poisoning, I sure wasn't making any calls," Brenda continued.

Brenda sounded so reasonable. And Kathy knew her intuition wasn't as infallible as she liked to believe. She put the phone down. "I guess that could be."

Brenda laughed. It sounded like a desperate attempt to be lighthearted. "Kathy, people do miss school sometimes and don't think to call. Amanda's still very young. And she's in love. I can tell you I skipped a lot of morning college classes to stay in bed with a guy."

Kathy nodded. "Guess I'm getting spooked. I don't know how I feel about Erin's brother. I can't explain. It's not even intuition, just a sense that something isn't right. Ever since I saw him with Amanda at his sister's memorial, something just doesn't square up."

"Ever considered that you're feeling jealous?"

She gave Brenda a sharp look.

"Kathy, think about it. I didn't work here when Erin was enrolled, but I know how much she meant to you. And I know what Amanda means to you now. You see her as your protégé—just like you saw Erin."

"Yes."

"So the brother of the dead protégé shows up and sweeps your current protégé off her feet. You're worried you're going to lose her, too, one way or the other. You've got competition for her."

Kathy smiled. The explanation had some truth to it. Her intuition was still screaming at her—Amanda's in serious trouble.

"If she's not here tomorrow, I'm calling the police."

"Easy enough to do," Brenda said. "Half the force seems to be hanging out here these days anyway."

70

Tuesday came. Amanda did not.

Kathy pulled back from a small classroom she'd peeked into after looking up Amanda's Tuesday class schedule. Amanda should have been in attendance.

As she walked down the hall, Kathy dialed Amanda's number on her cell phone again. The damn voice mail message answered again.

She was heartsick by the time she reached her office. Greg and his cohorts were in otherwise unoccupied classrooms interviewing students. Kathy fretted about her decision. She started dialing 911 just as Jim entered, swaying on his feet.

"I think Amanda's in trouble, Kathy."

She put the phone down. "I—I think so too, Jim."

"I went there."

"You went where?"

"Amanda's apartment. I knocked on the door."

"And?"

"I heard someone inside."

"Someone? Not Amanda?"

"No," Jim said. "Him."

"You mean Brad—Amanda's boyfriend?"

Jim clearly didn't like that word. "Yeah," he said.

"Then what?"

"They shouted go away, so I went."

"Amanda and Brad shouted at you through the door?"

"They shouted," he said.

He's completely dazed, Kathy thought. He seemed ready to fall but somehow he didn't go down.

"I'm calling the police right now."

"Okay," he said.

She redialed 911 and explained the situation as best she could. She looked at Jim and smiled nervously as she spoke. She finally felt like she was taking baby steps in the right direction. He smiled back.

"I'm going to go now," he said.

"Jim, wait," she began, still hopelessly stuck in the middle of her talk with the police. She couldn't simply hang up.

"Jim—" She tried one more time, but he was gone and the 911 operator was badgering her for more information. She heard a *thud*—it sounded like a body dropping. *Jim*? "Greg!" Kathy yelled by instinct, knowing he couldn't hear her. The operator said, "What are you saying, ma'am?" Too many things happening at once. Kathy found herself stuttering and sweating, thinking about Jim and Greg and Amanda. A few moments later she hung up, practically throwing the receiver onto the cradle and thinking she'd just gotten herself into huge trouble.

Amanda's in bigger trouble.

She pushed herself up from her desk, grabbed her purse, and ran out of the office. A few students in the hallway ducked out of her way and looked bewildered as her pace increased and she called Jim's name.

She got to the parking lot.

"Jim?"

Kathy scanned the lot. Then she saw him at his car and grew alarmed. Jim was leaning up against the trunk and close to doubled over.

"Jim?" Kathy said, approaching, "Why don't you step away from your car. I don't think you're well enough to drive."

"I've got to help Amanda."

"I know you do. So do I. The best way to do that—"

"They shouted for me to leave."

"I know. They shouldn't have done that. They need help."

He swayed again, collapsing against the side of the car. Kathy ran to him. He was holding his head and moaning. The bruise seemed to flare against his pale skin.

"We're going to call a doctor, Jim. We've got to get you better first. Then we'll be able to help Amanda."

"They said you'd say her name."

Kathy pulled back a little. "What? Who did? Amanda and Brad?"

He turned on her suddenly sure-footed and capable. She didn't even see his fist. He struck her dead in the face, knocking her cold to the pavement. She lay there for a moment, barely conscious. She heard the car door open and felt herself being lifted. Jim was throwing her across the back seat like a forty-

Jim went around the car and opened the passenger door and unlatched the glove compartment. A bottle of liquid and a rag were there. He opened the bottle and threw the rag on the ground and simply dumped the entire contents of the bottle over it. Ether splashed over his shoes and ran in rivulets against the tires of other cars. He kicked the bottle away and picked up the sopping rag, a trail of ether dribbling off it as he moved. He opened the passenger side rear door and look at her face.

There was light fluttering in the eyelids, and her mouth was opening, the lips forming little words. She was coming to.

He draped the rag across her face like a veil and shut the door.

71

K ATHY HAD A DREAM. SHE WAS ERIN, FACING HER KILLER IN the last minute of her life. The killer was not a man. It was regret. Regret for principles betrayed, time and love wasted, opportunities not seized. In her dream, she was dead before she was even killed, and she called Kathy her true murderer.

She woke and found herself bound on a wood floor and nauseated with pain. The first instinct to scream was defeated. She summoned every element of calm she could muster to keep that scream at bay. It echoed through her mind, but it did not escape her unrestricted mouth.

"They said, they said, no, you said, not I say."

Jim.

Cautiously she moved her head about. Her nose touched the ground and sent a bright flare of agony straight to the center of her mind. Her nose was broken. She closed her eyes, breathed heavily, trying for silence. At last the pain became manageable. She opened her eyes again and brought her head through an agonizing arc in order to scan the room.

Jim stood to her right at the front of the room several feet away. She wasn't angled for the best view. Could she attempt to reposition herself safely? She at least had to try.

She moved in centimeters, a delicate pivot of her body that only years of yoga practice let her accomplish so deftly. What she saw chilled her more than anything else. There was a massage table near where Jim stood. Crude modifications to it, mainly in straps and restraints, made it look sinister—and familiar. She'd seen these bindings before, when Allison Stockett's butchered body lay atop Erin's old table. The table now incarcerated a naked man.

Brad.

He's got them both.

"They said refer the pain."

Kathy blinked, listening. Jim's voice was different—deeper, more guttural. For a moment she thought she was listening to Judd Garvis.

Jim stood over Brad. "They said refer the pain!"

He struck Brad in the face. Kathy could just see Brad's head almost wobble on his neck, as if there were no spinal column to support it.

She couldn't stop herself. She screamed, "Stop it, Jim!"

"My head hurts," Jim said at Brad, striking him on the cheek with his right hand. His left caressed the bruise. "They say don't accept the pain, defer it."

Sadness, fear, and confusion struggled for supremacy in Kathy's thoughts as she watched. Refer the pain. The phrasing seemed familiar yet perverted, and she couldn't find its meaning in her scrambled consciousness. She stared at Jim, wondering how someone so unbalanced could function in society. But wasn't that the question asked of all serial killers? The world was a forgiving place. It could spare one a few hours of insanity here and there as long as they paid their taxes and smiled to the right people. She thought again of Judd Garvis. His problems had manifested themselves easily. But Jim…

Jim had a knife in his hand.

She screamed at him but nothing came out except a wail. Jim worked the weapon in grim repetitions across Brad's face. From her position, she couldn't tell how deeply he cut. Brad's complete lack of reaction chilled her the most. *He's already dead.* It was the only possible explanation.

Couldn't help Erin; couldn't help her brother.

She vomited, every muscle clenching in agony. She moaned so loud that when she finally gained control of herself, Jim had turned to watch her.

"Hi, Kathy," he said. He sounded like the hopeful young man who at his application interview had talked endlessly about his own experiences with massage and his desire to heal. Remembering it made her nausea spike.

"Jim, what—how—"

"My head hurts. That man was trying to refer his pain to Amanda, but I wouldn't let him. So he referred his pain to me. Now I referred my pain to him," Jim said, motioning to Brad. "You showed me how to refer my pain."

"I did?"

"Trigger points," he said. His innocent, explanatory tone infuriated her as much as it helplessly fascinated.

Kathy swallowed. The odor of vomit was still in her nose, making her gag as she tried to speak.

"Trigger points are inside you, Jim. It's the way muscles in the body end up transferring pain to other parts—because the body is a closed system."

"You said that. But they showed me trigger points are other people. One referred his pain to me. I referred my pain to another. Now I don't hurt as much."

"Is Brad dead?"

Jim stared as if he did not know the concept.

She stared back in disbelief and shock.

"No one wants you to hurt, Jim. We want to help."

"They said you'd say that."

"Who did, Jim?"

He stared hard at the floor as if he was trying to answer the question. Then he shrugged and just smiled at her.

"Jim, if I've caused you hurt in any way, I'm very sorry. People do things without realizing it sometimes."

"I know. Sometimes I do too."

"That's right." She swallowed again. *Just talk to him. Just keep talking even if it is insanity.* "Did you realize it when you tied me up like this?"

"I…"

He stared again, his head turned a little to the right. *Voices in his head*, Kathy thought. He looked like he was listening to something. Or someone.

Schizophrenia.

Madness.

Jim turned with great purpose, as if a decision had been made. Kathy's fright spiked again. *Where the hell are we?* It appeared to be an empty house—a run-down, nasty, empty house. She thought of Allison Stockett. The economy had forced so many to flee their mortgages, leaving a lot of abandoned, foreclosed houses. Bank appraisers probably hadn't looked at half of them, and they were not immediately suspect by the police. A killer's dream. She squinted, trying to see. The room stretched out too long, and there was one window, impossibly far away. Light outside. She could barely put two and two together at this point, but seeing sunlight gave her hope.

Back at the massage table, Jim unstrapped Brad's body and dumped it. *Oh no. Please no.* The sharp report of his body on the wood floor further suggested he was dead. She caught a glimpse of his face. She thought Jim had tried to carve the Reiki signs into his skin.

Oh God, I'm next—!

Jim walked toward her—then veered right, leaving the

room. Kathy heard the squeak of stairs as his footsteps muted. Alone, she began to struggle in earnest, getting a better sense of her bindings. He'd tired her with cord of some type, perhaps telephone wire. The bindings bit into her wrists when she moved them.

Jim's footsteps again. Labored. The steps really complained about the weight this time. Kathy heard something else. Resistance. Jim was struggling with his load. Now she heard high-pitched grunting and knew someone was crying out from around a gag. Kathy worked and flexed her body with more vigor, hoping for the slightest give in the bindings. The smallest slack and a little sweat would give her the escape she needed.

Jim entered half-carrying and half-dragging Amanda. She'd been bound more completely than Kathy, turned into an unwilling bride that Jim swept across the room like it was a honeymoon suite. This glimpse at her own fate caused Kathy to work harder. They still hadn't seen each other. Amanda was too busy screaming and pleading into her gag. Because of her restricted vision, though, she had not even seen Brad. Kathy dreaded how Amanda would react once she did.

Jim ignored her pleas and placed her on the table, slamming her down like meat. He showed her the bloody knife, and she began to scream again, roaring her terror through the cloth.

Kathy closed her eyes. A sudden *thud* made Kathy look again. Amanda began to flop on the table as if she were having a seizure. Kathy couldn't be sure. So much fear and adrenaline had to be shooting through her that her legs, though bound together, were doing anything to kick. Kathy twisted her wrists frantically as Amanda now went limp.

Jim worked without talking. Kathy only saw his back. Now he was leaning over Amanda, just stroking her hair. Amanda's eyes were open, her stare locked on Jim's face.

"Jim!"

Amanda reacted with a jolt at the sound of Kathy's voice. Their gazes met and Amanda's forehead creased into an expression of anguish, as if finding Kathy in Jim's clutches as well had dashed her last hope in the world.

"Jim!"

He turned, woozy on his feet. "Kathy?"

"Let her go, Jim."

"I love her."

"She loves you too, Jim."

His expression changed. It became petulant. "I gave her my love, and she referred it to him."

He kicked Brad's body in spite.

"I gave her my heart. I'll take my heart back."

Jim stormed off into another room, leaving the two of them looking at each other. "Help's coming," Kathy said, trying to control her voice. "You have to believe that, Amanda. Help is coming."

The cord around her wrists and ankles refused to give. She began to squirm along the floor, moving closer to Amanda in pathetic inches.

Jim came back with a different knife.

"No, Jim!"

Knife in hand, he resumed his old position by the table and bent down to stroke Amanda's hair again. Kathy meanwhile kept moving and writhing.

Suddenly, Jim gripped Amanda's hair and moved the knife against it in a sawing motion. Amanda's cries amped higher.

From the floor, Kathy called out in desperation, "Stop it, Jim! This is your teacher talking."

He did stop.

"My head hurts."

"So does mine. So does Amanda's, Jim. You can't refer pain to people who also have pain. Didn't I show you that?"

His face slackened. He was debating the point inside.

"They said—"

"Doesn't matter what they say. You listen to what I say. Cho Ku Rei, Jim. Remember?"

He dropped the knife and turned, the cut portion of Amanda's hair in his other hand.

"The symbol, Jim. The power."

"They said draw it for them."

"Draw it now, Jim. But for us. Protect us against them."

Jim teetered. Kathy thought he was about to collapse. She prayed he would collapse and die. Instead he looked around in confusion, listening to the voices—both hers and the ones inside. Kathy kept talking, competing, soothing. Her intuition told her this was the moment. Whatever insanity possessed him, he still had moments of clarity, moments when he was simply Jim, good-natured, good-hearted, eager but incapable. The voices inside were pressuring his sense of doubt, his feelings of incompetence. Her voice had to work with everything else.

"I've seen you draw the symbol, Jim. I know how good you are at it. Make it again."

"I don't understand the symbol. I just saw it once. But I stared a long time. They said it was important."

"They know if you draw the symbol for them, they can keep you down. Draw it for us, Jim!"

Still looking distrustful, Jim dropped to his knees and began to work. Kathy's nausea spiked anew when she saw how he drew, dipping his hands into Brad's blood like it was mere paint. He drew the symbol large, taking up a significant portion of the floor. The darker wood and lack of light made its progress hard to follow.

"Do you know the other symbols, Jim?"

He shook his head. "Sometimes I do. If they say."

"Let's make the one that will free you from them and leave you with Amanda forever. It's called Dai Ko Myo."

He focused immediately on the pronunciation of the first word. "Die?"

"Yes," she said quickly. *Talk as rapidly as you can, even if it makes no sense.* "Make them die. That's what you want, Jim. Make them die so Amanda can be the voice in your head from now on. The voice in your ear. Everything you need that they've been denying you."

"Show me!"

"Only a Reiki master can draw the symbol, Jim. We'll have to do it together."

"Direct me."

"Together, Jim. We can do anything together."

He squeezed his eyes shut and pounded his knuckles against his right temple. Droplets of blood stained his sideburns.

"They say no. They say kill you right now."

"Don't listen to them, Jim. You want to keep Amanda, don't you?"

His eyes open and he leered at Kathy. "Yes!"

"I need my hands. It's the most difficult symbol to draw. Its power is profound."

Jim moved fast, yanking her hands up. He reclaimed the knife and sliced the cords like they were mere scraps of yarn. Kathy started rubbing her wrists automatically, but Jim grabbed her and pulled her toward the largest pool of Brad's blood, her bound legs trailing after her like dead weight. Kathy retched as Jim forced her hands into the blood, already cool and thickening.

"Guide me!"

She did, with one furtive glance at Amanda.

Amanda had somehow freed her left arm.

Swallowing her disgust and terror, Kathy seized Jim's hand and they began to draw the symbol in large dimensions on the floor. There were two versions of the Dai Ko Myo, the traditional and the modern. The traditional was more intricate. Kathy decided to draw the modern incarnation because of its similarity to the Cho Ku Rei. It resembled one long spiral that made a two-pronged fork off to the right, so that it looked like a heavily stylized and italicized Y with a loopy, curlicue stem. Between the fork was a marking that looked like a thunderbolt.

She could not see exactly how well she drew. The wood seemed to take on the same color as the blood in the poor light. Jim's stare fixated on every motion. He had drawn the symbol himself at Allison Stockett's murder scene. Knowing this made Kathy suspicious of his attentions now. Was he faking not knowing the sign, or was the knowledge of it only accessible in some even darker recess of his personality? She made a quick glance at Amanda and thought, *Just keep drawing and talking*.

"Once the symbol is complete, you will be at peace, Jim. You will have all the power, and they will have none."

Jim's drawing pace quickened. He was panting now.

Behind him, Amanda silently sat up and unbound her legs. She ripped the gag out of her mouth.

She wasn't silent enough. Jim heard something—Kathy couldn't fathom it, with all the noise he was making—and looked up. "No!" he shouted, getting up and charging. Kathy reached forward and grabbed for his foot; she just snagged it. Jim's momentum carried him out of her grasp easily but sent him sprawling into the massage table.

The table fell sideways, spilling Amanda underneath it. Jim straddled the table, pressing the edge against her throat. In a weakening, gurgling voice, Amanda said, "Jim, I can't—I can't—"

Kathy dragged herself forward, cursing the leg bindings. She saw Jim's knife and cleaved to it. But she had none of Jim's deftness with it, and none of his physical strength. Where he had sliced the cords with a flick of his wrist, Kathy found herself reduced to tedious sawing.

Jim continued to press, bearing down and howling. Underneath him, Amanda gasped as the last oxygen was forced out of her.

"Jim! The symbol!" Kathy said.

He didn't reply. He kept up his pressure. His tears were flowing, falling onto Amanda's hair, glistening there like dew. He had sadness, and now it was her sadness. He had love, and now it was her love. He was referring all of himself into her. He said this over and over, just like they told him to.

Pain! So sharp and sudden and external he knew it didn't come from him. He staggered away from Amanda. Whose agony was this? Who was referring their pain to him? "Kathykathykathy," they said. "Give it back to her right now," they said.

"Yes," Jim said. He screamed as the pain came again, in a different place this time. He stumbled to his right and tripped. His back muscles locked up, his arms were stiff. Pain again! This time just below his shoulders.

"Don't let her kill us!"

Jim lay there, listening to many things.

"Amanda? Amanda?"

"Amanda," Jim said.

There was a sound. Her body was being taken off the table and placed on the ground. Amanda made no noise. Jim tried to speak again. All that came out was a gargle.

"One, two, three," he heard Kathy say. Followed by strange noises.

"I won't lose you, Amanda. Not like I lost Erin." Kathy sounded like she was gasping for air. "One, two, three." Strange noises.

"We're leaving you. No, we're not leaving because we're taking you with us," they said.

"Who are you?" Jim asked.

"Your pain," they said.

The last thing he heard was a new gasping, and mutual cries. "Kathy," Amanda's voice said. She sounded weak and in pain. Jim hoped she was okay. His own pain was fading into a cool black now. He felt it being referred out of his body and into Amanda. She would be able to conquer it.

He hoped her teeth did not hurt like his sometimes did.

Epilogue

Three weeks later, Kathy bent and touched the top of the tombstone. "Erin," she said.

"I'm finally getting in touch again. I'm sorry for the choice you made. I know you made it because you felt your back was against a wall. I wish you'd called me. Whatever your problems were, we could have found a solution. I should have called you. I thought about you often, wondering how you were doing, and I still didn't call. I put my students' photos on my wall and convinced myself that was good enough, like scanning their faces every day meant I was keeping up with their lives."

She stroked the tombstone like it was the side of Erin's face. Her own face was bruised and battered. She didn't cry. She hoped to be done with tears for a while.

Greg came up behind her and placed a hand on her shoulders.

"There's so much I just can't remember, Greg."

"That's a good thing."

Kathy looked at him and tried to smile. She failed. "Is it? I'm alive, but Brad isn't. I failed them both—brother and sister."

She looked at the new tombstone beside Erin's. Brad's was simple—all that Kathy could afford. *At least I was able to keep the two of them together.* She blinked twice, realizing her hopes were futile. She was not done with tears.

She wept.

Greg blanketed her in his arms. She cried against his chest, pressing her aching body against his. In the darkness of his clothes, she saw Brad and Amanda's faces.

"I missed both their funerals."

"Kathy, you're the strongest person I've ever met. You didn't fail either of them. And you saved Amanda's life. If you hadn't performed CPR—and in your condition, I can't imagine how difficult that was—then Jim would have killed another."

"She's still in the hospital," Kathy said.

"But she'll live."

She nodded only to appease him. Erin, Brad, Sharon—all of them. Jim. Right in front of her the entire time.

She had a brief flash of memory. She saw herself stabbing Jim in the back while he strangled Amanda. She didn't know how many times she'd stabbed him, but she did it more than once.

"Why didn't I see Jim for what he was? I could have stopped so much pain if I'd just realized—"

"He was very sick, Kathy. When and how the sickness started, we'll probably never know. If it helps at all, consider that it wasn't his fault. I don't think he wanted to do what he did. He was fighting demons the entire way. The voices were just stronger. He didn't understand. Probably you gave him the first real peace he's ever known."

She shivered and looked at her hands and felt she would never trust them again.

"What do we do now, Greg?"

He turned her to him and offered a shy, hopeful smile. "Love deeply," he said.

They held onto each other there for a long, long time.

About the Author

Sean Eads is a writer and librarian living in Denver, Colorado. His second novel, *The Survivors*, was a finalist for the 2013 Lambda Literary Award. His latest novel, *Lord Byron's Prophecy*, was a finalist for the Colorado Book Award and the Shirley Jackson Award.